FOREVER KNIGHT™

INTIMATIONS OF MORTALITY

In Aeternum

SUSAN M. GARRETT

Sm M. Garrett

1-18-98

D1324372

BOULEVARD BOOKS, NEW YORK

For the members of
ForKni-L, FK Fic-L,
and my grandmother,
Mary Zahaver.

FOREVER KNIGHT: INTIMATIONS OF MORTALITY

Based upon the television series created
by James D. Parriott and Barney Cohen.

Produced by Paragon Entertainment Corporation in
association with TriStar Television.

A Boulevard Book / published by arrangement with
Sony Signatures, Inc.

PRINTING HISTORY
Boulevard edition / November 1997

The Putnam Berkley World Wide Web site address is
http://www.berkley.com

ISBN: 1-57297-313-7

BOULEVARD
Boulevard Books are published by The Berkley Publishing Group,
a member of Penguin Putnam Inc.,
200 Madison Avenue, New York, New York 10016.
BOULEVARD and its logo are trademarks
belonging to Berkley Publishing Corporation.

PRINTED IN THE UNITED STATES OF AMERICA

10 9 8 7 6 5 4 3 2

1

THE DEAD BROUGHT THEM TOGETHER.

Nick tried not to think about that too often, but it was something that just couldn't be avoided. He paused at the doorway to the coroner's lab and glanced around the room.

He was a Toronto homicide detective. Natalie Lambert was a forensic pathologist. They were connected by death; by murder most foul and unholy, by gunshots and powder stains, by signs of forced entry and bodily violation, by burned and torn tissue, wrenched cartilage and blood.

Mostly by blood.

The stench of it assaulted him. The stainless steel counters unrelentingly reflected the fluorescent light and the floor shone with a clean brilliance that dazzled, but his senses were still keen enough to detect the scent of blood. The smell of old blood lingered from bodies that had long since given up their secrets and now were interred in quiet earth in some distant graveyard. Another sniff and he scented newer, fresher blood from a recent arrival, the smell accentuated by the distant tang of gunpowder. It made his nostrils twitch, his senses sharpen.

It made his mouth water.

Natalie was scrubbing up at the sink, her most recent

1

"patient" lying to one side on a stainless steel cart, decently covered with a white cloth. That's where the smell of fresh blood was coming from, as well as the tang of gunpowder. How many bullets had it taken? One? Two? Natalie would know, of course. Natalie would tell him. That was her job, to help him protect and serve the fine and upstanding citizens of Toronto who slept better, knowing that their vigilant police force was on duty, chasing down the thugs and criminals, removing them from the streets.

And how well would they sleep if they knew that one of those vigilant defenders of law and order had been a murderer? That his hands had been covered with blood? That the urge to bare his fangs and hunt those fine, upstanding citizens through the darkened streets warred with the oath he had sworn?

Detective Nick Knight was a vampire. The secret was another thing he shared with Natalie Lambert, as well as his heartfelt desire to become mortal.

It took Natalie a few seconds to register his presence. When she did turn, she smiled, her hazel eyes warm and welcoming. But as she met his gaze, shaking her wet hands over the sink and drying them with a paper towel snatched from the dispenser, the light in her eyes dimmed and was replaced by a suspicious look. Removing the green surgical cap from her head, she locked her gaze on his, even when her chestnut hair fell into her eyes. Tossing it back behind her ears and shrugging out of the lab apron she was wearing over her green scrubs, she commanded, "Okay, spill it."

The shrug he managed was halfhearted. Inwardly, Nick cursed. He was better than this—he'd spent a good portion of the last eight hundred years masking his feelings, letting his face betray nothing to mortal or vampire alike. At first it had been something of a game to hide the predator in himself from the prey until the last moment, until they were trapped and within reach of his fangs and blood lust. For many centuries more, he'd hidden the monster out of shame

2

and fear, wanting to be part of the mortal world that lived and breathed and decayed around him.

Sometimes it worked. Sometimes, for an hour or an evening, he could pretend that he was as mortal as any man, that he could stand in the sunlight without harm, could dream of having children and watching them grow to adulthood, could hold a woman in his arms without feeling the overwhelming desire to drain every drop of blood from her body.

But it was pretense, nothing more. The beast was still there, lurking within him. He'd learned to mask its presence and tried to learn to mask his feelings as well, his hurt and anger and disappointment. Sometimes that worked, too.

Under Natalie's relentless scrutiny, it wasn't worth the effort. Nick shrugged again, avoiding direct contact with her eyes. "We've had a rough couple of nights."

Natalie's eyes clouded for a moment, and she looked down at the clipboards arranged on a trolley in front of her—the cases he and the others at the precinct had covered while she was gone. "The jumper?" she guessed, after a moment's hesitation.

There were times when her perception amazed him. "He wasn't a jumper." Nick shook his head slightly, then turned away, examining the tile, the ceiling . . . anything.

He could still see the crime scene in his mind. The frozen ground had crunched beneath his feet as he'd walked from his '62 Cadillac to the tower. The chain link fence had bent slightly beneath the weight of the recent ice and its own age. He'd paused briefly, noting the absence of snow at the top and in certain handholds and footholds. The tracks up to the fence were clearly marked, sneakers and boots, blurred slightly on the other side where they'd landed. He could almost hear the boys' voices as they dared one another, running up to the fence, scrambling over it and into the deserted park.

Nick had looked up to see the tower . . . and his

partner, Detective Tracy Vetter. Floodlights had been placed at the scene, and her blonde hair appeared almost as white as the snow around them. The place seemed eerily silent— Tracy's voice was low as she interviewed an older man, probably the one the kids had gone to for help. The other three boys, the lucky ones, were sobbing as they were led to an EMT van.

Taking care not to disturb the tracks, he'd walked over to the bottom rung of the ladder that led up to the bungee tower platform. He'd heard Tracy approach, but kept his attention on the snow, noting the bits of ice and dirt that had come off a pair of boots or sneakers that had climbed the ladder to the top.

"It was a dare," Tracy had said, tucking her notepad into her coat pocket.

Staring down at the evidence in the snow, he could see it all in his mind's eye—the four boys laughing, exchanging words lightly, then more seriously, the feet kicking back and forth in the snow until someone took the dare, walked up to the ladder, began to climb. . . .

He'd moved onward, to the area beyond the tower. The body was already bagged—Tracy was the primary on the scene; she'd have given them permission to take it. The white snow was splotched with red, the ground churned up by the man who'd come when the boys had called for help, arriving too late to do anything.

Tracy had followed him. "Nick, maybe we should head back to the station. There's nothing to this. It was an accident."

"An accident," he'd echoed.

The story was there, recorded in the snow from the first to the last. When the snow melted, even that bit would be gone. If he listened, he could imagine the sounds—the skid of rubber on ice, a faint and disbelieving cry as gravity took hold, followed seconds later by a wet thud.

The worst of it was that he couldn't quite bring himself to

4

care. There was only a numb ache in his heart that he couldn't excuse as the cold, and the flare of hunger in his chest at the sight of fresh, red blood wasted and cooling in the snow.

How could so little of it appear on the black-and-white printed page in Natalie's hand?

"He went up the bungee tower on a dare. The ice got him at the top." Nick nodded toward the clipboard. "Whatever that tells you, we've got witnesses to confirm. Although we won't be able to interview the kid who made the dare until he comes out of sedation."

Natalie lifted the clipboard and scanned it. "He couldn't have been more than what—sixteen?"

"He was *stupid*." The anger that had been building in him, the frustration of despair, finally escaped in that single word. Nick took a swing at the trolley, but stopped himself in time—not quickly enough; his hand grazed the edge of the cart, and sent the clipboards flying. Instantly, he dropped to a crouch and began to retrieve them. "I'm sorry," he muttered, handing two of the clipboards up to her and reaching for a third. "I've got no right to take this out on you—"

"You're right." Her hand covered his as he rose and handed her the last clipboard. "It's an occupational hazard in our business, you know that. A waste of life is always tragic. It's going to affect us."

Nick forced his eyes away from hers, slipped his cold hand from the comforting grasp of her warm fingers, and turned away. "But some of us don't know what a tragedy it really is. To throw his life away—his humanity—on something so stupid—"

Natalie's hand caressed his shoulder; her touch was gentle even if her words were sharp. "It's not your fault, so take off the hair shirt. He was a kid. He made a bad decision. Accidents happen. You didn't do anything stupid when you were younger?"

"Yeah." He turned his head to meet her gaze, almost flinching again at the regret he saw in her eyes; she'd realized too late what she'd said. "But he won't come back as a vampire, will he? For him, at least, it's over."

Her lips parted, but Natalie looked away without saying anything further. She lifted the clipboard in her hand and stared at it. He could almost hear her mind racing, trying to think of some words to comfort him, some retort to shock him back to himself. That was one of the reasons he'd come here at the end of his shift, hoping she could goad him out of the depression that he'd been unable to shake since the boy's death. His dedication to his goal of finding mortality was beginning to crumble.

The other was that she'd been away. He'd missed her.

And his self-pity was a great "welcome home."

Nick cleared his throat and walked away from her, across the tile floor of the lab. Distance was always safer. "How was the conference in New York?"

"Okay, I guess." There was relief in her tone; she was grateful that he'd changed the subject. "The same old stuff. There are only so many ways you can cut into a corpse. Although there's a new exploratory laser I'd like to get my hands on. And I borrowed the slides from a spectacular lecture on liver dissection, if you're interested."

His revulsion must have shown on his face when he turned, because she laughed. The sound helped to ease a little bit of the darkness that had settled over his soul. He wondered, for a moment, whether the past few days of senseless death had so disturbed him because Natalie hadn't been there. "Thanks, but I'll pass."

"You don't know what you're missing." Natalie walked over to her desk and opened a drawer. "I think you'll want to take a look at this, though."

"You got it?" In his haste, he moved to her side in a blur of motion too quick for her to see. Natalie started, but he placed a hand on her arm to steady her, the other hand lifting the small, white cardboard jewelry box from her palm.

"Uh, yeah." He could sense her eyes on him, but for a moment all he could do was stare at the box . . . it was completely and utterly ordinary. "That woman was strange."

"She lives in Greenwich Village."

"That's an explanation?"

"It used to be." He debated whether to open the box there or drop it into his pocket and leave, but Natalie's curious eyes told him that he wouldn't make it to the hallway without being tackled. He did owe her that much, after sending her on the mystery errand.

A flick of his finger removed the lid. Inside was a small wicker doll; the eyes and mouth were painted dots, its clothing consisted of a piece of red and gold patterned cloth, and the hair was painted brown. It was no larger than his thumb. "Any instructions?"

He looked up, to find Natalie staring at the doll in puzzlement. "Yeah," she managed, after meeting his eyes. "She said to keep it with you. That it would lead you to what your heart desires most."

"That's all?"

"Hey, isn't that weird enough?" Her eyes narrowed. "Nick, this isn't another quick fix, is it? We've talked about this before. If we're going to find a way to reverse your condition, it's not going to be through eye of newt and wart of frog."

"Science doesn't seem to be doing me much good, does it?" He regretted his words when he saw Natalie's gaze lower to the floor, her lips setting in a firm and disapproving line. "Nat—I'm sorry. I know you're doing everything you can, but protein drinks and vitamins haven't gotten us anywhere."

"Would you like me to fast-track this?" She looked up, eyes flashing. "I'll bet researchers all over the world would

7

drop AIDS and cancer in a heartbeat if they heard what we're working on. A cure for *vampirism*?"

"Nat—"

He dropped the box onto the desk and moved closer, reaching out his hand to touch her arm, but she jerked it away. "If what I'm doing isn't good enough—"

"It's not you," he said firmly, this time managing to grab her hand and entwine his fingers with hers as he pulled her closer. "It's . . . me."

Some of the fight left her; her eyes widened a little and she said softly, "We've come close—"

"But not close enough."

"You've got time. More time than anyone could—"

"But you don't."

His gaze met and held hers, letting the awful, brutal truth that he saw in her eyes slip between them again. He lifted his hand, brushed the hair from her face, and imagined her features in ten or twenty years. Then again, he wouldn't *have* to imagine. Without a cure, he'd continue to be a vampire and Natalie *would* age, as mortals did. "I don't want to waste your time."

"It's mine to waste." She bit her lip slightly and shook her head. "No, that's not what I mean."

"I know what you mean." Nick squeezed her hand, then released her. He walked back to the desk and picked up the box containing the doll again—for some reason, it reminded him of a small, white coffin. He'd never thought he'd ever see one, and yet here it was. And now that he had it, did he even have the heart to use it?

He looked up as Natalie walked toward him. "The woman who gave me that—have you ever met her?"

Nick replaced the lid and closed his fingers over the box. "No. She was . . . a referral."

"I guessed as much." When Nick gave her a questioning look, Nat smiled almost guiltily. "Well, she's gorgeous. She's got this black hair and almond eyes and this dress that—well, it's green. She stood in the door of the shop and watched me leave. It must have been ten below and there wasn't a goose pimple anywhere on her—believe me, in that dress, I would have seen it." Her eyes narrowed. "She isn't . . . one of you, is she?"

"I don't think so." Caught off guard by her question, he considered the possibility that the woman who'd obtained the item for him might be another vampire, then shook his head. "No."

Natalie sighed, and it was only then that he realized she'd been holding her breath. "That's reassuring."

"Why?" Tucking the box in the pocket of his leather jacket, he seated himself on the edge of her desk. "What was wrong with her?"

"Wrong with her? Nothing. Half the people in Hollywood would give their souls to look like her, and the other half—" She shook her head, a taut smile appearing on her lips. "It's just that, well, I asked her to do a tarot reading for me. And she wouldn't."

Nick raised an eyebrow in mock horror. "Dr. Lambert! I *am* surprised."

Natalie tapped his shoulder with the back of her hand as she passed. "Well, she had cards sitting on the table. Her door said she was an 'adviser.' I thought it would be good for a laugh."

His hand went to the box in his pocket and his fingers closed around it again. He didn't much believe in the cards or the fortune-telling tricks of charlatans. Then again, he'd met people who had seen and known things. . . . "Did she give you a reason?" he asked, with what he hoped was casual interest.

"She said I knew more than I should." Natalie's fingers closed over one of the clipboards. "Then she showed me the door." Carrying the clipboard to a filing cabinet, she turned her head to look at him. "You don't think she knows what you are? I mean, she doesn't—?"

"No," Nick said firmly. He rose to his feet and walked toward her. "There's no way she could know. I've had no direct contact with her; someone else made the arrangements."

"And you're willing to trust . . . that?" She inclined her head slightly, indicating the box in his pocket.

"I'm willing to *try* anything," he corrected. "Don't tell me the empirical Dr. Lambert is frightened of a little dream doll?"

"The empirical Dr. Lambert has seen a lot recently that would have sent other coroners into the loony bin," she reminded him. "It's just that—" She shivered, turning back to the filing cabinet. "Never mind. It's just a doll; it can't hurt you. As usual, I came back just when the office was hip-deep in bodies, and I'm cranky."

"Well, at least things can't get much worse."

"Yeah." Closing the filing cabinet, she smiled at him— but the smile was forced. "See you tomorrow."

His answer was noncommittal as he turned and left, his fingers again searching out the box in his pocket, his hand closing over the cardboard protectively. As Nick headed to his car, he thought about what he'd told Natalie—for centuries he'd tried everything that crossed his path, hunted the length and breadth of the known world, dug into the archives and ruins of the past searching for something that might cure him and return him to mortality. Nothing had worked. Eight hundred years later, he was still a killer, a vampire.

His thoughts as dark and cold as the predawn sky, Nick found himself swinging by the Raven, the club that his master, Lucien LaCroix, now owned. It was located in one of Toronto's less fashionable warehouse districts, but the club was one of the darker bright spots of the city's nightlife.

Not that LaCroix would have noticed. His ownership of the club was only a diversion, a convenient means of passing time within the mortal world. The Raven flourished in spite of his disinterest, or because of it.

As a mortal LaCroix had been general of a great Roman army, his victories earning him the acclaim of the Senate, the goodwill of Caesar, and the life of a noble in the city of Pompeii. As an immortal, a vampire, his fascination with conquest had continued. He'd dabbled in the lives of mortals throughout history, played kingmaker and merchant, aristocrat and politician, pitting his intellect and his mania for control against the adversities of nature and the will of those he would have used as pawns and puppets.

His interest in such games of power had paled over time, and LaCroix had focused the daunting combination of his experience and abilities on the one thing that had continued to elude him—Nick's insistence upon maintaining the mastery of what was left of his own soul and his refusal to accept the inevitability of the nature that LaCroix had bestowed upon him. Perhaps LaCroix saw the club as a means to his ends, although it was equally possible he was using it merely as an expedient tax dodge.

The bouncer never even blinked as he passed by, and Nick nodded to some of the regulars as he entered—with Natalie out of town he'd found himself drawn here often during the past week. For a reason he had yet to fathom, something about the place numbed the despair in his soul—the music was loud and raucous, the dancing was frenetic, and even the secluded tables were lit by bright candelabra. A number of the vampires of Toronto drank their fill of wine-laced blood there, and he couldn't help but approve of that, especially since it meant there were fewer homicides due to blood loss that he'd have to investigate.

The place had changed during the time he'd been in Toronto. He paused at the railing along the upper landing just inside the door, missing the mystique that Janette had imparted to the club, the air of mystery and sensuality that her presence had ensured in the decor and clientele.

She was another of LaCroix's children in blood, brought across into her life as a vampire almost three centuries before LaCroix had offered the same gift of immortality to Nick . . . using his beautiful, raven-haired offspring as a lure. They'd traveled the world together, the three of them, and if there had been any joy in the decades he'd spent trying to escape the mastery of LaCroix's will, Janette had been the source of it.

Curtains of chains had been shifted, wood replaced by chrome, artwork hinting at the erotic taken down in favor of the blatantly sexual—both he and the club had suffered the loss of Janette when she'd disappeared from Toronto six months ago. Of the two, only he had been affected by her brief return to the city not too long before. The crowd that had been drawn to the change in decor and atmosphere continued to dance, to drink, to meet and mate and part in a haze of alcohol and dulled senses, oblivious to the loss that he, and Janette, had suffered.

Scanning the crowd, Nick paused, catching sight of a black leather jacket and an unkempt tumble of dark hair. Their gazes locked, then Javier Vachon backed away and disappeared into the crowd. Nick frowned, took one step toward the dance floor, then stopped.

No. He had no beef with the young and generally insolent vampire, other than to warn him that he might be seeing a bit too much of Nick's partner, Tracy Vetter—a Homicide detective who happened to be pretty, eager, and very mortal. Vachon was the type who'd take such a warning as a challenge; he'd been a conquistador, a soldier in the army of conquest Pizarro had brought to the New World from Spain, and the intervening centuries had done little to temper his headstrong nature. The last thing Nick wanted was to have to prove to Vachon just how much stronger the three-hundred-year difference between their vampiric ages made him.

Nick let his gaze wander around the club for a moment, and his eyes met those of one of the dancers briefly. It was

Urs, one of Vachon's friends. LaCroix had once called her a goddess, and among vampires or mortals she might seem so; she was blonde, with a Marilyn Monroe quality about her, a combination of innocence and sexuality wrapped in a deceptively charming, bloodsucking package. Her smile to him was sad but knowing, as she returned her attention to the dance she was performing on the raised, lit platform to one side of the club. Nick found himself smiling as well, as he caught her looking around, and guessed that she might be trying to find Vachon, to warn him of Nick's presence. Well, he didn't feel like bothering with either of them tonight—he'd leave them to their own business.

Vampire business.

He took a seat at the bar. The vampire bartender on duty knew him by sight—he picked up a bottle, poured its contents into a glass, and left the drink on a coaster in front of Nick before moving on to other customers. He left the bottle on the bar.

"Slumming?" asked LaCroix, from beside him.

Tall and dressed entirely in black, LaCroix fit in well with the mixture of Goth and garish fashion that he'd fostered in the dance club. Nick had watched him move among the patrons with a silent step, an eternally vigilant predator guarding and protecting the boundaries of his tiny kingdom. Mortal and vampire alike, the crowd parted before his aristocratic bearing, whether knowing enough of him to fear him or out of the instinctive mortal dread of the dark. LaCroix allowed his clientele their fun, within limits. And if those limits were delineated by no more than a sharp look from the proprietor, they were observed as religiously as if they'd been inscribed on every brick that comprised the structure.

Nick concentrated on the glass, lifting it carefully to his lips—he wasn't up to dealing with LaCroix tonight. He was never in a mood for one of LaCroix's lectures, and now was no exception. Coming here had been a mistake.

But where else could he have gone, other than back to the loft apartment he currently called home?

"You seem to have become a regular," noted LaCroix, echoing his thoughts. His voice held more than a hint of amusement. "Every night for an entire week, Nicholas? There's hope for you, yet."

The glass contained cow blood—the smell told him that much. He took another sip, pretended that it was enough.

But it wasn't. It kept his hunger barely under control, never sating it completely. Only human blood could do that.

He'd given up killing, given up the drinking of human blood, almost a century before. He'd had enough of murder, of innocent blood on his hands, on his soul. With a grimace, Nick took another sip of the animal blood and found he couldn't stand the taste. What had it gotten him, this self-imposed abstinence from human blood? A hundred years, and he was no closer to mortality.

Taking the glass from Nick's hand, LaCroix set it aside. Making the briefest gesture toward the bartender, he met Nick's eyes with a even, gray gaze. "Do I detect the beginning of a crack in your tedious moral foundation? Has this benighted quest for redemption finally begun to bore you?"

"Don't you have a show to do?" Nick asked flatly, refusing to give in to his master's taunting. He gestured over his shoulder toward the soundproof booth that had been installed in the back of the club, where LaCroix delivered his nightly soliloquies and philosophy to the late-night radio audience of Toronto in his persona as the Nightcrawler.

"I've just signed off." LaCroix favored him with a look of mock sympathy as he leaned forward to grasp the fresh bottle and glass delivered by the bartender. "Don't tell me that you missed it? I was on my mark this evening. The topic was self-delusion—something with which you're intimately acquainted, I believe."

LaCroix opened the bottle, then dropped the cork on the

14

bar. Nick caught it before it could roll to the edge, and felt the remnants of human blood still clinging to it soaking through his skin. The aroma was heady, enticing after his steady diet of cow.

Natalie had suggested that it was his consumption of blood, *any* blood, that had kept him from regaining his mortality. Despite her attempts at substitutes—protein shakes and other hideous concoctions—the beast within him, the vampire, still craved blood. The animal blood was a form of appeasement; it was a token offering of sorts, a means by which he could keep his nature under control.

That it was a poor substitute had never been debated. Both he and the hunger that rose within him knew better than that. Human blood was their true source of nourishment, combining all the sensations of life that their nature denied them with the utter bliss of fulfillment. No matter how much cow blood he drank—and he tried to limit that to the regimen Natalie requested—the beast longed for the taste of human blood.

"I opened with a quotation from Sartre," said LaCroix, pouring the contents of the bottle into the glass. "There were a number of calls this evening. I might even continue the topic tomorrow night—"

Nick was only half listening to LaCroix's words, his senses focusing on the blood in the glass. The scent of it called to him, luring him closer. His mouth was dry, and he licked his lips; the red liquid gleamed through the glass even in the dim and smoky interior of the club. What could it hurt, to have a glass? He'd followed Natalie's prescribed regimen for months without a break . . . well, more often than not. He'd swallowed protein drinks, taken vitamins, cut down on the amount of blood—cow's blood—that he consumed. He deserved this. He owed himself this.

"Life *is* really a matter of self-delusion, isn't it? People tell themselves that this or that will make them happy and, when they finally have their heart's desire, they find that they're no different at the end of their journey than when they began."

Nick started at the mention of "heart's desire"; his hand dropped into his jacket pocket, fingers clutching the small white box that Natalie had brought back from New York. But his eyes remained fixed on the liquid within LaCroix's glass, the scent of human blood holding his attention.

"It's really nothing more than a matter of knowing exactly what you want." LaCroix lifted the glass to his lips, then hesitated, the shadow of a smile lingering in his expression. "Do you know what you want, Nicholas? Or do you merely *think* you know?"

"I know—" Nick raised his gaze from the glass to meet LaCroix's unfathomable stare. With an effort, he looked away, turning his back to the bar and facing the dance floor. "I know that I don't want *this*."

"And would mortality be so very different, do you think?" The glass made a "clink" as LaCroix set it on the bar. "Yes, mortality has a finite end, whereas our existence is, nominally, eternal. But still . . . would it really be any different? Would *you* really be any different?"

Nick licked his lips again, hearing the glass being slid along the bar toward him. All he had to do was reach out and take it. But he wouldn't.

He couldn't.

The music suddenly seemed too loud, the crowd too noisy and garish for his tastes. And his mouth was still dry.

"I have to go." Nick pulled his wallet from his jacket, opened it, and threw a handful of bills on the bar.

"Yes. I know." His master met his gaze with a cryptic smile. "But where, Nicholas, will you go from here?"

LaCroix's words echoed in his ears as he hurried out of the club, pushing his way past the mortals and the vampires who mingled unobtrusively among them. Halfway up the steps to the door, he paused and looked out over the crowd.

He could see the warmth of the mortal bodies, their heat

16

shining from them like small suns, glowing within—a sharp contrast to the colder and darker blues and greens of the vampires' bodies. Predator and prey seemed to coexist peacefully in this place, but it was all an illusion . . . LaCroix's illusion. In the modern mortal world, identities had to be carefully constructed to endure meticulous scrutiny and victims chosen from among the refuse of society, but in this one place the vampire still ruled. This was a hunting ground, a place to keep senses sharp, to indulge appetites.

He didn't like it here.

He didn't *want* to belong here.

As he turned to go, he caught sight of LaCroix at the bar, still watching. LaCroix raised the blood-filled glass to him as if in salute, mouthing the word "Where?"

Nick's fingers closed around the box again as he tucked his hands in his pockets and hurried out of the club. He returned to his car, slipped behind the wheel, then paused, looking up at the night sky through the windshield.

For so long he'd thought that when he became mortal, he would find what he was seeking. That had become his goal—to cross back into the world where he could walk beneath the sun without burning, where he could love a woman and not kill her, where he could have children and grow old . . . and die. But his dream of becoming mortal seemed even further away now than when he'd started. And even if he did manage to achieve his goal—what if there was no place for him there? What if LaCroix was right, that he'd become human and find that he was still, at heart, a killer? A beast encased in mortal instead of immortal flesh?

Nick dropped his hand in his pocket to pull out his keys, but his fingers found the box again. He withdrew it, then opened the lid carefully.

The doll remained as he'd last seen it, the tiny painted mouth frozen in a perpetual "o" of surprise, the dotted eyes staring into eternity. It was ordinary beyond belief, the work of some South American native craftsperson. He'd spent what many would consider a small fortune to purchase this trinket, although he probably could have found one for the amount of change in his pocket at any small shop in half a dozen border towns. Was this what he'd come to, pinning his future on a worthless toy, some superstitious nonsense?

Nick tilted the doll from the box and onto his palm, smiling sheepishly at his folly. Perhaps LaCroix was right, he was a fool. Maybe he didn't know what he really wanted— how many people could truly say that they did? At least he knew what he *didn't* want. He didn't want to be a predator. He didn't want to be a vampire.

But did he truly want to be mortal? Was he willing to reenter that finite world of sunlight and love and laughter . . . and pain and accident and death? The waste of that boy's life, to have fallen to his death on a dare, still weighed upon his soul. How fragile it all was. How pointless.

The doll still stared up at him, the expression frozen in time. Nick dropped it back into the box and closed the cover, hiding its face. It was only a toy, after all. Superstitious nonsense, as LaCroix would have told him. In fact, he could easily manufacture a mental image of LaCroix's disdainful sneer accompanying the comment.

Yet all the way home, it was the forced smile on Natalie's face that stayed with him. And it took him the rest of a sleepless morning to identify the shadow that had lurked behind her eyes when he'd left her.

It had been fear.

2

THERE WAS A RED FLARE OF PAIN FROM THE BACK OF HIS HEAD. Nick opened his eyes to darkness, stunned for a moment that the world was nothing more than a blur of shapes and angry whispers. With his darkly perfect vampire vision, he should've been able to see everything clearly, but it was as if a black netting had been placed before his eyes.

"Here he is," said Vachon's voice, in not much more than a whisper. "Nick? You okay?"

What was Vachon doing here?

Where *was* here?

Strong hands supported him, helping him to his feet in the near-black void. He leaned against a wall, the plaster cool against the warmth of his forehead, and realized that he'd been sprawled on the floor. "Where am—?"

Fingers touched the back of his head lightly, and his question faded into a groan at the pain the searching pressure evoked.

"There's blood here." Vachon's voice was more than a little alarmed. "He's hurt—"

A scream rent the air—something inhuman and ear-splitting. A rough hand grabbed his shoulder, then his upper arm—Vachon?—and he was dragged away from the brief comfort and support of the wall. He stumbled and recovered, fear giving his feet more coordination than he would have thought possible. Something was behind him, chasing him.

The solid black and deep shadows gave way to bands of lighter gray as he moved through the dank hallway. There were brief glimpses of a pattern on the peeling wallpaper and unmentionable stains accompanied by the acrid smell of urine. Trash and rubble were strewn across his path, and he stumbled over them. Vachon—he could see the silhouette ahead of him—was dragging him through a darkened basement corridor. When they seemed to reach the end, Nick tripped on concrete steps going upward, despite Vachon's relentless tug on his arm—or because of it. He caught himself with his free hand and found the stair carpeting beneath him, torn and threadbare. Just as he looked upward, a door opened above him.

Daylight flooded through the opening, engulfing and blinding him.

Nick pulled back instinctively as Vachon tugged him forward. "The light!" he croaked, his throat dry. "Vachon—the light!"

Another hand reached down, the callused, twisted fingers grasping his forearm and unceremoniously hauling him upward into the blinding light. Nick blinked in the brightness, unable to make out objects, or even shapes. He teetered on the edge of the steps, terrified, waiting for the burning to start, for his vampire flesh to begin to smoke and crackle and char beneath the light of the sun.

But he didn't burn.

He stared down at his bloodied hands, scraped and dirty, and felt only the heat of the summer sun upon them. The air was fresh, moist with humidity. He began to tremble at the shock of it and almost fell back down the steps, into the darkness.

Then something hit him from behind, sending him

sprawling face forward onto the ground. Nick twisted as he fell, and something or someone fell on top of him. Talons clutched at his throat, trying to squeeze the breath from him. His sight was coming back, but all he could see was a pair of gold-red eyes and fangs bared in an inhuman snarl.

With scarcely any thought, he locked his elbows and pushed upward in an attempt to throw off the attacker—but nothing happened. The vampire strength that he'd relied upon for centuries was gone.

Instead, there was a weary ache in his abused and battered body. The fangs drew closer, and the thing reached up a hand to push his head to one side. He couldn't breathe, couldn't move, frozen in fear as he felt the breath of the vampire on his neck.

Nick grunted as that other body was suddenly pushed down against him, the hands releasing their unbreakable hold on his arm and shoulder. The eyes above his face turned from furious gold to a surprised brown and the mouth opened wider in a scream, deafening him. The thing began to struggle, the fingernails raking down his face and neck, and he tried to scramble away from the vampire.

Again hands caught his shoulder, dragging him out from under his attacker. He saw that the thing—what was left of a woman wearing a beige sweater and skirt—was writhing in agony and howling, pinned to the asphalt by a broken piece of wooden fencing that had been thrust through her chest. She was burning as the waning light struck her, skin sizzling as she screamed in pain and frustration, still clawing the asphalt of the street as if to follow him. The stench was like a combination of barbecuing meat and burning rubber. He choked when a well-placed breeze hurled the smell into his face.

Nick tried to move his arm across his eyes so that he wouldn't see the agony that was assaulting his ears. The grip on his shoulders was removed and he fell, catching himself just before he landed heavily on his left arm. As it was, he scraped it across the warm sidewalk. It stung, adding a harmonic note to the pounding at the back of his head.

"That was *stupid*, Nicholas," said a familiar voice.

Leaning his elbows against the warm concrete beneath him, Nick saw the outline of a silhouette against the sun. Work boots, khaki pants, sleeveless T-shirt, sweat running in dirty rivulets against skin, light brown hair close-cropped—but it wasn't until he turned that Nick matched the profile features to his memory. "LaCroix?" he whispered in horror, the word coming out as little more than a croak.

There was movement beside him and his elbow gave way—but a strong hand under his arm kept him from crashing onto the concrete. Vachon's dark hair tumbled over his eyes, escaping from the leather tie that bound it into a tousled ponytail, as he squatted beside Nick. His tanned face, which should have been pale, was covered with streaks of grime and rivulets of sweat.

Nick stared at Vachon in wonder—another vampire in the sunlight? His clothing wasn't that different from LaCroix's—a T-shirt and jeans, with lighter leather boots, but flashier. "I was right—he smacked his head when he hit the wall." Vachon stared into Nick's eyes, then held up two fingers. "Can you see me? Are you dizzy? How many fingers do you see?"

He tried to answer but couldn't, choking instead. His throat was dry from dust and fear.

"Here." Nick looked up to see LaCroix pull a flask from the belt at his hip and throw it to Vachon. "Give him that. Would serve him right if he's concussed himself."

"He pushed me out of the way."

"You shouldn't have been *in* the way."

He heard Vachon fumble with the flask cap, then felt the rim at his lips. Greedily, Nick drank the cool water, sucking it into his mouth and down his throat without a breath. He pushed Vachon's hand away from the flask and tipped it on end, then sputtered, spitting water as he choked.

Water.

"Easy," cautioned Vachon, taking the flask from him. "You can have more later. We've got to get under cover." He looked worriedly up at the buildings, silent black shadows on either side of the street, and the reddening sky beyond. "Not much light left."

LaCroix turned at his words, looking up at the sky, then back down at them. Fixing Nick with a measuring stare, he asked, "Will he be ready for his shift?"

Vachon threw the flask back at LaCroix, hard. "Why ask? You'll send him anyway."

"That's up to Nick, not me," answered LaCroix coldly. He caught the flask easily and slid the strap onto the belt at his waist without missing a beat. "I doubt a cracked skull will stop him." Glancing back toward the skyline, he added, "We've got half an hour until sunset. And we can't send him off to work with that open head wound—they'll be on him like a pack of rabid dogs."

What was going on? Nick rubbed the back of his hand across his mouth and watched the pair of them, knowing that Vachon's angry scowl should mean something. But that mattered little compared with the raw ache of his head, the wound throbbing in time with his heart. Why hadn't it healed? Why did his senses seem dull, his reflexes slow, his muscles unresponsive?

And how were they out here, exposed to the sunlight, without burning?

But neither Vachon nor LaCroix seemed disturbed by the fact that the three of them should have been piles of ash.

"Can you walk?" Vachon asked, eyes watching him carefully for any sign of weakness.

This time he didn't try to speak, settling for a nod. With Vachon's help, Nick gritted his teeth and rose from the ground despite the protest of his muscles. At first it seemed that Vachon would support him, but then LaCroix slipped an arm beneath his shoulder, pushing Vachon to one side. "Scout ahead," he told Vachon, gesturing down the street with his free hand. "It's too close to dark to take any chances we'll be caught by a police patrol."

Vachon's scowl returned. He opened his mouth as if to answer LaCroix, then met Nick's eyes, paused for a moment . . . and turned away. "Hurry."

"We will."

Nick looked at LaCroix, hearing an odd note of strain in his voice. By the time he looked back to where Vachon had been standing, he'd disappeared into the shadows of the buildings on the far side of the street.

As LaCroix helped him turn, Nick caught sight of the loose clothing wrapped around the fence post stuck into the warm asphalt of the street, the ends of a skirt lightly billowing as a warm breeze rushed past. The ashes from the vampire were already beginning to disperse, scattered by the wind. His stomach churned at the smell that lingered, even though the corpse was gone.

But LaCroix didn't seem to notice the grisly landmark. He moved forward slowly, allowing Nick to put his weight on him as they shuffled across the deserted street and onto the far sidewalk.

"Good work," said LaCroix, barely loud enough for him to hear. "Vachon was right—you saved his life. That thing would have taken his head off if you hadn't distracted it. Next time, though, remember to duck. I can't afford to lose either one of you right now."

Mumbling a feeble assent, Nick managed to keep pace with LaCroix as they made their way down one alley and then another. Fighting to carry as much of his own weight as possible, despite the throbbing in his head and the steady burn of the scrape across his arm, he stumbled along and ignored the odd dips and turns the surrounding world seemed to take. The sun was low in the sky, well behind the buildings on either side of them. He knew that it should have been the beginning of rush hour on Yonge Street.

Nick stopped, startled, as he realized they were in the heart of downtown Toronto, yet the streets were empty except for the occasional speeding car. He hadn't thought about the one that had passed them a few moments before, but took note of the second—it contained two young men, their expressions and faces blurred by the speed of their vehicle.

"Idiots," said LaCroix, his tone quiet but derisive as he spat at the ground. "Fools. They know what time the sun sets. They shouldn't be out."

"Like us?" Nick almost regretted the remark when LaCroix glanced at him sharply, but his hoarse comment earned him a grim smile.

"At least we're working for a cause, instead of scavenging." He matched his steps to Nick's pace. "There's one less vampire feeding off the streets."

"One less . . . *vampire*." Nick tasted the words and found them odd, but vaguely familiar. He met LaCroix's defiant gaze.

"That, too." LaCroix's smile sharpened. "One less criminal parasite feeding illegally from our people *and* one less vampire. Convenient, wouldn't you say?"

As the sun set, the city began to prepare for the appearance of the night people. Nick stared into the storefront windows with open curiosity. Of the half-dozen former restaurants they passed, not one was open. The grocery stores seemed closed or were closing, except for the ones that carried signs advertising the availability of blood. The owners gave them hurried, suspicious looks as they lowered protective awnings or locked their doors, mopped the sweat from their brows, and scurried away in the prelude to twilight.

There were too many windows darkened or boarded up, too many buildings that were little more than silent sentinels. With the exodus of the shopkeepers who traded only with mortals, the streets were becoming even more desolate. Yet Nick felt eyes watching them from the buildings as they moved through the hot, sunlit streets. A steady hum filled the air from the machinery that kept the interiors of the buildings cold and dark during the daylight hours.

For *them*.

Nick was surprised at the vehemence of the thought, the bitter bile that rose at the back of his throat. He wanted to ask a hundred questions—a thousand questions—about why vampires like he and Vachon and LaCroix could stand in the sun without burning, why his senses seemed dull and his muscles weak.

There was only one answer that made any sense.

Somehow he—they—had become mortal. It explained the wounds that hadn't healed, the dullness of his senses, and the loss of the strength he took for granted as a vampire. It explained his ability to walk in the light without burning. But how that had happened, and when, and why all of this seemed so natural to him remained a mystery. Maybe it was the blow to the head—had his memories been scattered by his injury?

Nick barely noticed when Vachon appeared again, waving an all-clear about a block ahead of them before disappearing around another corner. Forcing himself to concentrate helped, but the pounding in his skull grew louder and more insistent. He needed to rest, to sleep. . . .

LaCroix tightened his grip on Nick's shoulder and whispered, "Just half a block more. You can do it—I've seen you do better. Then again, that was when you had one of them at your back, trying to rip out your throat. Another block, and then you'll rest."

It was at least three blocks before they turned down a side alley—LaCroix had stretched the truth more than a little. Nick rested his weight against the wall, waiting while LaCroix knocked on a heavy metal door. He closed his eyes and leaned his head against the side of the building, then was dismayed to find that even the brick was warm. Sunset wasn't bringing any relief from the oppressive heat, and sweat was running down his back and face in small streams. It would be good to get inside, to sit down, to close his eyes and—

The series of raps on the metal door was in a sequence that seemed all too familiar and didn't ease the pounding in his skull, booming like thunder. Nick opened his eyes as he heard the door scrape open, and lurched toward the beckoning darkness. LaCroix grabbed his arm, as did someone else who darted out the door, the pair catching him and preventing him from falling to the ground. Between them, they dragged Nick inside, out of the heat and fading sunlight.

It was cool and dim in the basement of the building. Once inside, Nick felt a wall against his back and slid down to the floor; the distant smell of a stew cooking made him nauseous. The heavy metal door groaned as it was pushed back into place, and he looked up as he heard sounds indicating that long metal pipes had been dropped into holders on either side of the door frame. Nothing short of an explosion would make it through that door until those pipes were removed.

Vachon squatted beside him and thrust a flask into his hands.

The water was lukewarm. Nick grimaced after the first swig, then handed the flask back. He met Vachon's eyes, but Vachon only smiled. "No beer; you might be on duty tonight. Can't have you arrested for DWI, now can we?"

Before Nick could answer, a shadow fell across them— LaCroix. He reached a hand down to Nick. "No rest for the weary."

"Or the wicked." Nick took LaCroix's hand and was hauled to his feet. His free hand went immediately to the wall, bracing himself as the world seemed to tilt on him again. He closed his eyes, his stomach churning with the sudden vertigo.

"See!" protested Vachon sharply. "There's no way he's going out tonight. Have him call in sick. He can't even *stand*, for God's sake."

"He has to go—for *our* sake," was LaCroix's firm but quiet answer. "There'll have been a report by then. They'll never suspect him if he shows up for his shift. We need him on that shift tonight. You know that."

"What if they know about that vampire today? What if they know about all this? About everything?"

"I'll be *fine*," snapped Nick. He opened his eyes, pushed himself away from the wall, and pretended to be far more steady on his feet than he felt. He met Vachon's frankly disbelieving gaze with a glare. "I'm going in."

"What if they know . . . about you?"

"They don't. And they won't," answered Nick with conviction. He grinned at Vachon. "Don't you trust me?"

"You—yes." Vachon cast a quick look at LaCroix over his shoulder, then met Nick's gaze again. He seemed about to say something more when LaCroix placed a hand on his arm.

"Get Urs," ordered LaCroix. "I want her to take a look at that head wound."

Vachon froze, then deliberately shrugged LaCroix's hand off his arm. His dark eyes held Nick's for a moment. "You take too many chances."

Then he turned and headed down the corridor at a run.

Nick started to follow Vachon, but LaCroix placed a hand on his shoulder, stopping him. "You've got work to do. Ready for the gauntlet?"

Nick raised an eyebrow and glanced at LaCroix, then down the corridor, not knowing what to expect.

"You're a hero to them," said LaCroix. "Remember that."

Nick slowly made his way down the corridor, supported by LaCroix's grasp on his left bicep. A few wan fluorescent lights flickered here, revealing faces of all ages and sexes that were vaguely familiar. Nick couldn't attach names to them, but he knew that this child and that had been orphaned, this woman had run from a husband who had turned, and that man, conscripted for "blood work," had fled here to escape his fate. There were so many refugees here, in corridors and basement rooms, and other places, that he couldn't know them all. He rarely saw them, working as he did on the night shift at the police station. No matter how many he tried to meet, there seemed to be more each day.

Many more.

Even though they appeared adequately fed and wore clean clothing, the eyes of a few still burned angrily, defiant to the last; the rest were mostly the same—hollow and glazed, shell-shocked.

Except when he passed. For an instant he saw a flicker of life return. The children smiled or stared at him wide-eyed, stopping their play in the middle of the corridor and backing away. A woman paused in a doorway and mouthed, "Bless you"; a child clung to the tails of the man's shirt that she was wearing. Another man, reading what passed for a newspaper these days, looked up from a chair at another doorway and gave Nick a grim nod, which he returned.

It occurred to him that they knew what he had done that afternoon, that he'd helped to kill a vampire. And that tonight he planned on leaving the relative safety of this place to work among and for the vampires in an attempt to keep this safe haven intact for a little while longer. To them, he was a symbol. As LaCroix had said, a hero.

He didn't feel like much of a hero. Nor did he want to be one.

It seemed an eternity until they paused. LaCroix pushed open a door, flicked on a light, and led him inside a stark room that contained a chair, a bed, and a small chest of drawers. Nick stumbled to the bed and sat heavily on the mattress, nearly falling over when it sank beneath him.

Sitting on the edge of the bed, his head in his hands, he closed his eyes and wondered why all of this seemed so strange . . . and yet so familiar. He dropped his hands from his face when a hand touched his arm—LaCroix.

Squatting beside the mattress, he eyed Nick suspiciously. "Are you well enough to go in?"

Nick wondered, for a moment, if he might tell LaCroix the truth—this was not where he belonged; he had no idea what had happened, how they had become mortal. But the memory of those faces in the corridor and the ones unseen, the lost fathers and mothers, sons and daughters, gave him pause. He knew these people. Hell, he'd been the one who'd saved Vachon from a donation center when the boy was fifteen and had been caught throwing Molotov cocktails into vampires' resting places. He had a history here. He had a life here.

Was the other world, a world of mortals in which he was a vampire, just a dream? A delusion due to a crack on the back of the head?

There was a sound at the door—he and LaCroix looked up at the intrusion. Vachon stood against the door frame, hands in his pockets, his expression sullen. Beside him stood Urs, blonde, bright, and cherubic, a large leather bag hanging from a strap that rested over her shoulder. "Heard you boys had a little trouble," she said brightly.

"A little," admitted Nick, as Urs crossed the room to his side. "But nothing Vachon couldn't handle."

Refusing to meet Nick's eyes, Vachon looked down at the floor. "At least I know how to duck."

The bed shifted beneath Nick as Urs placed one knee on the mattress, the bag falling open beside her. "Head and shoulder?" There was a pull on the back of his T-shirt and Nick caught the bright gleam of scissors out of the corner of his eye just before he heard the snip of cloth. "This doesn't look too bad," she added a moment later. But then her fingers lightly investigated the back of his scalp and Nick winced. "Nothing broken—just a scrape."

He looked away when he smelled the antiseptic, knowing that the head and arm wounds would sting like crazy. His gaze turned to LaCroix, who had risen to his feet, was watching him carefully . . . and was still waiting for a response.

That's when he knew he could give only one answer. Oddly enough, his head was starting to clear—he didn't feel dizzy any longer, and the pounding had lessened. "I'll have to show up for my shift. If I'm not there, they'll check on me. We don't want them looking at this place too—oww!— closely."

Urs grinned as Nick swung his head around to look at her. Brandishing the antiseptic and a bloody cotton pad, she held her hands up in mock surrender. "Do you want to walk into work bleeding from a head wound, or not?"

"Not," he decided, after enough of a moment's pause to cause her grin to widen further. Then he turned his attention back to LaCroix, suddenly making sense of Vachon's earlier protest in the hallway. "You've got something planned tonight, haven't you? Today wasn't enough?"

"Nothing to concern you." Clasping one hand into a fist, LaCroix appeared to be examining the thickness and odd angle of his twisted fingers as they curled. "We have to get as many of them as we can before that artificial blood plant comes on-line. After that, we'll only be a nuisance to them. And you either hide nuisances . . . or you exterminate them."

"But they'll need us for replacements . . . well, accidents *do* happen," Vachon retorted, shifting his position against the door frame when LaCroix smiled at his sudden delicacy. "And they'll need to keep their population constant. Which means they'll have to keep us around."

"They'll try—as slaves, not as equals. And you forget the hunt provides a certain amount of pleasure for them. They'll want to keep a few of us on hand for that. Not to mention thugs for daylight activities."

Nick raised his hand and said, "Guilty," in a light tone, then paused in wonderment. Why on earth had he said that?

But LaCroix didn't seem to notice his lapse of memory. Nodding, he met Nick's eyes. "Yes, but for how long? You've been too good at what you do—the fact that they took you off day patrol and put you on night duty so quickly should tell you that much. Vampires in power have started to notice you. I wouldn't be surprised if they offered to turn you. And soon."

There was a startled gasp from Urs. She looked away when they glanced at her, pretending to repack the medical kit. "You're fine. I put some sealant on it. It'll be tender, but they shouldn't notice anything out of the ordinary. Your shirt will hide the patch on your arm. A fall down the stairs will probably cover any questions."

He caught her hand in his, allowing his fingers to intertwine with hers. "Thanks."

Smiling sadly, she pulled her fingers from his grasp. "If you'd be more careful, I wouldn't need to patch you up so often." Snapping the kit closed, Urs rose from the mattress, then paused and eyed Nick thoughtfully. "Be careful tonight."

"I will," he promised.

Her smile was even sadder, and he knew she'd recognized the lie—he'd do what he had to do. Just as they all did. Personal safety wasn't an issue when the lives of so many were involved.

Urs walked over to Vachon and lightly ran her fingers along his bare arm. "Walk me out?" she asked softly.

Ignoring LaCroix's murmur of impatience, Nick met Vachon's gaze. "You can hang for a bit, can't you?" He was the one who had saved Vachon, had raised him like a younger brother. There'd been no time to talk lately, not when so many rogue vampires like the one they'd destroyed this afternoon were hunting mortals indiscriminately. There was something Vachon wanted to tell him, wanted to talk about.

But Vachon's eyes went to LaCroix; then he looked at the ground again. "I don't think I want to hear what's going to be said," he answered, almost angrily. His dark eyes met Nick's again, this time filled with sadness and edged with fear. "Be *very* careful, Nick. Walk in the light."

"I will," he answered, but Vachon was already gone, his arm around Urs's waist, their voices, soft in conversation, echoing from the hall.

"He'd be devastated if anything happened to you," said LaCroix, as Nick's eyes followed Vachon's departure from the room. "But he'd survive. Out of all of us, I think he's the one most likely to make it through this—or turn at the first chance they give him."

"No," said Nick reflexively, glaring at LaCroix. "Vachon would *never* turn—"

"Most of them would, if given a chance. Remember that, Nicholas. Remember that, when you're standing among your 'friends' on the force, trying to ignore their jokes about mortals, their hungry eyes and their hard stares. Remember that the people whose lives we guard can be trusted only so far—and no farther."

Still holding his gaze, Nick thought back to the people he'd seen in the hallway, their eyes. . . . "There are some I'd trust with my life."

"Never trust anyone with your life," warned LaCroix, sharply. "Anyone."

"But Vachon—and you—"

"Not Vachon. And not me." LaCroix smiled, his lips drawing into a thin, grim line. "Especially not me. But for God's sake, don't trust any of *them*. They're predators, Nick. Remember that, too. And when they make you the offer—"

"They won't."

"They *will*," insisted LaCroix, his eyes burning. "When they offer to turn you, think about it."

Nick looked down at the floor and shook his head. "You can't be ser—"

"Think about it." LaCroix placed a hand on his shoulder to get his attention, his smile still grim. "You'd better get washed and dressed. You'll be going on shift soon."

Their conversation faltered as they became aware of a presence at the door.

The girl was no older than eight, hair braided in small, neat cornrows accented with tiny red ribbons. Her clothing was clean, though well worn—a Blue Jays T-shirt and denim shorts against dark skin. Wide-eyed, she had one hand on the door frame, as if she were a skittish bird ready to fly at the first sign of danger. She was one of the casualties in this war—the mortal child of the vampire police captain Nick served under, Captain Reese.

"Come in, Lindy," said LaCroix. He gestured toward Nick. "He's fine."

A lopsided smile lit her face as Lindy took a step into the room, her eyes glued to Nick. He noticed that she left a wide berth between herself and LaCroix. "Momma said they brought you in. I was worried."

"I'm fine," repeated Nick. To prove it, he managed to rise from the mattress without wincing, though a quick glance at LaCroix told him that he hadn't fooled everyone in the room.

But at least she smiled, shyly. Then her eyes grew dark and serious. "I wanted to know—you're gonna see Dad tonight, right?"

LaCroix sighed and took a step toward her, his hand raised to place on her shoulder. "Lindy, we've talked about this before—"

Nick saw her flinch and wedged his way between them, placing his own hand on Lindy's shoulder. Meeting LaCroix's

34

gaze, he nodded toward the door. "I'll see you when my shift's over."

"All right." LaCroix hesitated for a moment, glancing down at the girl, then turned on his heel and stalked out without another word.

Nick felt Lindy's shoulder relax beneath his hand. Gesturing toward the mattress, he said, "Have a seat."

She sat down, looked toward the door, then back to Nick. Shaking his head, Nick rubbed his chin with his hand. "Lindy, I understand why you're angry at LaCroix—"

"He wants my Daddy dead," she answered sharply. When he met her eyes again, she looked away. Her hands were clasped tightly together in her lap, and she dug at the cement floor with the toe of her sneaker. "It wasn't Daddy's fault. He didn't want to turn. Even you said so."

The eyes that fixed on his wanted comfort, reassurance. Seating himself beside her, Nick met that gaze evenly. "I'll say it again. A lot of the police didn't want to turn, Lindy, your dad among them. But they'd passed the new laws. With more and more vampires being made each day and more and more of us getting killed . . . somebody had to take the job. He wanted you and your mom to be safe."

"I know." Lindy looked down as her sneaker scraped the concrete. "Mom cries a lot. She tries to pretend she doesn't, but she misses him."

"At least you know where your dad is. And that he still loves you and your mom. Some people aren't that lucky."

Her chin moved, and he realized that her gaze had gone to the doorway. "Like him?"

"LaCroix?" Nick hesitated, but when her eyes sought his again, he nodded. "Yes, like LaCroix. His family, all of his family, were killed back in the first uprisings. That's why you're here, why we're here. He wanted to make sure that didn't happen to anyone else."

"And that's why they hurt him?"

Nick winced at her words, glad that her eyes weren't on

him. How simple it sounded from a child's lips—the crushing of a concert musician's hand as punishment for hiding refugees had gone deeper than "hurt." They'd taken his wife, his child, his brother . . . even his music . . . but they hadn't killed him. And that had been their one mistake.

"That's why." Her eyes met his again, and he wondered if she really understood. He and Lindy and Lindy's mom saw their situation in shades of gray—knowing, trusting, even loving those who had been turned. But they were outnumbered by LaCroix and those who had been all but destroyed by the vampires in a hundred different ways. For them, it was a war, the survivors being mortals or vampires. There could be no compromise.

And yet . . . LaCroix wanted him to consider being turned, if the offer was made.

"Oh," said Lindy suddenly, her hand going to the pocket of her shorts, "I was s'posed to give you something." She pulled a small wicker doll from her pocket and placed it in the palm of his hand. "It's a good luck charm."

Nick started, knowing that he'd seen something like it before. "Where did you get this?"

"Some lady—one of the ones passing through." Lindy's wistful expression let him know in no uncertain terms what her feelings were about the ones who "passed through" the number of sanctuaries they'd set up in the city. There were places the law of the vampires hadn't reached yet, rural areas where mortals were still in control and arming themselves against this new world order of the night.

Nick turned the doll over in his hand—it was small, with a brightly colored cloth for a dress, black painted hair, two dots for eyes and a small red circle for a mouth. He had no idea who it might be from. Unless . . . Janette?

His breath caught in his throat when he thought of her—Janette had brought him to LaCroix back in the beginning, when the panic became worldwide. Riots were the order of the day, food was scarce, and the vampires hadn't begun to reorganize society in their own image. Blood ran through the streets—human blood by night and vampire blood by day.

He'd been alone then, his mother and sister gone, just struggling to survive. It was Janette who had stumbled across him, Janette who had taken him into her bed and her heart, Janette who had led him to LaCroix and the great work of the resistance and protection of the mortal refugees.

And Janette who had disappeared, without a trace, not so very long ago.

"What did she look like?" he asked softly. He didn't want to hope, didn't dream of hoping that she might still be alive. . . .

"Really pretty lady. Her dress was green—it matched her eyes—and she had dark hair. She said it was a good luck charm."

Not Janette, then. Janette's eyes were blue. Very blue.

Oblivious to his disappointment, Lindy reached over and touched the doll with her finger, flipping it onto its back so that it rocked in the palm of his hand. "I asked Mom if I could have a green dress like that when I grow up. She said yes. But she cried."

Nick looked up at the child's face, seeing her puzzled frown. There wasn't a mother here who didn't cry, knowing that she couldn't promise her children anything, not even that there'd be a tomorrow. This was why he took the risks. This was what he'd tell Vachon—that it was for the children and the widows, the dispossessed and the lost that he took the risks.

But was Vachon right? Was he foolish to risk his life on LaCroix's crusade to rid the world of vampires? How many of these people could he really save before he was caught? How many of these children, who trusted him completely, did he endanger each time he walked into that police

37

precinct, not knowing if he was going to be arrested for participating in the vampire resistance movement?

Lindy looked up at him. "Nick . . . will you see Dad tonight?"

Swallowing the lump in his throat, he gave a noncommittal shrug and tucked the doll into his pants pocket. "Maybe."

"Will you tell Dad—tell him I love him? And that I'm okay. And Mom's okay."

"I will," he promised, mentally crossing his fingers. The less Joe Reese knew about the whereabouts of his family, the better it was for all concerned.

Lindy frowned, seeming to sense his hesitancy. "Cross your heart?"

"And hope to die," he responded, crossing his chest with his finger, then holding it up in a pledge.

That seemed to satisfy her. She nodded, then grabbed his hand with her own. "I guess you'd better get going, huh?"

"If I'm gonna make it to work on time."

Impulsively she hugged him, then turned and ran from the room.

Nick sat a moment, then sighed and pressed his protesting muscles into action. He headed down the corridor to the fire stairs. Cautiously making his way past the booby traps, he slipped down the rear service corridor, then took another set of stairs up to his apartment. With the sun going down, he had no fear the few other tenants who didn't know about the refugees in the basement would be around—this building housed only mortals, and no mortal with any sense went outside after sunset. Even if they questioned his coming and going at this hour, he'd made a habit of being seen jogging before work.

Nick fitted the key in the lock of his apartment door, entered the foyer, and glanced around to make certain nothing had been touched. The windows were blocked and boarded from the inside, but he didn't bother hitting the lights as he wandered through the living room to the bedroom. As far as vampire surveillance would know, he'd been in all day. And no mortal was going to contradict the story of a cop . . . even if that cop happened to be one of the few mortal day-patrol members on temporary night assignment.

The sight of the made bed and the scent of the clean cotton sheets when he entered the room brought a smile to his face—Mrs. Reese's work, no doubt. She'd adopted him as her special project, and no matter how much she grumbled about his bachelor habits or her own workload, she considered it a source of pride that he could always expect clean sheets and a clean apartment. He often thought it was one of the things that kept her from going completely over the edge. Captain Joe Reese had been a lucky man— when he'd been mortal.

Nick walked to the bed and threw himself on it, planning to grab the few minutes' sleep he could before he had to shower, shave, and dress for his second job—in the night world. But before his head could hit the pillow, the buzzer on the alarm clock on the bedside table sounded, the noise insistent enough to wake the—

Nick sat up in bed, the black silk sheets sliding from him. He stared wildly around at his surroundings, leaped to the floor, then knocked the clock off the table with one hand as he made his way to the bedroom door.

The buzzing stopped when the clock ricocheted from the wall and crashed to the floor, shattering into plastic and metal bits. Ignoring it, he threw open the bedroom door and walked to the upper railing of the loft.

Everything in his home was where he'd left it before he'd gone to sleep early this morning—the shutters were still drawn against the daylight, the latch on the elevator access remained locked, the message light was not blinking on his answering machine. It was still dark and quiet.

He was still a vampire.

Wearily, Nick ran his hand across his eyes and yawned, trying to get his bearings. He felt like he'd been hit by a truck. Whatever he'd dreamed, it hadn't left him at all rested.

The memories flooded back, swirling in his conscious mind like a sudden tsunami—oppressive heat and the smell of burning and decaying flesh, the tepid water, the eyes of frightened children. He grabbed the railing for support, dizzy, then felt the top edge of it bend beneath his hand as his vampire strength easily twisted the metal. Alarmed, he released the rail in panic and backed into the wall—but that brought back the memory of waking in the dark, his head throbbing.

His hands at his temples, Nick stumbled back into the bedroom, barely noticing the bits of broken clock that he brushed out of his way or that cut his bare feet. Two worlds collided in his mind, melded, and became one, the contradictions tearing at him.

Then he spotted the dream doll sitting on the bedside table. He picked it up.

And the memories receded. There was only this world, the world in which he was a vampire, the world in which he worked as a detective in a police department, the world that was ruled by mortals.

Closing his eyes, Nick breathed deeply, able to think clearly again. When he opened his eyes, the room was still the same. Numbly, he sat down on the bed, staring at the small wicker doll in the palm of his hand.

One leg was bent upward at an awkward angle, toward the chest. Gingerly, Nick tried to move the leg back down—he was certain it had been straight when he went to sleep last night—but it wouldn't budge. After a few seconds, he gave up and put the doll to one side, afraid he would break it. As soon as he showered, shaved, and dressed, it was going back in the box. A call to a delivery service would take it back to New York and out of his life forever.

Not that he believed the doll had anything to do with his dream. It was his own unease that had caused this, his own questioning about who he was and where he truly belonged that had brought about the nightmare. It was gone now.

But getting rid of the doll wouldn't hurt.

By the time he got out of the shower and was dressed, he was late for work. Nick hurried down the stairs, the doll in his hand, then saw the blinking light on his answering machine. Cursing under his breath, he checked the downstairs clock and realized just how late he was.

The message was from Tracy, his partner; he must have missed it while he was in the shower. "Nick, we've got a call at fifteen-o-seven Westmore. It sounds like a domestic dispute gone bad. I'll meet you there."

Nick fast-forwarded the message tape but that was his only call. "Fifteen-o-seven Westmore," he repeated, shoving the doll into his pocket and heading for the door.

3

AT OTHER TIMES, NICK MIGHT HAVE ENJOYED THE DRIVE TO fifteen-o-seven Westmore. The neighborhood was residential, barely within his jurisdiction. There was something soothing about cruising the empty streets at night: lights glowing from behind curtains and blinds as the inhabitants ended their day with a meal, conversation, or, what seemed to be even more likely, several hours parked on a couch, watching the flicker of a television screen and enduring a laugh track or movie or sports program.

He'd even stopped and parked once or twice, when he'd had a night off and had decided to spend it driving aimlessly. Then he'd get out of the car and walk, block after block, envying these people their simple, ordinary mortal lives. A dog would bark now and then, perhaps a blind would be raised and an elderly woman dressed in a housecoat, curlers in her hair, would peer nervously into the street, then drop the blind hurriedly if he waved and smiled.

They had no idea what they had—comfort, security, family . . . unconditional love. And if they worried about mortgages and credit cards and orthodontists' bills, what of it? He would have traded his abnormally acute senses, his longevity, his experience, his strength, even the ability to fly for the peace of a normal, mortal life.

But he didn't have that option. When he'd accepted LaCroix's offer of immortality eight centuries ago, he'd left humanity and all that it offered far behind. These people were right to bar their doors and cover their windows, hiding from the darkness. Somehow, perhaps instinctively, they knew death lurked outside their snug homes. The well-dressed, well-groomed man who strolled their sidewalks had blood on his hands— he was a killer.

How could he ever become one of them again?

But the dream lingered. As he drove through the early evening darkness, he glanced down at his hands, remembering them scraped and warmed by the sun. It had only been a dream, after all, taunting him with what he could never have. Perhaps that was the message of the dream doll: that if mortality was his heart's desire, it would always be beyond his reach.

Yet another reason to pack the thing in an envelope and send it back to New York, before it sapped all of his hope. Perhaps this was one box that even Pandora would have known enough to leave tightly shut.

There were a few sawhorses connected by yellow crime scene tape at strategic points on the snow-covered lawn. Despite the cold, he saw several neighbors lingering, coats thrown over pajamas and robes, some with towels or scarves or hats on their heads, their warm mortal breath exhaled in wisps of white, chilled smoke as they spoke among themselves. The police were still there, navy blue uniforms stark against the snow. The photographer's flash punctuated the scene as he snapped pictures of the two bodies. Nick saw Natalie exiting the house as he drove by, then spotted Tracy's car . . . but there was no sign of Tracy.

After parking the Caddie, he was hurrying to the crime scene when a snippet of conversation caught his attention— Tracy's voice.

". . . can't tell me you think they'd be better now than when they were—?"

Pausing, he glanced casually left and right, trying to pinpoint her position by using his heightened sense of hearing. There—half a block away. He could see her fawn-colored jacket and white scarf, the blonde of her hair bright against the darkness of the evergreen shrub behind her. Someone else was with her, a shadow in black leather and jeans who moved just enough so the streetlight illuminated his face—pale skin, *very* pale, a mass of unruly black hair, and a scruff of a beard.

Vachon.

"They'd have to be better now," was Vachon's response. "Tracy, they were *kids* back then—they were lucky they knew more than one chord."

"I really *would* like to see them perform live." He heard the regret in her voice. "My dad, well, you can guess that no little girl of his was going to any rock concert. And by the time I was old enough to get out on my own, they weren't touring anymore."

"We'll go, then."

"*You* can get tickets? But they're sold out!"

"Trust me." Vachon's voice was smug; he placed a hand on Tracy's shoulder, pushing her back with a light touch. "Tickets aren't a problem. You want floor seats, right?"

"Floor seats?" Tracy's voice positively squeaked in disbelief, then it lowered and she moved toward him. "This isn't some sort of . . . ? I mean, you guys don't have your own Ticketmaster? It's not like one of the band is a—"

Nick tucked his hands in his pockets and hurried across the sidewalk to the crime scene, slipping between the taped sawhorses. The chill that had run through him had nothing to do with the cold—his body normally wasn't that sensitive to his environment.

Tracy Vetter was his partner. She'd worked her way up through the ranks, helped along by promotions pushed by her father, the police commissioner; but she was still young, still inexperienced in the ways of the streets, in the hard lessons that one learned about life and death when homicide was a nightly occurrence. She was mortal.

And she knew that vampires existed. She didn't know that *he* was a vampire—he'd managed to keep his true nature secret from her—but she knew more than enough about them through her continued association with Javier Vachon.

Nick managed a grim smile for the officers he encountered, then stepped as close as he dared to the first body. Natalie Lambert was kneeling in the snow on the other side, bundled up in her coat but not wearing a hat. Her hands were in latex gloves as she reached down.

The first thing he saw was the blood, the smell striking up at him like a knife through the clear, crisp air. The victim was female, late middle age, but he barely noticed the wide, staring eyes and the open mouth, except for the specks of blood that were scattered across the pale and cooling skin. It was her chest that drew his attention, a gaping, bloody mixture of flesh and organs and bone dotted with black specks.

"Shotgun at close range," said Natalie almost absently. "My guess is she walked out the door onto the front steps and turned. He shot her, and the blast threw her out here." She glanced up at him, then her eyes narrowed and she started to rise. "Nick? Are you—?"

"Fine," he answered, his words clipped and sharp. "I'm fine." He turned as he spoke and raised his hand to his mouth. He couldn't escape them—the onlookers were all around the perimeter of the crime scene, perfectly ordinary people.

Just like the woman lying on the ground with a hole blown through her chest. The difference, of course, was that she was dead, her flesh and blood growing cold.

The others were still warm.

He heard Natalie remove her latex gloves and then her hand was on his arm. She led him to one side, but he could still see both of the bodies. "I assume the—husband?—shot her," guessed Nick.

"That's the theory. I heard Tracy taking statements from the neighbors." She gestured over her shoulder toward an elderly woman and man speaking with a uniformed officer. "They heard an argument—didn't seem to be anything out of the ordinary for these two, lately. But it got loud. The neighbors were about to call the police when they heard the gunshots. Her, then him."

A glance in the direction of the other body was enough— part of the head was missing. "Gun in the mouth?"

"Suicide," said Natalie sadly. "He had an old service revolver. Dropped the shotgun, walked back inside, picked up the handgun. . . ." Then she started and looked around. "Where's Tracy? She should be telling you this. There she is!"

Tracy was trudging across the lawn, her boots sliding slightly on the snow, until she reached the shoveled walk, then sliding again as she walked toward them across another expanse of snow. She met Nick's gaze with a guilty expression, then gave a shrug when she arrived. "Sorry—I was meeting with a snitch. Natalie fill you in?"

"I thought that was supposed to be *your* job."

"That's my cue," said Natalie quickly, backing away. "This one's cut and dried, guys. If you need anything, like the autopsy reports or a referee, let me know. I'm in the book."

Tracy's cheeks were flushed, and she glared at him. "I'll accept an apology."

"That would be nice—if I were offering one." He turned and walked even further from the scene, knowing that she would be following, then paused as she drew abreast of him. "Have we got a motive on this?"

"Hang on a minute—we're not done yet." Tracy moved so that she was standing in front of him. "I've got a right to meet my informants when and where I feel I have to meet them."

"Not when you're the primary at a crime scene. Stories change, you know that. We've got to get here and get people to talk as soon as we can, while it's still fresh in their minds and before they have a chance to change their story."

"I know that. So does everyone else who's finished the interview techniques course at the academy." She still glared at him. "I was having a meet when I got the call. He came along."

Nick raised an eyebrow. "You brought your informant to a crime scene?"

She was wrong. They both knew she was wrong. Tracy looked away. "Okay. So maybe it wasn't a good idea. I couldn't get rid of him. I'm sorry. It won't happen again."

Tracy turned to head back to the scene, but Nick caught her arm, stopping her. "You couldn't get rid of him?"

She stopped, waited until he dropped her arm, then glanced over her shoulder at him. "Yeah."

"That guy—" He paused, as if searching his memory for the name, then met her gaze. "Vachon?"

Her eyelashes flickered and she looked away. "You saw him?"

"He's the only one of your snitches I've met." Nick dropped her arm. "Be careful with him, Tracy. I've—I've used him in the past. He's not completely reliable. He's not . . . safe."

She looked back at him quickly, and he saw the question in her eyes—did he know Vachon's secret? Did he know that Vachon was a vampire? "What do you mean, *not* safe?"

"I mean that maybe I'd be careful to check everything he told me—twice. That I'd meet him in a public place, or near a public place if he's skittish. That I'd watch my back." His voice was quiet and certain—he wasn't trying to hypnotize her, just warn her off. "I'm not saying you don't know what you're doing, but you've got to be careful. Sometimes we

48

get caught up in the lives of informants. It's a business transaction—information only. Anything else . . . and somebody's going to get hurt."

He knew that she wanted to come back at him—one of her gloved hands was clenched into a fist. But she wasn't a spoiled little girl—she was a cop. She gave him a faint smile and the benefit of experience. "Okay. I'll be careful. If you promise to stop protecting me like the baby sister you never had." There was a curious look in her eyes as she regarded him. "Assuming you *didn't* have a baby sister."

He'd always been careful not to talk too much about himself, his past, his family. It was safer that way, easier to make certain that his explanations matched the facts on his meticulously forged documentation and records. He remembered some vague reference somewhere about Detective Nicholas Knight not having any living relations. That, insofar as it went, was true.

"I did have a sister," he admitted. "But it was a long time ago." With a sigh, Nick raised his head and looked over the crime scene again, ignoring the curiosity in her eyes. "Let's clean up here and get this one back to the station."

Tracy nodded, trying to match his pace through the snow. "Senseless, something like this. They'd been married thirty years."

"Thirty years?" Nick paused as two of the coroner's attendants walked past them, carrying a bagged corpse on a stretcher. He looked down at the place where the body had lain, marked by spots and pools of blood in the snow and on the shoveled walk.

It was a blink of an eye to him, but almost half a mortal lifetime. Thirty years of companionship ending in an argument, two gunshots, and a neighborhood spectacle.

"I want to know why this happened," he said softly. "I need to know why."

Within a half hour, he knew. Or knew as much as anyone could know, the participants having been bagged and taken to the coroner's lab in no condition to speak with anyone. Tracy had gone and Nick pulled his car away from the curb, his thoughts focused on the fragility of human life, on blood on the snow, on a dare that had sent a young boy off a tower and into the darkness.

He pumped his brakes lightly at the next stop sign, leery of skidding on the icy road. Vachon appeared out of nowhere, standing in the road in front of the car. With a muttered curse, Nick spun the wheel to avoid him, the car skidding slightly to the left.

Vachon never turned a hair. He stood there for a moment, grinning. Then he approached the right side of the car.

Leaning across the seat, Nick rolled down the passenger window and barked, "Get in."

For a moment he thought he was going to get an argument. Vachon planted his fingers on the roof of the Caddie and leaned in at the window, his eyes angry. But then he shrugged, opened the door, and slipped onto the seat beside Nick.

"Close the window," Nick ordered.

"Afraid you'll catch a cold?"

"Close it."

Again there was an instant of hesitation, of defiance. Nick knew that he had no authority over Vachon, had no right to order him to do anything. Their first encounter had been a matter of old-fashioned physical intimidation—Nick had drawn on the weight of eight hundred years of vampire strength and menace and there'd been no contest. After that they'd become acquaintances, camaraderie verging on friendship from time to time.

He was willing to risk that, to destroy that if need be. Tracy's safety mattered more.

Vachon rolled up the window. "I heard what you said to Trace—look, it *was* my fault. I wouldn't get out of her car and—"

"That's not the point." He glanced at Vachon, then pulled

the car back onto the street. "You're supposed to be protecting her."

"Do I look like anybody's guardian angel?" Vachon turned innocent eyes to him, holding out his hands—he was wearing leather biker's gloves with the fingers missing. "Hell's Angel, maybe."

"You know what I mean."

Vachon slumped low in the seat, his knees resting against the glove compartment and the dashboard. "None of the Enforcers have come sniffing around, asking questions. In fact, nobody's taken a second look at her. And Tracy's got enough sense not to be sticking that pretty little nose where it doesn't belong."

"So you're saying she's safe from the community."

"I'm saying there's nothing to protect her from."

"Except you."

Now the soles of Vachon's boots were flat against the glove compartment, his knees tucked close to his chest as he slid a little higher on the seat. "Meaning?"

"You know what happens when we get close to mortals." Nick turned the wheel of the Caddie hard, cutting short a turn and slamming Vachon against the passenger door. "You've been seeing her."

Vachon planted his feet on the floor and leaned his back against the passenger side door. He rubbed the side of his face with his hand, but the bruise from his unexpected contact with the door was already fading. "That's none of your business. You're not Tracy's keeper."

"I'm her partner," Nick said sharply, giving Vachon a cold glance to emphasize the word. "As far as you're concerned, I *am* her keeper. Up to now you've been keeping an eye on her for me, and I appreciate it. But she knows all she should about vampires. Too much, maybe. Discussing vampires can't help."

"We don't talk just about vampires," defended Vachon.

51

He grinned when Nick looked at him, and folded his arms defiantly. "Sometimes we don't 'talk' at all."

"I want you to drop her."

"Drop her?" Vachon's voice was incredulous. "Off what, the CN Tower?"

"If you care about her, you'll let her go. And if you don't care about her, it won't be any hardship to stop seeing her, right?"

"I can*not* believe that you're serious." There was a pause, then he heard Vachon chuckle. When he looked over, the vampire had slumped back down again, arms folded across his chest. "Now *this* is rich. You and Dr. Lambert have had a thing going for—how many years? I walked in at intermission, remember?"

"This isn't about Natalie. This is about you and Tracy," said Nick, with more than a hint of annoyance. He glanced out the driver's side window, then coaxed the car into another turn at an icy intersection. They were almost there. "There's no comparison." He glanced at Vachon, and seeing a wide-eyed stare of disbelief, added defensively, "There *isn't.*"

"You can't see it, can you?" Sitting up, Vachon turned his body so that he faced the car door. "No, you wouldn't."

"All I'm asking is that you let her down soon. Just back off. Stop seeing her."

"And what if she doesn't want to stop seeing me?"

"I'll deal with that."

Vachon chuckled again. "You'll try."

Nick pulled the car to the curb across the street from the boarded-up, abandoned church in which Vachon was living. "I'll deal with it," he repeated. The passenger side door opened, but before Vachon could escape, Nick grabbed the elbow of his jacket. "She's a mortal—you know how dangerous that can be. It's got to stop before it goes too far."

For a moment, Vachon met his eyes, then he glanced down at the restraining hand on his jacket. Nick released his grip and lifted his fingers slowly, knowing that he was probably in danger of having several broken if he didn't let go.

"Thanks," said Vachon, his voice low and without any sign of gratitude. "As far as this going too far, I think that ship's sailed. Say hi to Dr. Lambert for me, will you? I never got to thank her for what she did for Screed. And me."

The door slammed shut before Nick could move. There was a small blizzard outside the passenger window when Vachon lifted quickly into the air, taking the latest loose dusting of snow with him . . . until the flakes were slowly drawn down and settled to the ground one last time.

Nick slammed his fist against the steering wheel, then noticed a smudge on the passenger side window. Leaning closer, he realized that Vachon had drawn a heart in the ice on the window and placed a line through it, like an arrow. There were initials in the heart, but he pretended not to notice them. Unclipping his seat belt, Nick leaned across the seat and ran his hand through the smudge on the glass, destroying it.

For an instant he felt the chill of the icy water against his hand. Nick stared at the unexpected redness of his fingers, the color quickly fading beneath his gaze. Then he buckled up again and headed for the station.

He cursed himself in languages living and dead as he drove to the precinct, knowing that Vachon was right—he'd waited too long to separate him from Tracy. When the fever plague had swept through the community not so long ago and Vachon had fallen ill, he'd watched the two of them together. Hidden from view, he'd seen Tracy say her good-bye to someone she thought she'd never see again. And it had gladdened his heart for both their sakes that he'd been able to bring Natalie's cure to Vachon in time, however late it might have been for Vachon's friend Screed.

That's when it should have ended. There'd been no cost for the cure, no fee requested or exacted; he should have demanded that Vachon maintain the illusion of his death for Tracy's benefit. She was only mortal after all, fragile and easily broken. Why allow her to waste her time pursuing a relationship that could end only in her own destruction? Because that was the only possible outcome—a mortal who became involved with a vampire walked away, or was killed, or was brought across.

Tracy was his partner. Partners watched each other's backs, that's what his first partner, Don Schanke, had always said. Because he hadn't watched Schanke's back, Schanke was dead.

He wasn't about to lose another partner.

When he was parking his Caddie at the station, he again began to feel the effects of a day of unrestful dreams. Nick leaned his forehead on the steering wheel and yawned. It was so tempting to just nod off in the car—no one would even think to check on him out here. Just a catnap. . . .

But he still had the better part of a shift to get through, and the paperwork was piling up on his desk. If there had been any times in the past when he'd felt kinship with his mortal friends as they griped and groaned about the daily grind, right now would jump to the top of the list. With an effort, he opened the car door, then winced at the blast of cold air. It was just enough to rouse him, and he stumbled up the steps and into the 96th Precinct, already counting the hours until his shift was over and he could return to the comfortable darkness of his loft, slip between the black satin sheets on his bed, and pass out, dead to the world.

Every step of the walk into the building and through the bullpen felt like a mile. Not even bothering to peel off his frozen leather jacket, Nick fell into the chair behind his desk, leaned back, and covered his eyes with his hands. Then he heard Captain Reese call, "Knight?"

He fought back the groan that rose to his lips, forced his eyes open, and tried to look alert as Reese approached with a file folder in his hands. "Yeah, Cap?"

Reese looked him over, frowned, and backed up a step. "What happened to you? You look like hell."

"Feel like it, too." Nick wiped his hand across his face and suddenly noticed that Tracy wasn't at her desk, although her coat and scarf were hanging over the back of her chair. "And Tracy is—?"

"Powdering her nose." Reese seated himself on the edge of Tracy's desk. "She said the Westmore call wasn't a problem."

"For us, no. For the Torsiellos—?" He picked up a pencil lying on his blotter and replaced it in the pencil cup. "Husband and wife, married thirty years. Just another argument. No one took notice until a neighbor called in a report of gunshots. By then it was too late."

"That's a damn shame. Thirty years, huh?" Reese shook his head and tapped the file against his knee. When Nick looked down at it pointedly, he stared for a moment, then handed over the file with an even deeper frown. "You're not gonna want to see this right now, but we got a return from the Crown Attorney's office." When Nick grabbed the side of his desk in annoyance and started to leave his chair, Reese placed a hand on his shoulder and pushed him back. "No—sit. They want a little more detail on your pursuit statement."

"Detail?" Nick pulled the file from Reese's hand and opened it, flipping through the pages until he found the one he wanted. "Three pages. Three. And they want *more* detail?"

"They said they need it to make the resisting arrest charge stick. We don't give it to them, the perp'll walk on that one. Not to mention the fact that you used a 3379 form instead of a 3390—"

Nick stared at him a moment, looked down at the file, flipped a few more pages . . . and froze. They were right—he'd spent two hours filling in the wrong form. This time he didn't bother to stifle the sound of exasperation as he tossed the file onto his blotter.

Reese rose to his feet and pointed toward the file. "Don't let that sit—they need it tomorrow morning. The arraignment's at ten. Which means you get it done before the end of shift."

"Yes, Captain."

"Thirty years, huh?" Reese shook his head again. "It's a damned shame." Then he cleared his throat. "Which reminds me, I've got to pick up some flowers for Denise on the way home. Take it easy, huh, Nick? See if somebody's got some cold medicine or something they can give you. Gotta catch these things as soon as they hit, or they'll knock you flat."

He wanted to tell Reese that he didn't get sick—until their recent bout with the fever, vampires had never known an illness that could affect them. But he nodded and said, "I'll keep that in mind." Reese, like his other coworkers on the police force, believed that he was mortal. None of them knew that vampires existed.

Except for Tracy.

Sighing, Nick pulled his chair up to the desk, opened a drawer and removed the appropriate forms, still fighting back the urge to act on the smell of blood that lingered in his nostrils from the crime scene. He couldn't shake the thought of the blood in the snow twice in two nights, red on white and glistening in the darkness.

Another scent suddenly assaulted him, something so heavy and thick that it made his stomach churn. Nick nearly dropped the forms on the floor at the noxious odor, then recognized it as coming from the steaming cup Tracy held in her hand as she returned to her desk.

"Still green?" she asked. The cup of hot chocolate in one hand and rice cake in the other left no suspicion as to where she'd been since returning from that call—the coffee stand in the break lounge. Tracy set the hot chocolate down on his desk. "What you need is better eating habits. Like me."

"The last I heard, rice cakes were *not* a food group." Nick winced at the crunch as she bit into the rice cake, then added, "Especially the caramel-covered ones."

"Have some hot cocoa, at least. You look frozen—it'll warm you up."

The smell nearly caused him to turn his head in disgust at the suggestion. But Nick surprised himself by staring at it, just for a moment, before pushing the cup toward her. "No, thanks. And I don't need the captain coming down on me because *my* reports are covered with sticky rice bits."

"Suit yourself." Tracy sank her teeth into the rice cake again, then perched on the edge of her desk, legs swinging against the side of it. She stared into space thoughtfully as she chewed. "You know," she said, after another swallow, "I don't think I've seen that big a mess at a crime at a crime scene since. . . ."

"Last night?" offered Nick.

Tracy stared at him a minute, then nodded. "Yeah, I guess you're right. That one was just as nasty, huh?"

"Please!" Nick held up his hand and half rose from his seat to meet Tracy on eye level. "Just do me a favor, okay? Let's leave off the blood and guts business for now. I'd *like* to get some work done."

"Okay, okay," s͏ʳ Tracy. But as Nick returned his attention to his pape. .vork, he felt Tracy's eyes studying him.

Throwing down the pen, he looked up. "What?"

"Don't take this the wrong way, but you look like something the cat dragged in."

"There's a *right* way to take that comment?"

"No, I'm serious." Putting what remained of her rice cake on his desk, Tracy reached out and touched Nick's forehead. "You don't feel feverish."

Nick slapped her hand away lightly, remembering to use

a lot less force than he might have. "I'm fine. I didn't get much sleep today." He turned his shoulder to Tracy and covered his work with his arm, trying to shut out his partner's attention.

But Tracy didn't get the message, still watching him with concern. "Have you eaten since yesterday?"

"No. I haven't." Again, he threw the pen down on his desk. "I overslept. I ran out of my place and straight to the scene." Which was true, for what it was worth—although Tracy wouldn't have understood that all he needed was half a bottle of the cow's blood in his refrigerator. But even the thought of that turned his stomach. He stared at Tracy. "Are you done? Can I get back to work?"

But there was no twinkle in Tracy's eye, no hint that she was joking. "That boy last night. That's it, isn't it? The bungee tower?"

Nick met his partner's even stare and tried to lie, tried to think of some quip, or joke, or comment that would change the subject. But he was having the same problem he'd had with Natalie—these people were beginning to know him too well. And he trusted and respected them too much to lie all the time. Nor did he want to.

He shifted in his chair and looked away. "It was a waste of a human life. It shouldn't have happened."

"Like the four-car pileup on Friday. Or the cash machine holdup on Sunday. And now, tonight, a man shoots his wife after thirty years of marriage because she burns the chicken?" Tracy nodded slowly. "It's the busiest we've been since I transferred in. We've seen a lot of blood this week."

Nick tried to fight the wan smile that came to his lips. How could he tell Tracy that he'd seen blood flow like a river from a battlefield, corpses stinking with plague and decay piled high in the streets, and sights that would make the carnage of the last few days seem less notable than the swatting of a fly on a midsummer's evening? He should have been immune to a few more corpses, *had* been immune . . . but each and every death had been senseless.

He looked up at Tracy and met those all-too-mortal eyes filled with concern. "Didn't it get to you, too?"

"I was starting to wonder about you," said Tracy softly. Picking up the rice cake, and then apologetically wiping the crumbs off his desk, she half smiled. "There's been more than a couple that have gotten to me since I transferred in. A couple of times, I thought about sneaking off for a cry. And then I'd look at you and you'd be standing there like—well, like it would take a forklift to move you." When he chuckled, she added sharply, "You know what I mean. You take it all in, and you care—I'm not saying you don't care—but it's like it doesn't touch you. Most of the time." She looked over at him with a faint, sad smile. "I thought *you* had the answer."

He sobered, and shuffled the forms he'd placed on the desk. What could he tell her? That with all that he'd seen in eight centuries, most of the time it didn't affect him? Death was death was death; the dead were to be avenged by catching their killers and serving justice. But these deaths had been so unnecessary, so wasteful.

"I don't think there *is* an answer," said Nick, after a moment's hesitation.

"But we can still hope, can't we?" There was something in Tracy's manner that touched his heart, something of the little girl who still clapped her hands for Tinker Bell and believed that pixie dust could make you fly. Then she snapped her fingers and half turned, leaning across her desk to pick up a pink slip of paper. "And speaking of answers—there was a phone message for you at the front desk. It's from Natalie."

Nick stretched out his hand, expecting Tracy to give him the message. But she unfolded the pink paper and glanced at it. "Speaking of whom—"

"Tracy—," he warned softly.

"What is it between you guys? You should take her out to

dinner sometime. You're not getting any younger, you know."

Nick snapped his fingers, his hand still outstretched, hoping his glare would be as sufficient warning that his patience was wearing thin.

"And Natalie isn't, either. But she looks *great* for her age," added Tracy hurriedly, when she realized what she'd just said. "And if you *ever* tell her that I—"

Springing up, he grabbed the note from Tracy's fingers and returned to his desk.

"You're welcome." With a relieved smile, Tracy sat down behind her desk after shifting her coat and scarf to one side of her chair. She suddenly seemed too intent on her computer screen.

The message was brief—nothing more than a notation that Natalie had called. Crumpling it in his fist, Nick tossed it into the trash with a frown. His hand hovered over the receiver for a moment, but, realizing that Tracy was watching his every move, he abandoned the idea of returning the call. She was just checking up on him, no doubt. And after the business in the lab last night . . . why was this getting to him? He'd seen—and *caused*, if he was being truthful—more horrible deaths in his eight hundred years than he'd seen in the last few days.

Maybe Tracy was right. Maybe it was cumulative—too much too soon, and all on his watch. The couple tonight had been the capper.

"Um . . . Nick?"

He looked up, but Tracy's gaze was fixed intently on her paperwork. "What?" he asked wearily.

"I know you're a little protective." She glanced at him, then back at her computer screen. "Okay, so you're a lot protective. But you've gotta let me run my own informants. I know what I'm doing. Maybe I was wrong bringing him to a crime scene, but I think you were out of line—"

"You're right," admitted Nick. "I was. I'm sorry."

The grim look on Tracy's face faded into wide-eyed near-astonishment. "You were? You *are*?"

Nick wheeled his chair to the edge of his desk, closer to her. "You run your informants the way you need to run them. But you also keep them at arm's length." He heard her heartbeat speed up. "If you tell me that Vachon's your informant and there's nothing else to it, that's fine. You walk your side of the street, he walks his, and nobody gets hurt."

He saw it in her eyes, the desire to lie, the need to convince him that everything was all right, that he didn't have to worry about her. But Tracy was too young, she hadn't learned that kind of lie yet. At least, not one that she could pass off on someone with his experience. And, then again, maybe she *didn't* want to lie. Not really.

"There *might* be something more to it." She looked down, and Nick began to understand the boundaries of Tracy's life, that she *would* lie to him to protect Vachon, to protect the secret of what he was. "He's . . . different. Different from any guy I've ever met."

Nick took a breath, hearing the fascination in her words, in her tone. Too long, he'd let this go on *far* too long. But there was still a chance, if he made it part of the job, a professional matter. "Tracy, a snitch who turns into something *more* than a snitch isn't a snitch anymore. He's got an angle. You can't trust him, you can't trust his information. You've got to cut him loose and develop other sources, other interests."

Tracy scrunched up her nose. "You sound like my dad."

"I'm your *partner*."

"You're going to be my *dead* partner if you don't go home and go to bed," said Tracy sharply. She rose from behind her desk, then walked to his and picked up the cold cup of cocoa. "I think I'd better nuke this—it looks like sludge. Can I get you coffee? Juice? Decongestant?"

He chuckled, leaned back in his chair to get out of the way as she shifted the cocoa, then realized that it didn't smell that bad when it had cooled. "No, I'll be fine. And I'll leave as soon as I get this case file cleaned up—the Crown Attorney wants it by the end of shift."

"Don't they always?" asked Tracy in annoyance, carrying the cup of cocoa out of his range and, he hoped, out of his life.

It was quieter after she left, but concentration still eluded him. Nick stared at the paperwork in the file—it wasn't making sense. The numbers and words were running together, and he was having difficulty reading his own fairly legible handwriting. Sitting back in his chair, he closed his eyes and yawned. Just a few seconds' rest, that was all he needed. A few minutes of shut-eye, and he'd be fine. . . .

4

"NICK? THE DAYS ARE FOR SLEEPING, THE NIGHTS ARE FOR *working*."

Nick forced one of his eyes open as he leaned back in his chair, then closed it again as Tracy came into view. He didn't remember ever being this exhausted. "Just resting my eyes."

"Yeah. And maybe that's *all* you're resting during the day." She shrugged out of her suit jacket and fixed it carefully over the back of her chair, then gave him a sly glance. "Your friend—what was her name . . . Uma?— she was a *big* hit in booking."

"Urs," Nick corrected absently. Then his eyes flew open and he sat up in his chair, staring at Tracy, still caught up in his dream. It had been something about snow . . . and blood?

Nick pulled his chair closer to the desk, nearly knocking over his cup of coffee. He picked it up and took a sip, trying to come up with some sort of answer—then nearly choked when he got a sudden flash of drinking something else, something thick and warm and salty.

But the coffee went down easily enough. And the taste . . . it was as if he'd never really tasted coffee before. A little sugar took the bitter edge off it.

"Do you think this is too much? Or too little?" Tracy grinned and turned, giving him a mock runway twirl. She was wearing a pale yellow sleeveless top and what could best be described as tan walking shorts. "I don't suppose the perps will care that the department's suspended the dress code for detectives until this heat wave lifts."

Nick matched her smile and leaned back in his chair for a moment, eyeing her outfit. "It *may* cut down on pursuits. The outfit screams 'Freeze!' louder than you can."

"I talked to Dad last night—he didn't agree with the dress code suspension. He says we're all vampires now, so we should be able to take the extra heat." She pushed her chair away from her desk and shrugged, giving him an apologetic glance. "Present company excepted."

"Thanks." Loosening the collar button on his short-sleeved shirt, Nick tried to turn his attention to the paperwork on his blotter, although either action was a token concession to his situation. Even though the air conditioner in the precinct was running at its highest setting, his dress shirt and T-shirt were plastered to his skin by sweat, as were those of the two or three other mortals present. The vampire members of the force, like Tracy, always looked cool and comfortable . . . despite the fact that many of the uniformed officers ignored the dress-down rule by remaining in full uniform. It seemed like another way they could set themselves apart from the mortals that they supposedly protected and served.

The case file on his desk was doing nothing to take Nick's mind off the heat—one mortal who'd stabbed another during a theft from a food store. Few mortals seemed able to find employment in anything but menial positions, and their economy had degenerated into barter and theft. The paperwork was a moot point; he was more than certain that the murderer had already been processed through one of the local "donation" centers. But it still had to be filled out. Paperwork made it seem as if the status quo were being maintained, as if civilization weren't crumbling around them.

Or so the vampires seemed to think.

Tracy was at her computer, typing in a report. He glanced at her from time to time and could tell by her frown that the system was slow, probably due to the heat. Even computers weren't as resilient as the vampires.

"Just wondering if you know she did wonders for your reputation."

"Um?"

"Bringing Urs to the open house. Dad wasn't real happy about opening up the station to mortals, but I think it's a great idea, don't you?"

Nick smiled inwardly at her optimism. One of the attempts of the new regime to acclimatize the mortals to vampire–mortal joint rule had been an open house at the police stations across the city. "Tracy, we were the only mortals who showed up." And he had shown up only because LaCroix had forced him to take Urs and Vachon, so they'd know the layout of the station in case of an emergency.

"I know." She frowned and then slapped the side of her computer terminal impatiently. "I think they should try it again, but make it mandatory. I think your friends and families would feel safer if they saw this place from the inside."

"You think so?" Urs had charmed the vampire officers, but he'd kept her close to his side the entire time, holding her hand when her trembling fingers belied the seductive smiles she'd passed around the squad room.

"Of course. They'd feel protected, more secure." Giving up on a response from her system, Tracy leaned back in her chair and turned her full attention toward him. "And I *really* liked meeting Vachon."

"Yeah, well, I'm sure he liked meeting you." Nick shook his head for a second, not wanting to add that Vachon probably would have liked plunging a stake through her heart even better. It had taken him hours to convince Vachon that the firebombing of a police station filled with vampires might *not* be a good idea, his argument being that during an open house, dozens of mortals might be killed. If there was anyone who hated the vampires more than LaCroix, anyone more willing to do anything in his power to ensure their destruction, it was Vachon.

Tracy was about to say something more, then her eyes widened and she shook her head slightly, as if trying to warn him. When Nick glanced up, he saw Captain Reese walking toward them and knew that she had sensed the approach of another vampire. Which, he conceded to himself, might be a handy talent when the vampire in question was your boss and you were goofing off on the job.

There was a handful of vampires around whom Nick had begun to grow comfortable, and Reese was one of them. He looked after the people who worked for him, whether they were mortal or vampire. It didn't seem to matter to him. His clothing was just a size too large for him, a holdover from the days before the vampiric transformation had changed his body from that of a paunchy, dark-skinned mortal to that of a more muscular predator. Physically, vampirism seemed to bring out the best in mortals, making them sleeker and enhancing their positive characteristics.

LaCroix had explained it once in terms of Darwinian selection; even among the vampires, it was the strongest, the fastest, and the most beautiful who were able to attract and hold their mortal prey. Although they were supposed to subsist on the allotment of bottled "donated" blood, it was the vampires with the killer instinct, the most efficient hunters, who would always thrive.

"Vetter, Knight." Reese wrapped the fingers of his left hand through the leather belt on his waist and tugged upward on it, a habit he'd acquired as his pants daily seemed in greater danger of ending up around his ankles. "Anything on the vigilantes on the Sykes case?"

A chill went through Nick, and he scribbled something innocuous in the file on his desk blotter, knowing the case referred to was the vampire he, Vachon, and LaCroix had destroyed that afternoon.

Tracy patted a file on her desk. "All we've got is the day shift report. I didn't think there was much sense in us going out there yet." She glanced at Nick and shrugged. "We're still catching up on yesterday's paperwork. You know how Dad is about that."

"Yeah," agreed Reese, with a long-suffering sigh. "I know."

"Do we have anything to indicate that it *was* a vigilante action?" asked Nick, forcing himself to meet Reese's eyes and hoping that the increase in his heartbeat wouldn't reveal his complicity.

"Other than the fact that the victim's been cited half a dozen times for assaults on mortals and unauthorized donations?" Reese shook his head and stared at the floor. "I hate to stick you on an assignment like this, Nick, but I think we need a mortal perspective. I know if I was still mortal, and there was a vampire in my neighborhood who was trying to pad his blood allotment with a little midnight snack here and there, I'd be moved to do something about it."

Nick continued to meet Reese's gaze, trusting the captain not to hypnotize him or force him to admit something against his will. It was against current department policy, but that hadn't stopped a number of vampires on the force from using their hypnotic abilities on the mortals who served with them, the intent having ranged from generally harmless but embarrassing practical jokes to self-incrimination.

How much did Reese know? Did he suspect that Nick might be part of the resistance LaCroix had organized?

Nick took a breath. "Like you said, Captain—the victim was cited *six* times, but she was still out on the street. Wouldn't you say we've already had our shot at her and we blew it? Maybe they're not vigilantes. Maybe they're just cleaning up the cases we let fall between the cracks."

Reese nodded slowly. "Vetter, do me a favor and take a walk."

"But Captain, I—"

"Take a walk," ordered Reese, his tone nonthreatening but giving Tracy no room for challenge.

Nick met her worried gaze with a smile to let her know that he'd be all right, then looked back to Reese. Moving closer, Reese pushed aside the "in" basket on Tracy's desk, then seated himself on the corner, waiting until Tracy left before speaking.

"I know you're gonna get tempted, if you haven't walked into this sort of stuff already. All I can tell you is that it's not worth it. We've gotta keep the peace. There's a hell of a lot of people who respect what you're doing, a mortal working with vampires to keep law and order for both. Don't mess this up, Nick. There's a lot more riding on you than you know."

"I know," answered Nick, as quietly as he could. He glanced past Reese, at the other officers absorbed in their daily routines, any one of whom could be listening. It was common courtesy to pretend that the enhanced senses that accompanied their transition to their new lifestyle were there only when necessary. But the police department was, as it always had been, a family. Gossip was one of the main forms of recreation. That was one of the reasons LaCroix had pushed the issue of getting him assigned to this precinct—more than half of what he'd heard through here had helped the resistance form plans and evacuate in advance of raids, and had saved lives.

Mortal lives.

Reese clapped him on the shoulder in a friendly manner—it seemed the lecture was over for now. "You should bring your friends in again, show them around. That

68

girlfriend of yours certainly made a big splash the last time she was here."

"She'll be flattered you noticed. Although your wife would take your eyes out if she got wind of it," Nick quipped. Then he looked away quickly, realizing what he'd said. "I'm sorry. I didn't get a lot of sleep this afternoon—"

"It's okay," said Reese, his tone subdued. "It's not like Denise and I are still legally married, right? 'Til death do us part. And since I've got the paper to prove it—"

Nick glanced up, hearing the hidden anguish in the words. "Captain—"

"It's so quiet there, without them," Reese said, so softly that Nick almost couldn't hear him. The captain's eyes focused elsewhere, moving from the boarded windows of the station to the water cooler, and back again. "Lindy and Sarah were always making some sort of noise or the TV was on too loud. Denise and I never could agree what to watch on the tube—she always wanted one of those science fiction shows and I'd have to fight for the hockey game—usually lose. She left most of her clothes and stuff, you know. I was going through them last night. I found her diet pills. Denise's always had a thing about her weight. But, now I'm thinking I've got the solution—"

"Captain, don't do this to yourself—"

"Because if she went on a permanent liquid diet . . . *and* she'd be young forever. No face-lifts or anything." His eyes moved back to Nick, the moisture at the corners bloodred. "Have you see them? Spoken with them?"

Nick swallowed the lump that rose at the back of his throat. Captain Reese couldn't know that he saw Mrs. Reese and their daughters on a daily basis. If he knew where they were, there'd be too much temptation to try to see them. And then, the inevitable would happen, as had happened to so many families when one member was turned . . . blood would be shed. He'd heard from Mrs. Reese how they'd talked before Joe had been turned. Lindy and Sarah were definitely too young to be condemned to an eternity of physical childhood, and Mrs. Reese feared the loss of the light. But they'd continued to try to live together as a family. It had lasted a week before she'd taken Lindy, Sarah, and the clothes on their backs, never to return.

And now he was faced with his captain, a man who'd been forced to choose between the law and his family, who'd chosen to uphold his oath to protect and to serve, even if it meant the loss of his wife and daughters.

"At least tell me that they're safe. I know you must hear stuff."

"Yeah." Nick nodded slightly. "I've heard that much. And there was a message passed on from Lindy—she loves you and she wants you to be careful."

"Thank you." Captain Reese turned away, pretending to rub something from his eye as he wiped away the bloody tear. "That helps, a little."

There was a call from across the room. "Captain?"

Reese rose from the desk and walked over to another officer, who handed him some papers. "Faxes for you, sir."

Knowing that their discussion was over, Nick was about to return his attention to his case file when Tracy arrived, a coffee cup in her hand. She moved behind Nick and leaned over his shoulder, asking softly, "He didn't ask about me being late for shift, did he?"

"No." He glanced up at her, caught a whiff of the warmed blood in her coffee cup, then leaned over the file on his desk. "How many times this week?"

"Only four."

"In four days."

"You've been counting."

Nick watched her as she walked back to her desk, her gaze on Reese's office door. Tracy took a long swig from the coffee cup, then, when Reese hadn't called them, seemed to relax. She lifted her jacket from the back of the chair, shrugged into it, and buttoned it, seemingly oblivious to the heat inside the station. "We'd probably better head out. The night's not getting any cooler. And we've got reports of four more attacks on vampires to check, in addition to the Sykes case."

Inwardly, Nick groaned. The rising temperatures during the abnormally hot summer were leading to more frequent and violent vampire–mortal confrontations. His shirt was still plastered to his back, and the makeup Urs had used to cover the abrasion on his head was starting to itch. Still, duty called. He struggled up from his chair and reached over to get his suit jacket from the rack.

"Come on," needled Tracy. "It hasn't even topped ninety yet."

"Yeah, like you'd feel it."

"Knight? Vetter?" It was Reese, down to shirtsleeves now but, like Tracy, looking none the worse for it. He stood in the doorway to his office and gestured for them to join him.

"We were just heading out," said Nick, slipping on his jacket.

Reese's eyes widened slightly, but his grim expression never changed. "My office. Now," he commanded, stepping back and waiting just inside the door.

"I think the thermometer just went up a couple of notches," said Tracy.

Nick smirked, and gestured for his partner to enter first. "For once, this heat's gonna affect you just as much as it affects me." Not being suicidal, he dropped the smirk after Reese closed the door and stood behind his desk. "What's up, Captain?"

"If it's about showing up late for shift, I can explain—"

Reese raised his hand, quickly cutting off Tracy. "We'll deal with that later. Now if it were Nick, I could understand. You look like hell. What's the problem, can't get used to the night shift? It's been six months."

Nick shook his head. "Just a lack of sleep. Maybe I'm not all that nocturnal."

"Well, maybe you'd better start thinking about getting used to it—on a full-time basis." Reese picked up a page from his desk and handed it to Nick. "Your papers came in—the brass okayed the promotion. Congratulations."

Something cold and hard fell into his stomach as he accepted the papers from Reese, and Nick was pretty certain it was his heart. LaCroix had been right—how the hell had he known? The form was straightforward, a promotion. But with it came a change of lifestyle. Or, rather, deathstyle.

Tracy clapped him on the shoulder. "That's fantastic! I don't think anyone's ever been brought across without being on shift for at least twelve months."

"Eighteen," corrected Reese, beaming. "But it's well deserved. Sit down, Nick. Take five."

"Thanks." He all but fell back into the chair, still staring at the paper. Forcing a smile, Nick looked at Reese and Tracy. "I don't know what to say."

"Say you'll take care of it this weekend, so I'll have you back by the end of the month." Reese glared at Tracy. "Anything on Knight's roster that you can't handle?"

"Contrary to popular opinion—no," said Tracy sharply. When Nick glanced up, she smiled. "We're pretty much caught up on the paperwork, and the few outstanding cases we have . . . unless someone walks in with a confession, I don't think there's any rush on them." Then she turned to Nick and said slyly, "Now comes the fun part—picking a sponsor."

Reese cleared his throat almost uncomfortably. "As a matter of fact—" He passed another sheet of paper to Nick. "Somehow, word got around before the official memo came down—I think the secretarial pool had something to do with it. It's not usual department policy, but here's a list of potential sponsors."

"Each and every one a volunteer, probably." Tracy craned her neck to see the list, but Nick took it quickly from the captain's hand and folded it, not even glancing at the names. "Is a certain coroner's name at the top?"

"Easy, Tracy," warned Reese. "Give the guy some air." His eyes narrowed, and the ghost of a smile flitted across his face. "Let me guess, Knight—you were the only one in the building who didn't see this coming?"

Nick nodded, and swallowed again. Hard. "Guess I'm out of the loop," he muttered by way of explanation. "Captain, I—how long do I have to decide?"

"Decide?" Reese stared at him. "Nick, it's not optional. The brass likes your style, and they want you on board as fast as possible, but they don't give second chances, even to up-and-comers. If you turn this down, they won't drop you back to day shift. You'll be off the force. And there's no way you'd get another offer to turn legally."

"I know." He stared down at the paper, the legalese hiding the horror of what he was being ordered to do. "It's just that . . . I need to think about it. I've seen"—he met Reese's gaze—"I've seen what happens."

"Yeah," Reese answered, "but you don't have any family. That's one of the reasons the brass put you on the fast track." Reese sat down behind his desk. Reaching into his pocket, he withdrew his badge and threw it on the desktop. "We all know what we said when they handed us one of these—to protect and serve. The law is the law. It doesn't matter if they're vampire or mortal, our job is still that— protect and serve. We're one of the few things standing between day-in, day-out business-as-usual and blood in the streets. The way things are going, this isn't going to change in the near future. Now we've got two types of predators on the streets. And we're going to need the best people we can get to keep the status quo. Nick, you're a good man. *And* a good cop. We need both."

"I appreciate the confidence," said Nick. "But I've got reservations—*especially* about the status quo. You see what's happening, like with the Sykes case. If 'justice' becomes 'just us,' I want to be able to walk away. And this would make it a damn sight harder to do that. Maybe even impossible."

"I respect that. And I'd be sorry to lose you, if that's your choice. It's your decision." Reese gestured toward the paper. "That's dated tomorrow. The brass won't expect your answer until the day after."

"Thanks. I appreciate it." Nick turned to Tracy. "Aren't we on call?"

"Protect and serve," answered Tracy lightly and with an obvious interest in getting out of there as quickly as possible. Her hand on the doorknob, she said, "See you later, Cap."

"Just a minute." Reese rose from behind his desk and walked around it. "You"—he pointed at Nick—"I'm finished with. Out. But you"—he glared at Tracy—"I think something was said about coming in late for shift?"

"See you later, partner," Nick whispered in Tracy's ear as he slipped out the door. He closed it behind him and headed for his desk, his pleasure at one-upping Tracy dissipating almost instantly. The paper in his hand felt like a lead weight.

A tap on his shoulder startled him and he whirled, just as a voice said, "What's a girl gotta do to get arrested around here?"

Despite the heat, something in his soul froze. No mortal could move that quickly. And if the voice belonged to Natalie—

It did.

Her hazel eyes were bright and her smile charming; her teeth gleamed like mother-of-pearl. Dressed in a stylish tweed suit, she had a self-presence that somehow surprised him, although she was always like that. She cocked an eyebrow at him, as if expecting an answer.

Nick turned his back to her and continued toward the desk. "You might try dressing like a hooker."

"Is that any way to talk to your sponsor?"

He froze again, hands on the back of his chair. There had been a lightness in her tone, but suddenly she was beside him, a hand on his shoulder, apology in her voice. "Nick, I'm sorry. I guess I shouldn't have said anything. I assumed you . . . you *do* know, don't you?"

Placing the paper flat on the desk, he ran his hand over it to smooth it out. "Reese just told me." He dared to meet her eyes, then handed her the list. "And gave me this."

"Typical, me showing up and putting my foot in it." Natalie unfolded the sheet of paper as she spoke, glancing at it. "I'm sorry, Nick. I wouldn't have said anything but—that *cow*! And . . . the name of every woman in the station must be on here."

For a long moment, he only half listened to her comments about the various names on the list, content just watching her. Being a vampire agreed with her. She radiated a confidence that charmed as well as impressed. The best of her features had been highlighted, especially her eyes. They seemed darker than the night at times, and shone silver or green, depending on the light, at others. That was the way it worked, just as it had with Reese—transformation of the prey into the predator by making the plumage brighter, the lure more difficult to resist.

But there was also something hard and sharp about her. There was some phantom of memory with which Nick suddenly found himself comparing her, perhaps an image of what she might have been like as a mortal. Some of the softness that he might have treasured in her manner and her smile must have disappeared along with the light.

She tossed the list back at him. "I hope you're not serious about interviewing everyone on that list."

"I'm not interviewing anyone." Her smile faded when he added, "I'm not taking it."

He didn't think it possible, but those dark eyes grew darker. Catching his arm, she steered him into a corner.

75

"Nick, are you crazy? Do you know what that would mean? To your career? To your life?"

"That's the choice, isn't it—life or death? Well, I'm choosing life."

Her hand dropped from his arm and she took a step back, biting her lip lightly, a gesture so familiar it tugged at the phantom memory in his heart. "Look, if it's me, if I came on too strong just now . . . I'm sorry. I was just so—I didn't think it would happen this soon. And I thought you felt the way I—" He could see her distancing herself; then she looked away and said softly, "I was wrong."

Nick reached forward to touch her cheek. Her eyes met his, hesitant and fearful. "Nat . . . you weren't wrong. It's just that—this is a decision I have to make."

Her hand covered his. "It's not that bad," she whispered, taking a step closer to him, all but in his arms. "Nick, you know I'd never hurt you. And after . . . we'd take care of each other, forever. It's the only way we can be together."

After carefully dancing along the various boundaries for six months—coworkers, public servants, friends—it was the one dance they'd never tried, the one boundary they'd never crossed. It was just too dangerous—they'd both agreed. And even if he'd had the inclination to let her turn him, which he hadn't, it would have been unsanctioned and illegal.

But that was no longer the case. He couldn't hide behind that excuse any longer. And he wasn't certain he could make her understand why he couldn't accept her offer.

"Daisies," he answered.

Natalie stared at him. "Excuse me?"

Extricating himself from her arms, which had somehow tangled themselves around his shoulders and drawn him into range of her perfume and eyes—both equally intoxicating—he held her at arm's length. "Daisies," he repeated. "You said you regretted that you'd never see the flowers in your mother's garden again. Especially the daisies, the way their petals open and move when the sun touches them."

She blinked and looked down at the floor. He took her hands and moved closer to her, whispering in her ear. "How can you ask me to become what you've become, when you regret it? Every hour of every night, you regret being turned. And you want to find a way back."

Natalie straightened and shifted, as if to move away from him, but he slipped his arms around her shoulders, standing behind her and holding her close. The muscles of her neck were tight. He had a feeling she was trying not to cry. "And you're asking me to do this, to make the same mistake, so we can be unhappy together?"

"I'll never understand how someone so sensitive can be so cruel."

Releasing her, he stepped back. "I'm only telling you the truth."

"That's what I mean." She turned toward him. "You use it like a sword, hack and slash away anything that isn't real, that isn't honest. You can't even leave dreams alone."

"I've had a good teacher," Nick said, chalking up yet another thing he owed LaCroix.

"But dreams feed hope. And we can't live without hope." Natalie looked away. "At least, I can't. That's why I'm looking for a cure. There's got to be a way back."

"And when you come back, I'll be waiting."

The hardness returned to her eyes as she looked at him. "Will you?" Then, frowning sadly, she dropped her gaze to the floor. "I don't think you'll live that long."

Nick didn't know what to say, so he settled for nothing. After a moment, she gestured toward the files on his desk. "There are the two autopsies. And the photo results on the vampire murders."

"Thanks."

"There's been nothing on . . . the other thing."

77

He pulled her toward him and asked softly, "No sign of her?"

"No. Nothing." Natalie placed her hand over his when he tried to move away. "But that's a good sign. If Janette's name isn't on any documentation, she hasn't been picked up. It means she's still alive out there."

"All it means is that she wasn't *officially* picked up." Walking over to Tracy's desk, he lifted the file folder that contained the Sykes case and handed it to her. "Like this one."

She opened the folder and started flipping through it.

"Virginia Sykes was cited six times for assaulting mortals—no names of victims listed, though." When Natalie looked up at him, her eyes sad, he added, "How many more mortals did she drain and drop in the lake? You know how many floaters you've had to deal with in the past six months. We're up to—what?—maybe ten a day, twenty? Every one of them drained."

"I give them names, Nick," she said firmly, almost defensively. "Or I try. I work from dental records, finger-prints, clothing, whatever we can find. But it doesn't work the way it used to. The backlog of missing persons is just too large."

"And the ones who can't be reported missing because someone in authority might start asking questions?" asked Nick, when she glanced away. "How many people just disappear because there's no one left to look for them, because everyone they know or who would have known them is already dead and buried or in the lake or listed as a 'donor'"?

He gave the word the venom it deserved, but when Natalie flinched, he regretted it immediately. "Look, I didn't mean—"

"No. It's okay. I understand." Her smile was bitter as she took a step back from him. "Believe me, I understand. I'll let you know as soon as I hear anything."

"Thanks." As she tried to walk past him, he reached out and grasped her upper arm. Natalie paused, then he leaned forward to kiss her softly on the lips. Drawing back, he added, "I mean that."

"I wish to God you did."

It took no effort for her to shake his hand from her arm. She stalked out of the station without a backward glance. For a long moment he considered following her, but a look at the files on his desk convinced him otherwise. Whether Janette was lost or found, whether he'd just been ordered to become a vampire or chose to resign from the force instead, for the moment he was still a police detective in the 96th Precinct, and there was work to do.

Tracy finally emerged from Reese's office, closing the door softly behind her. Noticing that she seemed only slightly subdued, he waited until she returned to her desk before asking, "What's the verdict?"

"I'm getting docked unless I stay an hour past shift tonight and tomorrow to cover it," said Tracy unhappily.

"You'll still make it home before sunrise."

"Yeah, but I'll have to make a phone call." She plopped down in the chair at her desk and then shot an annoyed glare at Reese's door. "Maybe I should have let him dock me."

"Someone's waiting for you? Or will be?"

Tracy started to nod, then stopped suddenly. A very faint flush of pink touched her cheeks, fading almost immediately when she turned toward her computer screen to cover her embarrassment.

"That's why you've been late a lot lately," said Nick. He smiled as the flush returned to her cheeks, and knew he was on the right track. "You've been seeing someone."

"No, I haven't." Her words were clipped and brittle, which only confirmed his theory. Then she turned and said softly, "Look, I'll make a deal with you. If you don't tell anyone about this, I won't tell Natalie about that list Reese gave you."

79

He couldn't help but smile. "She already knows."

"She—"

Nick tapped the files Natalie had left on his desk. "The autopsy records. She was here when I came out of Reese's office." Pausing, he ran his hand through his hair, still somewhat bewildered. "She knew about the promotion. And so did—" He stopped himself before saying LaCroix's name, then added sheepishly, "Everybody knew about the promotion . . . except me."

Tracy leaned forward, smiling. "Did Natalie say she'd be your sponsor? You two are good for each other. You know you are. You can trust her."

Nick managed a wan smile in response to her excitement, then asked, "Trust . . . that's important, then?"

"Oh, definitely. It doesn't always work. You've seen the ones they've brought in." Her enthusiasm dimmed as she shuddered. "The bloodline might be bad, or . . . something doesn't go right. There's nothing we can do for them, except lock them up until they—" She stopped suddenly, then turned her attention back to her computer screen, unable to continue.

He understood why—the failures were one of the vampires' dirty, little secrets. Some of the converts went crazy, tearing their own flesh and anything else in their path. Their pain only increased their frenzy to the point where the last threads of sanity finally snapped and they collapsed in exhaustion. Each precinct was now required to have a "disposition room" that was accessed by a single door, the walls, ceiling, and floor impenetrable. The failures were locked away until they battered themselves into oblivion— then a coroner would declare them officially "dead" and wooden bullets would be used to shatter the heart and the brain. Staking them previous to that point would be murder, so the farce preserved the propriety of the vampire adherence to "law and order."

He'd seen it happen once, the time Natalie had drawn the lot requiring her to examine and sign off on the case.

80

Afterward, he'd spent the day in her apartment with her. She'd shivered in his arms for hours, sobbing uncontrollably at times.

"But that won't happen to you," said Tracy. Nick looked up and found her staring at him worriedly. "Not if Natalie brings you across. You can trust her."

"What about you? When you came across, who sponsored you?"

"My father." She turned away, her eyes distant as she added, "With my dad it was really . . . formal. It was a good career move—I remember he kept saying that, repeating it the whole time. And how he wouldn't have to worry about me anymore. My mom—they were having a bad time. He offered, but she said no. That's when she left. She begged me to go with her, begged me not to turn, but I couldn't. I couldn't let him down." There was a faint smile on her lips when she repeated, "He's my dad. I couldn't let him down."

Nick met her gaze with a knowing smile. It was how he'd felt about LaCroix in the past—anything to please the man who'd saved him, had saved thousands and hundreds of thousands from becoming blood donors or simply disappearing. He couldn't let LaCroix down. He would have to accept the promotion.

But . . . he didn't want to become a vampire.

"We'd better hit the road," Nick reminded her as he closed the files on his desk.

"I guess so." With a weary sigh, Tracy picked up the stack of new case reports and a clipboard. "Guess we—"

The ring of the phone on her desk cut off her sentence. Tracy picked up the receiver. "Detective Vetter, Homi—Where?" She met Nick's eyes, then said into the receiver, "We're on our way. Yes—every car you can get us for backup. Thanks." Before the phone was settled in the cradle, Tracy was on her way through the bullpen, Nick behind her.

"A bomb just went off at the DayClub," she called back to him.

Nick caught up to her at the door by the front desk of the station. "All units?"

"All the backup they can get us. It's a vampire club. Mostly vampires, anyway." She hesitated, meeting his eyes. "I was going to meet—"

"Who?" Nick pressed, when she paused.

Tracy seemed to reconsider, then shook her head as she headed out the door. "Never mind."

Sirens wailed around them as patrol cars headed for the scene. Nick moved toward his car, but Tracy grabbed his arm. "No—we'll take mine. It's faster."

Her Ferrari was the sharpest car in the lot, as well as the most expensive. Nick opened the door and slid into the passenger seat. The door had barely closed before he'd buckled himself in place, then hit the siren and turned on the flashing lights.

Tracy's door closed behind her. The engine purred, then roared when she hit the gas. "Would you believe," she shouted, over the wail of the siren, "I used to drive a Honda?"

Nick grinned. "What brought this on, then?"

"A . . . graduation present. From my dad. This is what I got for being a good girl." Her expression turned grim as she guided the car out of the lot behind the patrol vehicles, then onto the street. "I can't have children. I can't grow up and grow old. I can't die." She rubbed the flat of her hand against the steering wheel and added, "If anyone *ever* touches this car, I'm going to rip their heart out."

The drive to the club was proving to be a nightmare— most of the traffic congestion now occurred between sunset and sunrise, which made getting around Toronto easily by car nearly impossible, especially in the summer. Many of the vampires flew to their destinations, of course, but they'd yet to work out the transportation of luxuries, necessities, and anything else without the use of cars, trucks, and vans.

As the adrenaline rush started to wear off, the lack of sleep caught up with him again. Nick closed his eyes and allowed his mind to drift, hoping that Tracy's vampire reflexes would get them through the circus of squealing brakes and blaring horns intact.

Almost falling from his chair, Nick snagged the edge of the desk like a drowning man grabbing a life preserver and stared around wildly. There were no boards on the windows of the police station, and he could see lattice-shaped traces of ice on the glass. The room and the people in it were all too normally human, handling ringing phones, civilians at the desk, and paperwork as if it were just another evening. Tracy was sipping her cocoa at her desk with a self-satisfied smile.

It had been a dream, *another* dream.

But it had seemed so real! And yet. . . .

Nick rose from the chair and tried to hide a yawn behind his hand.

"Catnap didn't help, huh?" asked Tracy sympathetically. Putting her cup down on her desk, she gave him an appraising stare, then nodded. "You *still* look like hell."

"Thanks." Tracy was right—he felt even more weary than before his little nap. There was a crick in his back from sleeping in that awkward position. Nick stretched, mild wonderment accompanying the pain—he wasn't supposed to feel things like this. So why did it hurt? "How long was I out?" he asked, trying to gauge time from the relative positions of the various officers and personnel milling around the room.

"Ten minutes. Maybe fifteen."

"Fifteen—?" Nick shook his head, bits of the dream coming back to him. It had seemed like . . . hours. "You're wrong. It must have been longer than that."

Tracy held up her coffee cup. "Couldn't have been more

83

than fifteen minutes—this is just starting to get cold. Well, I *did* nuke it to within an inch of its life," she admitted. "And nobody spotted you sleeping—I covered for you. That's what partners do, right?"

For a moment, Nick stared at her. "Yeah, right." Rubbing his eyes with his fingertips, he shook his head again. What was happening to him? Was he going mad?

"Go *home*," pressed Tracy. "Wait a minute—there's the captain." She rose from her chair and turned, calling Reese over with a wave. "Will you tell Nick to go home? He won't listen to me."

Nick held his hands out in front of him, hissing, "Tracy, no," but it was too late.

Reese ambled over, his suit jacket off and shirtsleeves rolled up. "You still here?" he asked, studying Nick with a squinting gaze. "Tracy's right—you don't look so hot."

Making a dismissive wave with his hand, Nick backpedaled a step. "Really, Captain, I'm fine."

"Like hell. You look like something we should send to the morgue." Lowering his voice, Reese added, "Take a sick day, Nick. For God's sake, Personnel said the cash you've got in accumulated sick time is killing our budget. Do us all a favor and go home."

"All right!" he relented, grabbing his coat from the rack. "I'll go. And I *can* drive myself," he added quickly, as Tracy set down her cocoa and got to her feet, already starting to make the offer.

"Good." Reese nodded again, then squinted toward Tracy. "You finish up that file the Crown Attorney sent back. Maybe they'll settle for your version of the pursuit in addition to Nick's. It leaves this office by the end of shift, and it's not my butt in the sling if they don't get it bright and early. Got it?"

"Yeah," said Tracy, falling back into her seat with a disappointed look when Nick almost cheerfully passed the file folder from his desk to hers.

"Good." Again, Reese nodded, as if punctuating the

comment. Clapping Nick on the shoulder, he added, "Get some sleep, will ya? You really do look like hell."

"Thanks." He forced a smile for Reese's benefit, then reached into his pants pocket for his car keys, but they weren't there. Shrugging into his coat, he dropped his hand into another pocket.

His fingers closed around a small, hard object. He took the dream doll from his pocket and let it rest on his palm—it had escaped from its box, which was still in his pocket. *Both* of the legs had curled inward.

Unaccountably, a shiver ran through him, jostling the doll from his hand. It fell onto Tracy's desk, and before he could do anything, his partner picked it up. "Hey, cute!" she said, examining the brightly colored wicker doll. "Although I think you're kinda old to be playing with these things."

Nick moved to take the doll from Tracy, then stopped himself, his hand frozen in midair. He didn't want to touch it. "I, uh, picked it up in the parking lot," he explained quickly. "Do me a favor, toss it in the trash."

"This little thing?" Tracy touched the folded legs of the doll gingerly. "Too bad it's broken. Although you can fix stuff like this if you soak it in water—softens it up. That's what my arts and crafts counselor told us at summer camp. Maybe I could fix it for you."

"No!"

Tracy shot him a look, surprised at his sudden vehemence, and Nick forced another smile. "Who knows where it's been?" he said, in what he hoped was a sensible explanation. "Just . . ." He dropped his hand into his coat pocket, pulled out the empty box, then held it toward Tracy. "Just toss it in here, okay?"

"If that's what you want." Shrugging, Tracy dropped the doll into the box, but her eyes widened when he produced the box cover from his pocket and fixed it in place. "Just what parking lot did you find this in?"

Nick reached past her and grabbed a rubber band, then

another one. He wound the rubber bands around the box in two directions. Only then did he return the box to his pocket, certain that he was relatively safe from the doll.

"Nick, if you've got a minute before you head home——?" Tracy gazed up at him almost nervously. "About Vachon. I've been thinking about what you said."

Any thoughts of the doll and even his weariness disappeared instantly. Nick backed up a step, then seated himself on the edge of her desk. "And?"

"You're right. I think——I think I've let this go too far. I'm not going to use Vachon as an informant any more."

There was a certitude in the way she answered him, but he also heard something else in her tone, as if she were looking for approval. "And you're not going to see him again, right?" When Tracy hesitated and looked away, Nick leaned closer to her and repeated, "Right?"

"Yeah." She looked away, as if admitting something to herself reluctantly, then met his eyes again. "Yeah. Okay. That's what you wanted to hear?"

"That's *exactly* what I wanted to hear." Smiling, Nick nudged her shoulder lightly with his fist. "You know it's for the best."

"Yeah, I know."

"And if he gives you *any* trouble——"

"You'll climb out of your sickbed to rescue me?"

"I'll be sleeping with my cellphone, just in case."

She made a face at him, and Nick smiled. He put his hand down on the desk, levering himself to his feet, and nearly knocked over the cup of cocoa. He caught it in time, but some of the cocoa spilled over onto his hand.

It wasn't hot—barely lukewarm, in fact. Absently, he raised the side of his hand to his mouth and licked off the spilled liquid. It didn't taste anything like he thought it would—sweet, but not sickening. In fact, he kind of liked it.

On an impulse, Nick stuck his finger in the cup of cocoa,

86

then into his mouth. Only when he saw Tracy staring at him in horror, then at her violated coffee cup, did Nick realize what he'd done. He wanted to explain, even as the rich taste of the liquid lingered in his mouth, but there *was* no rational explanation.

"Ick!" cried Tracy, picking up the cup and holding it at arm's length.

"Going," Nick whispered distractedly. He headed for the door, still licking the chocolate from his hand. However tired he was, he felt like a weight had lifted from his shoulders. Tracy wasn't going to see Vachon any more.

"And if you're going to act weird, take tomorrow off, too," Tracy called angrily from behind him.

Holding his hand up in a wave, Nick didn't bother to answer. Now that the doll was secure in its box, he'd get rid of it and he'd be able to get some real sleep. But first he had a small errand to run on the way home.

And that meant heading to the Raven.

5

THE MUSIC IN THE RAVEN SEEMED LOUDER THAN IT HAD THE NIGHT before, the dancing more frenetic, and the attitudes of the dancers even more callous, as if motion helped to momentarily remove them not only from the worries and cares of the working world but also from themselves. Nick had little sympathy for them, roughly pushing his way through the mass of people to reach a clear place at the bar.

The bartender, a large men with a rat's nest of hair approached him. "Vachon?" asked Nick, afraid that he might have to shout to make himself heard over the throbbing of the music.

After a shake of his head, the bartender shrugged, then moved on to the next customer. Nick turned, annoyed, and scanned the crowd, but there was no sight of the familiar leather jacket. He could go to the church, of course, but that was as hit and miss as the Raven. Vachon seemed to wander aimlessly from place to place, going wherever fancy took him, somehow managing to stay beyond the addresses and answering machines that tied a soul to a place and identity in the modern world. It was easier to be found by Javier Vachon than to find him.

The scent of the blood in the glasses held by many of the

vampires present did nothing to ease his hunger. If anything, Nick felt slightly nauseated by the heavy, cloying smell that permeated the air wherever vampires clustered together in the club. Tucking his hands into his pockets, he wandered away from the bar and closer to the dance floor. Nick leaned against a wall, barely giving the dancers a second glance as he tried to decide just where and how to contact Vachon.

An arm slipped through his, and he felt a body beside him. Urs tossed her head, her short blonde curls falling saucily over one eye, and she smiled at him. "Lost, nowhere else to go, or just looking for someone?"

Her comment was a little too close to LaCroix's words the night before. Nick shifted, and Urs leaned the length of her body beside him. The move was casual, sensual, and not at all unpleasant.

"Vachon," he said, watching her expression.

"Oh." Her attention suddenly seemed centered on the dancers; there was only the barest flicker of an eyelid in response to the name. "He's not here."

"I noticed." Having pressed his back to the wall, Urs was now leaning against him. He placed his hands on the bare skin of her upper arms and rubbed them lightly. "Know where I might find him?"

Her eyes clouded, and her head rested against his chest. "No."

It wasn't the truth and it wasn't a lie; it was something in between. Nick brushed her hair with his fingers, the strands soft and yielding. "But you'd find him, if I asked?"

"Yes."

And that, for a moment, was all that needed to be said. Nick rested one hand in her hair and thought for a moment, knowing that Urs could probably locate Vachon through the thread of blood that bound them to one another . . . but only if he wished to be found. Vachon was her master; he was the one who had made her a vampire and brought her across, into the darkness.

He felt Urs's heart beat, tremulous and soft, audible to him despite the thunder of the music and the sounds of the crowd. Once every eleven minutes, that was the rate of a vampire heart, which could afford to be slow and patient. It had eternity, after all.

But it could still be broken so easily.

There was a commotion across the floor—a slight scuffle. Nick looked up with interest, hearing fragments of words the other dancers pretended to ignore.

"She's with me."

"I asked the lady if she'd like to dance."

"Steve, don't!"

"I said the lady was with *me*!"

The pretty brunette and her escort were mortals; the interloper, a clean-cut, young male vampire wearing jeans and a plaid shirt. Nick was already looking around for someone to intervene when he saw the vampire raise his hands before him, palms out in surrender, and back off. He faded back into the crowd, as did the two mortals.

Urs shifted against him, and his thoughts returned to her and the sadness he sensed. "What about you?" Nick asked, touching her chin with his finger, so that she turned her head to look up at him. "Lost, nowhere else to go, or just looking for someone?"

Urs smiled faintly, but with gratitude. "All three." Then her smile grew broader and she pushed herself away from his chest. "Wanna dance?"

Letting her lead him onto the crowded dance floor, Nick was amused at her sudden spirit. There was a bright, engaging quality in Urs's nature, a vitality he'd seldom seen equaled in any vampire. But then, she was still relatively young, barely over a century at most, and had yet to grow weary of the sameness of the world.

The music was still loud, but the tempo changed to something stronger and slower, more seductive. Urs's arms

91

slipped around his neck and his hands fell to her waist as they swayed in time to the music.

"We've been seeing you a lot here, lately. Are you becoming a regular?" she asked, gazing at him with a bright smile. Then the smile softened and she raised a hand to his cheek, brushing it softly. "You look tired."

"Thanks for noticing." He could feel the coolness of her skin beneath the thin, clinging material of her blouse. Drawing her closer, he thought of Janette, the vampire who had brought him to LaCroix. The two were different shades of darkness, one fair-haired and one with midnight tresses, but both were vampires, exhibiting the physical perfections of their gender, sultry and seductive in differing styles that were equally effective. He knew barely anything of Urs, having met her only recently, but he'd shared countless moonlit nights dancing with Janette and even more daylight hours in her arms, as they'd slept hidden from the destructive light of the sun. Since Urs had arrived, Janette had left and returned and left again, days meriting barely a blink of an eye in their accounting.

That was the way among their kind, to love and part and love again, as decades and even centuries passed. Eternity was a long time. If he failed to become mortal, he would see Janette again. He'd try to make up for what he'd done. And they'd dance like this a hundred years from now in another place, wearing different clothing and listening to music unimaginable.

There was another conversation going on nearby; he recognized the mortal voices from the earlier argument.

"Went to the men's room, for God's sake. You didn't—"

"He asked me to dance. You don't own me. *Nobody* owns me."

"She's wrong," whispered Urs against his shoulder, her hearing as sensitive as his. "We're all owned, bought and sold."

"Mortals aren't bound by the blood," he reminded her. "They're masters of their own fates."

"They're bound by their hearts, by their love and their hate." Lifting her head for a moment to meet his gaze, Urs smiled sadly again. "But . . . so are we."

As her head returned to rest on his shoulder, Nick's thoughts drifted again to Janette and a conversation they'd once had. They'd talked about their lives as "children" of LaCroix, for Janette had been brought across by LaCroix as well, and had spent almost three hundred years walking the night before Nick had even been born. Although LaCroix had often tried to keep him on a tight leash because he rebelled, while Janette was given freer reign, she also felt the restraint of the blood that bound them, the limitations of their "captivity." If he became mortal, he'd be free of all that. He'd be free to live and love as he chose. Choosing *would* make it different, wouldn't it? Or was Urs right, were mortals as captive to the desires of their hearts as vampires were to the bonds of their blood?

Urs had fallen quiet, and he glanced down at her. Her eyes were distant and unfocused, and he realized that just as his thoughts were of another woman, hers were probably of another man. "Thinking about Vachon?' he whispered in her ear.

She started in his arms, then smiled guiltily and leaned her head against his shoulder again. "Does it show?"

"Let's say it was a lucky guess." Nick tightened his hold on her, wanting to protect her from the sadness he could see in her eyes. "Why don't you tell him?"

"Because he knows." Urs sighed despairingly and looked down at the floor. "And because it doesn't matter. Not really. He has other things on his mind right now."

"Like . . . Tracy?"

He felt a shiver run through her and he saw fear in the quick glance she shot at him before she looked away again. Nick let his arm fall around her waist and walked her off the dance floor, to a corner of the club. Urs turned once, trying to get away, but he held her arm tightly and her attempt at flight was over as suddenly as it had begun. She was no match for him; he was older, stronger, and more powerful than she. They both knew it.

Urs pressed herself into the corner of a niche, her back flat against one wall and her hands against the other, as if she felt safer. "Maybe you should go," she said softly. "Or maybe I should."

She looked like a trapped animal that had despaired of escape. Nick backed out of the niche, then leaned against the wall beside it. "If you want to leave——"

"I have nowhere else to go." He felt her hand leave the safety of the niche and touch his shoulder, resting there. "I'm frightened for him, for Javier."

"I don't want to hurt him."

"But you will. That's how it works." There was a sad but knowing quality to her voice. "He doesn't want to hurt her, either—Tracy. But he will. Then you'll hurt him. And then I'll be hurt because you've hurt him."

Urs grabbed his arm tightly with both hands, her expression serious. "If you hurt him," she threatened softly, "I'll kill you. Or I'll try."

It would have been no contest between them, but in that moment he saw just how much Vachon meant to her. Nick gathered her hands together in his, holding them. Her momentary resolve faltered and she looked away, tried to slip back into the niche, but he held her in place. "I won't hurt him," he repeated. "I just have to find him. I want to tell him it's over between him and Tracy."

"Is it?"

There was hope in her eyes when she looked at him. Nick nodded and smiled to reassure her. "I've spoken to Tracy. She's going to stop seeing him."

"Thank you." Urs squeezed his hands and then leaned her head against the side of his shoulder. "I was so worried about him. I wasn't jealous—not really. She's only mortal, after all. He's always done crazy things, taken risks—but for her? You know how it is, how dangerous it can be for us and for them."

The feel of her cool skin made him think of warmer hands clasped in his own, of Natalie trying to reassure him. He *did* know how dangerous it could be, how any mortal who knew about the vampire community was endangered by that knowledge. Looking out over the crowd, he wondered how many, or how few, were truly aware of the peril in which they'd placed themselves. They'd come here for a drink and a dance, to forget their problems and themselves. And if someone didn't behave or decided not to obey the rules, a few of those mortals might lose their lives.

The mortals he'd noticed earlier—Steve and his girl-friend—were arguing as they left the crowd and returned to their table. The young vampire in the plaid shirt was still watching, waiting for a moment to approach.

"Are you all right?" asked Urs, realizing that he was preoccupied.

"There." Nick nodded toward the couple at the table, then released her hands and met her gaze evenly. "Tell Vachon I want to see him. That's all—just that I want to see him."

Urs nodded, then bit her lip as she glanced over at the table again. "Someone should—"

"Someone is." Nick placed a quick kiss on her cheek, then started to make his way through the crowded club, heading for the problem.

The young vampire approached the woman, ignoring her male companion. "About that dance?"

The mortal, Steve, looked like a young professional trying to show he could have a good time without a suit and tie. The legs of his chair scraped across the floor as he rose, the fingers of his right hand curling into a fist. "She's with *me*."

It looked like a macho standoff was forming. Nick placed

95

a hand on the young vampire's shoulder and gripped hard to get his attention. "There's no problem here," he said, in his best "I'm a cop, don't mess with me" voice. A quick glance over his shoulder told him that the bartender was signaling the bouncer that there was trouble on the floor.

"You bet there's a problem," said Steve, swaying enough that he had to lean his hands on the table to keep himself upright. His eyes were bright but unfocused; he'd obviously had one too many. "This guy won't leave my girlfriend alone."

"I'm not your 'girlfriend.'" The woman eyed her mortal companion with a look that could only be called loathing, then picked up her handbag from the table and rose to her feet. "And I'm leaving."

The vampire Nick was holding tried to shake him off in an attempt to follow the woman as she headed through the crowd and out the door. When Nick didn't release him, he warned quietly, "I saw her first."

There was a glint of gold in the brown eyes. Every instinct within Nick roared at him to answer the challenge with fangs and changed eyes—but there were mortals present. He settled for pushing the vampire back a step, and said, "The lady wants to leave. So let her leave." When her drunken boyfriend tried to follow, Nick grabbed his arm just above the elbow and tossed the man into the seat the woman had just vacated. "Both of you."

The mortal was just drunk enough not to be able to offer any real resistance—the chair rocked when he fell into it, and he grabbed for the table to keep it from tipping over. The vampire took a swing, but Nick stepped aside and struck him on the back as he passed, sending him sprawling into the table. The glasses, napkins, and lit candle on the table tumbled toward the floor with the vampire. Someone managed to catch the candle before it hit, but the glasses shattered, scattering fragments over the participants and the onlookers.

The music had stopped at some point. Breathing heavily, Nick turned to see LaCroix standing behind him and holding another young male vampire in an armlock. LaCroix met his eyes, then pushed the troublemaker into the capable grasp of the bouncer, who then lifted the first vampire from the floor by the back of his shirt collar.

The table was righted, the mortal was escorted out, and a waitress appeared with a broom and dustpan, all within seconds. Nick wiped the back of his hand against his mouth and watched, amazed, as everything returned to normal and the music began again. Aware of the sharp glances from several of the vampires in the crowd, and not a few of the mortals, he almost took a swing when he felt someone grab his arm.

The grip on his elbow tightened and LaCroix drew him close, saying "Careful, Nicholas. Or you'll find your name in the paper tomorrow beneath a headline 'Police Detective Brawls in Local Club.'"

"Thanks for the concern." He shook off the grip, but followed LaCroix to the door that led to the office behind the club. A female vampire passed them in the short hallway from the basement entrance, a bottle in her hands. She eyed Nick with a predatory smile, showing the slightest indication of her fangs. He turned, watching her shapely hips sway in her spangled violet dress as she returned to the club.

"My concern is less for you than for *us*." LaCroix lifted a hand, gesturing at the retreating figure of the woman who'd passed them. Then he opened the door. "Much as I'd like to see your mortal reputation shaken, I'm not about to endanger my profits or our safety for so insignificant a gain."

Nick entered the office and closed the door behind him. "Then you should have taken care of it."

"Just as you should have been aware of the one behind you." LaCroix had turned on the lights and walked directly to the ornamental grate behind which bottles of the "house special" were stored. "Or do you attribute losing your edge to your lack of sleep." Pausing as he slid aside one of the heavy iron grates, LaCroix cast him a glance of mock sympathy. "You look like you had a restless day. It would be too much to hope that you spent it considering our last conversation."

"Don't flatter yourself." Nick took a deep breath and wandered over to the couch. He sank onto it and rested his head in his hands for a moment. LaCroix was right—he should have known the second vampire was behind him, he should have sensed *something*. He hadn't been in any real danger here in the club, but on the streets, following an armed murderer, would be another story entirely. It wasn't only his life, but the lives of Tracy and the other officers with whom he served—all mortals—that he could endanger.

"I thought your chivalrous gesture entertaining, at least." When Nick lifted his head, he saw LaCroix taking a bottle from the rack and examining it. With a frown, he replaced it and chose another. He picked up two wine glasses, then came into the room. "Although it was well in hand even before you decided to interfere."

"The woman?"

"Took a cab that I had the prescience to call—she left in full view of witnesses." LaCroix seated himself in a chair to the right of the couch, facing the door. He placed the glasses on the table, then proceeded to tear off the seal of the bottle. "My bouncer has instructions to pry the keys from the hands of any mortals who have indulged past the legal limit, so her friend is either on his way home in a taxi, off to another club, or sleeping it off in the gutter. I have no intention of ascertaining which option he chose."

"And the others?" asked Nick.

He wasn't certain whether LaCroix actually shrugged or

the movement was part of pulling the cork from the bottle. "They were escorted to the door with a strong suggestion that they would not be welcome if they returned." Lifting the cork, he sniffed it and smiled. He offered it to Nick, adding, "I trust that meets with your approval."

The scent of blood mixed with alcohol wafted from the cork. Nick waved LaCroix's hand away. "Someone should keep an eye on them. They may go after that woman."

"They've already forgotten her. They know the rules." LaCroix poured the mixture of blood and alcohol into a glass, looked at Nick as if asking permission to pour a second glass, then placed the bottle on the table when Nick looked away. "As do you. However inconvenient your intervention, I can't say that I'm not pleased with your attempt to maintain the status quo." When Nick raised an eyebrow, LaCroix added, "Each to his own kind. I believe that's the traditional phrasing."

Nick rose from the couch and started toward the door. "I didn't come here for a lecture on mortal–vampire relations."

"No," agreed LaCroix pleasantly. Leaning back in the chair, he took a sip from his glass. "You came here to find Vachon. He's not here. But Urs will deliver your message."

Nick froze, his hand on the doorknob. "You were listening."

"I'll admit to cavesdropping occasionally on my patrons, but only to avoid trouble. Like this evening." LaCroix's tone acquired an edge as he added, "But, no, I wasn't listening to your conversation. You rarely speak to Urs, unless you're looking for Vachon. In fact, you rarely speak to anyone from the community unless they've somehow drifted into the realm of your mortal identity." Rising from his chair, LaCroix carried his glass to the door and faced Nick.

"I'm a police detective—"

"You're a *vampire*. You've been one for eight hundred

years. I would have thought that you'd have understood that basic fact by now. As for being a police detective—" LaCroix walked back to the metal grate and slid it closed with his free hand, his fingers lingering on the tracery of the gold leaf ornament. "You've been an artist, a doctor, a teacher, a poet . . . you've dabbled in a number of professions over the centuries, Nicholas. You know how transitory they are. Let the mortals have their laws and their legal system; we have our own world. You should remember that."

"How can I forget it?" Nick leaned his hand against the door and stared at the wood. "We need to be part of this world, LaCroix. It isn't like it used to be. The world gets smaller every day. Sooner or later, they're going to find out about us." He swallowed, thinking back to his dream, and his hand went to his pocket, fingers closing around the small white box. "We're part of their world. We can't help it."

"And they're part of ours?" Leaning back against the metal grate, LaCroix paused thoughtfully, sipping again. "Which is why you attacked a man for trying to rescue a woman from a perfectly dreadful evening simply because he's a vampire and she's mortal? If they had all been mortals, would you have bothered to intervene?"

Forgetting the box, Nick stalked toward LaCroix. "They didn't know the danger—"

"Ah. So you felt compelled to 'protect' them from your own kind?"

It was an old argument, and he was too tired. Nick turned away and reached into his pocket for his car keys. As he pulled them out, the white box came with them, tumbling to the floor. For a second Nick paused, his breath catching in his throat as he stared at it, then he slowly bent to pick it up.

But LaCroix had seen his hesitation and scooped up the box before he could get it. "What's this?"

"It's nothing—"

100

LaCroix had placed his wine glass on the table and seated himself on the couch. Eyeing Nick, he removed the rubber bands that held the box closed, then flicked off the lid.

"It's just a toy," said Nick, trying to dismiss the whole thing. "It's just—"

The second leg of the doll was still bent, matching the first. He felt his breath catch in his throat again as he looked at it, then hurriedly walked away, shoving his hands and his keys into his pockets. "It's . . . nothing."

"Where did you get this?"

The odd note in LaCroix's voice made him turn. Nick walked back to the table, where LaCroix had placed the box. "Do you recognize it?"

"I've heard of them, although I've never seen one before." Lifting the tiny toy between his thumb and fore-finger, LaCroix studied it. "It's a dream doll." He looked up at Nick. "Another foolish attempt to regain your mortality, Nicholas? I'm afraid you'll find that it's only a legend. You'll do well to be rid of it."

Although his words held nothing but disdain, Nick noted that LaCroix handled the doll carefully, replacing it in its box. "Legend?"

"That it will show you your heart's desire." LaCroix put the top back on the box, then flicked the box across the table with his finger. "Nonsense."

Nick scooped up the box before it could sail off the edge of the table. The cover fell to the floor and he stepped on it, then kicked it aside. "I've had two dreams—one this afternoon and one this evening."

"Have you?" LaCroix scrutinized him for a moment, then sighed and rose to his feet. "About?"

"I fall asleep and then I'm in the dream. But I'm not me, I'm someone else." Nick swallowed, glancing down at the doll as it rocked back and forth in the box, shaken by the near rescue. "I'm mortal."

"What do you dream of, Nicholas? Wild west shows and pony races? Gardens or steeples or rivers of blood?" LaCroix lifted his glass from the table and sipped at it. "Even your mortal friend will tell you that what you're experiencing is wish fulfillment. They're fantasies, dreams. They have no substance to them, no life, no blood. And all of us, even you, need blood to survive." He took another drink from his glass. "It's almost time for my broadcast. You're welcome to stay."

Nick tucked the doll into his pocket and headed for the door. "If you see Vachon, I'm looking for him."

"Of course." There was the barest pause before he added, "And you'll dispose of the doll?"

"I'll think about it."

Nick didn't wait to hear LaCroix's answer. Closing the door behind him, he walked down the hallway and back into the club.

There were no signs of the earlier altercation—the table was back in place with a new candle and a new group of people laughing and drinking. The dance floor was crowded and the music was as loud as before, perhaps louder.

Nick spotted Urs standing to one side of the crowd, talking to a young man he didn't recognize. She nodded when she saw him, then turned back to the handsome youth beside her. It had been only a second when she'd nodded, and then again as she followed him with her gaze. He saw that the ineffable sadness was still in her eyes, hidden but not banished by her smile.

For a moment Nick hesitated, almost walked over to her . . . then ducked his head and pushed his way through the crowd at the doorway to the club. LaCroix was right—he had no time for Urs, or Vachon, or the other vampires. He knew that many of their kind thought him diseased, pathetic, or pitiable for wanting to regain his mortality. It would be better for the ones he knew or befriended if he wasn't seen with them. And better for him,

102

as well, not to be reminded of the better parts of the existence he was trying to leave behind.

He felt the box again when he reached into his pocket, but he ignored it. Keys in his hand, Nick headed to the Caddie and unlocked the driver's side door. He closed the door and turned the key in the ignition—his car didn't like the cold snap they'd been having, and warming the engine might keep it from stalling. On an impulse, he turned on the radio.

"Come to the night, my children," said LaCroix's voice. *"This is the Nightcrawler, joining you again. Tonight, we speak of dreams."*

Nick yawned, then rubbed his hands together in an attempt to warm them. When that didn't work, he stuck his hands in his pockets again. His stiff fingers encountered the doll in its box; he pulled it out and placed it on the passenger seat.

"Do you dream of falling? Spinning down into the darkness from a great height, limbs failing, heart pounding, knowing that you're going to hit the ground at any second—but then you awaken? You never do seem to strike the ground."

Glancing down at the doll, Nick yawned again and leaned his head against the headrest. He'd fully intended to get rid of the tiny toy, but if LaCroix felt so strongly about it, maybe he'd better hold onto it for just a little bit longer, if only to annoy his master. After all, LaCroix was right—it was silly. Nonsense. How could a little wicker doll be controlling his dreams?

"Some believe that if a man dies in his dreams, his body dies as well. We may never know if this is so—none have returned from the land of the dead to tell us that their dream of falling, and their lives, ended in a sudden, dull thud."

Closing his eyes, Nick barely listened to LaCroix's words. He was in no condition to drive, and he knew it. Better to take a quick nap here, in the parked car, than fall asleep at the wheel. It was warmer, now, with the engine running.

"*And so, my gentle listeners, it would seem a wise man shouldn't fear a dream of falling, but a dream of dying . . . in an instant of fatal, phantom gravity.*"

So much warmer. . . .

6

NICK OPENED HIS EYES AND BLINKED, STARTLED AWAKE BY THE CAR coming to a complete and sudden stop.

"This looks bad," said Tracy, unbuckling her seat belt. Biting her lower lip, she stared at the devastation. "This looks *really* bad."

Nick killed the lights and siren. He opened the passenger door, then stood there, experiencing the strangest feeling of déjà vu—he knew this club, knew it well, but the name hadn't been The DayClub. Staring at what remained of the facade of the brick building that was surrounded by empty warehouses and apartment buildings, he wondered why it seemed so familiar.

He had barely a chance even to think about it. Theirs was only the third car at the scene—thanks to Tracy's disregard for the laws of traffic, the city, and physics—and the impact of the explosion had yet to be hidden by white sheets and police barricades. Orders were being shouted, radios were blaring, and police tape was being strung between hastily placed sawhorses as he finally forced himself away from the car and into the thick of the scene.

The building was a burned-out shell, a blackened brick exterior with flames erupting through the ruins. Human limbs and torsos were strewn across the street and side-walks, along with building material, shredded clothing, and other debris. From the look of the area, the club had been crowded to capacity when the bomb detonated. At this time of night, if it had happened just four or five blocks north, the street casualties alone would have been phenomenal.

The onlookers were hanging back, mortal and vampire alike. There was nothing they could do to help, but many pale faces watched the spectacle with wide and hungry eyes. Nick wondered for a moment if he should ask one of the vampire officers to quietly caution the mortals at the front of the crowd and warn them away. He even turned to do that, catching a flash of navy blue from the corner of his eye, then stopped.

He watched the policeman walk past, pale skin made paler by the darkness of the uniform he wore, and knew that there was an even chance he'd be ignored. There were few, if any, mortal patrolmen anymore, the ones who could tough it out having been moved up through the ranks while the others simply walked away . . . or disappeared. In the station he had some authority, but out here—on the streets, where it really counted—he was treated as just another mortal.

That's when the smell of blood and burning flesh hit him. Pulling a handkerchief from his pocket, Nick covered his mouth and nose as he walked among the things that had been vampires and were quickly turning to piles of ash. Few of the bodies were intact. But of the ones that were—

He stopped, staring down at the corpse of a young blond woman, her hair piled elegantly atop her head, not a strand out of place. Part of her arm was missing, and a foot, but what had stopped him was the stake protruding from her chest and the fact that her head had been severed—her body was burning. It was a miracle the corpse hadn't disinte-grated yet. "Tracy!" he yelled.

His partner was at his side before he could blink. The

vampire took one look at the victim, then turned her head away, her hand to her mouth. "Oh . . . God. It's a vigilante action."

Nick stared, watching the corpse as it disintegrated before his eyes. "We need cameras," he said flatly. "Before the rest of them go. Natalie can't get a clue on the weapons unless she's got something—"

Tracy turned toward the uniformed officers who were making their way through the carnage. "Film," she called to them. "Take pictures of every intact corpse. Nothing fancy, just get us every shot you can before they melt."

Melt. Nick started at the term—it was what they used to describe what was happening before his eyes, vampire bodies turning to ash. It made gathering evidence for a homicide damn near impossible. Then again, how many causes of death could there be for a vampire, other than a stake and decapitation, or maybe fire? Weapons were what caught suspects now. Weapons . . . and a relaxation of evidentiary procedure. It was becoming easier to convict suspects, especially if the suspect was mortal and the victim had been a vampire.

Glancing around at the police officers combing the site, the handkerchief still over his mouth, Nick saw what the presence of blood did to them—how their eyes glowed red and gold and green, and their fangs extended. It was like taunting a hungry dog with meat. But *they* were always hungry, whether or not they'd just gorged themselves on their government allotment of human or animal blood. Before his eyes was the perfect illustration of what LaCroix had said again and again—it was us or them.

And he might have believed that, had one of *them* not been Tracy . . . his partner.

"Nick?"

He turned when he heard Captain Reese call his name, then hustled across the sidewalk, veering around bodies and piles of ash. "Yes, Captain?"

Reese put a hand on his shoulder and drew him to one side. "I'm sending all mortal officers back to the station."

Staring, Nick gestured toward the crime scene. "You're going to need everyone you can get out here. The witness statements alone—"

"There's too much to deal with here. Too much—" Reese wiped his forehead with his hand, then stared at the crimson droplets of sweat that clung to his fingers. "Too much blood," he added sadly. "There's no doubt in anyone's mind what this was—this attack was organized. I've called in riot teams from the surrounding three precincts. It could get bad." He met Nick's gaze. "This crowd'll be out for blood. *Warm* blood."

More barricades had been erected as the patrol cars had arrived. The crowd swelled against the yellow tape around the crime scene, threatening to break it in places. Nick noted that there was little mingling between the members of the crowd now—the vampires were gathering at the center of the group, while the mortals, their faces shining with sweat from the heat of the night and the fire, were clustered here and there at the periphery. Reese was right—this could easily turn into a riot.

"We've got to get them out of here," said Nick softly, nodding toward three men and two woman—all mortals—who suddenly seemed to have noticed they were surrounded by vampires and who looked distinctly uneasy. "Send mixed teams, ones you can trust. Otherwise. . . ."

"We'll have a blood bath." Reese pulled a handkerchief from his pocket and swiped his forehead. He winced at a sudden bright light from the edge of the crowd. "Great! The press is here." Nick started to walk away, but Reese caught his arm. "Nick, you've got your papers—somebody can bring you across whenever you want. Go back to the station. There's no sense trying to be a hero here. Mortal heroes get killed."

"Maybe we need some mortal heroes." Watching the

golden eyes and the fangs of the vampires in the crowd, Nick took a deep breath. He had to stay. He'd taken the oath to serve and protect. Smiling, he turned back and added, "Let me do my job, Captain. Our bomber's probably a mortal. Which means the suspects are going to be mortal. I'd like to keep them alive."

Reese met his eyes for a long moment, then nodded. "All right—go on. But stick with your partner. She should be covering your back anyway. Where *is* she?" He turned, calling, "Vetter?"

"Here, Captain." Tracy was kneeling beside the bloody remains of a mortal less than a hundred yards away. Rising to her feet, she tried to brush the dirt from the skin of her knees as she approached them. Her clothing was streaked with soot, dirt, and blood. "Bad fashion choice," she explained when she arrived, giving another half-hearted swipe at her knees in embarrassment. "I didn't know we'd have a bombing today."

"You're a police detective," admonished Reese. "You're supposed to be ready for anything. And you're supposed to be watching your partner's back. Especially here."

Tracy glanced at Nick with an almost sullen expression. "I had an eye on him."

"So does the crowd."

At Reese's comment, she looked up and seemed to notice the crowd for the first time. "I've been tagging victims," she explained, her voice shaking slightly as she took in the escalating situation. "Captain, with the cameras here—"

"I know—we were just discussing that. Any cameras come near you, it's 'no comment.' Be polite, but brush them off. You're not getting paid to talk to the press." He shot a glance at Nick, then at Tracy again. "I want suspects—living, breathing suspects. And I want them *now.*"

"Yes, Captain," said Nick, and Tracy echoed him a moment later. With a sigh, Reese turned away and headed toward the press crew, muttering something under his breath that sounded like "Goddamn vultures."

Tracy gestured toward the squad cars that had blocked off a section of the street—the bodies and debris had been blown a good distance. "They're over there."

The ten or twelve people either seated in the rear of the vehicles or standing around them under police guard were all mortals. Nick quickened his pace, and Tracy followed. "Witnesses or suspects?" he asked sharply.

"Does it matter?"

She was right—it didn't matter, not to the vampires on the force. A patrolman snarled as Nick approached—his name plate read "Bettes." In answer, Nick reached slowly into his pocket, then withdrew and flipped open his identification. "Detective Knight."

Officer Bettes eyed him carefully, as if memorizing his features, then stepped away. Nick watched the officer leave, making note of him—there was someone he'd have to warn Reese about. He started when Tracy bumped into him, then turned toward her.

"Sorry." She gestured toward the patrolman. "Nice guy, huh?"

He didn't answer, merely meeting her eyes for a moment. "You're my partner, *not* my baby-sitter," he warned her.

Her eyes widened, all innocence. "I'm just watching your back."

"Right." Nick approached another patrolman guarding the group. "What do we have so far?"

The patrolman cleared his throat. "Three waitresses and a bartender; the others were in the club. They're lucky to be alive."

"Where were they when the bomb exploded?" asked Tracy.

"The back of the club, the rest rooms, the stockroom." The patrolman lowered his gaze, then looked up at Nick. "We haven't found any vampires who survived."

110

"Then we'll keep looking." Nick glanced at Tracy, guessing that she, too, was thinking of the staked and decapitated body they'd seen, just one among many. Someone had made very sure that the only survivors would be mortals. "If they got out the back, they probably didn't see anything."

"Doesn't hurt to ask," said Tracy. She turned back to the patrolman. "I'd like to talk to them before you take them down to the station for a statement."

They weren't suspects, they were witnesses. They'd been victims of a bombing. And now they were terrified out of their wits, surrounded by police and flashing lights and vampires. One of the men was holding a sobbing woman in his arms. The two waitresses, their hose ripped and their uniforms torn to pieces, were half covered by blankets. The bartender beside them seemed belligerent, ready to defend them at a moment's notice.

"Trace?" said Nick quietly. He turned back to her and caught her arm, moving her to one side. "See if you can get them out of here. The press is going to be all over them."

She glanced over her shoulder at the group of witnesses, then turned back to him. "I'll have a unit assigned to them. Might be better to hold them at the station until after dawn. . . ."

"And provide a mortal police escort?" Nick matched her grim smile. "Good idea. I'm going take a look around back, see if I can come up with more witnesses."

"Or suspects? They haven't spotted anyone else—"

"Would you come out of hiding with this group around?"

Tracy frowned. "Good point." Then she poked him lightly in the shoulder. "Hey, I'm supposed to be covering you. I can't do that if I'm here and you're around back."

Nick grinned. "If anything happens, I'll yell. You'll hear me."

"I'd better." She glanced back at the witnesses. "It'd be a bad move, careerwise. I mean, my partner gets his papers

111

and then gets killed because I wasn't there for backup? What would my dad say?"

"That you'll do better next time?"

He was about to leave when he heard Tracy murmur something under her breath. Nick looked up and spotted Vachon, hands cuffed behind his back, being pushed forward by Officer Bettes. "I've got a live one for you, detectives."

Nick's heart stopped in his chest as he met Vachon's eyes—he didn't look more than slightly battered, no worse than any of the other witnesses. And he *had* to be classified as a witness. If they took him in as a suspect, they'd check his record. His fingerprints alone would tie him to half a dozen organized attacks on vampires, not to mention the solo efforts of his youth. He'd be arraigned, tried, convicted, and shipped to a donation center by dawn.

The fact that he was probably guilty of complicity in the bombing barely crossed Nick's mind before he dismissed the thought completely. That could be dealt with later. Right now, he had to save Vachon's life.

Before Nick could open his mouth, Tracy stepped forward. "Sorry, Bettes, but he's with me." She glanced at Nick guiltily, then nodded toward the patrolman. "We were supposed to meet here after shift." When Bettes hesitated, frowning, she added, "You think the police commissioner's daughter's going to be dating a vigilante? Just take the cuffs off."

Vachon didn't seem to know where to look, trying to avoid Nick's eyes. He gritted his teeth as Officer Bettes unlocked the cuffs, none too gently. The officer gave him a rough shove and snarled, "If you say so, *detective*. But I'm still logging him as a witness."

"I'll take responsibility," said Tracy, her back straight and a faint glow of gold in her eyes.

Backing down, Bettes turned away, muttering, "Yeah, sure you will. Commissioner's daughter."

Nick didn't know what to do for a moment. Vachon rubbed his wrists, then walked over to Tracy. "Thanks. Trust me to run into Officer Vamp-with-attitude."

"Hey, we're not all bad," she answered. Then she stepped forward and planted a kiss on his cheek, her hand grabbing his. "Are you all right? God, I thought I was going to find you out here, laid out in the street—"

Vachon's arm went around her waist protectively, then he turned, finally meeting Nick's eyes. "Well, here I am. I was at the pay phone in the back—heard the front of the place blow and ran like hell."

"You didn't run fast enough." Nick took a step toward Vachon, his heart a lump of lead in his chest. He looked at his partner, then back at Vachon. "Get out of here. Now."

Licking his lips, Vachon looked away and pulled Tracy toward him. "Nick, I was going to tell you. There wasn't any time—"

"Get out." Grabbing a handful of the leather collar of his jacket, Nick pulled Vachon away from Tracy. "Go," he said, his voice sounding cold and foreign to his own ears. "Go home."

"Nick?"

He felt Tracy's hand on his shoulder and shrugged it off, his gaze still locked with Vachon's. "Get out of here." He released his hold on the jacket and took a step back, exhaling. "Now."

"We'll talk later, okay?" Vachon hesitated, shifting his weight from one foot to the other. "Later. Bye, Trace."

Nick watched Vachon run toward the edge of the scene. When an officer stopped Vachon at the yellow crime scene tape, Nick raised his hand, signaling for him to be allowed past. He disappeared into the crowd a moment later.

"I wanted to tell you," said Tracy, still standing behind him. "But he said he had to do it."

"How long has this been going on?"

"Since you brought him to the station—the open house."

When he turned to stare at her, Tracy looked away—he saw the sparkle of red at the corners of her eyes, blood tears. "Look, it's our business, okay? It's just that . . . he really respects you. He didn't want you to think—but it's *our* business."

There was a cold, still place inside him. Nick no longer really felt the heat, or smelled the smoke drifting from the burning club. At some point the fire engines had arrived and there were hoses being turned on the flames—a fine spray of water drifted down upon him, carried by the wind.

It did nothing to cool the rage he was trying to contain. Nick remained silent for a moment, taking one breath at a time. "We've got a job to do," he decided. He looked around the crime scene, his gaze centering on the witnesses being held in protective custody. "Just get them out of here before something happens. I'm going around the back." Nick started to walk away.

"You can't control his life," said Tracy, defensively. "We *were* going to tell you—"

"When?" He glanced over his shoulder at her. "After you'd brought him across?"

She flinched at that, a guilty expression, then she turned away.

He knew then what LaCroix had said was true . . . Vachon *would* become a vampire if he were given the chance, the right offer. Could he blame him? The world belonged to the vampires now; they ruled the night, and the shadow of their absolute authority couldn't be dissipated even by the brightest sunlight. The only safety left was to embrace the darkness.

Walking among the bodies and the piles of ash, Nick thought about what the change would mean to Vachon. He'd still be wild and reckless, fighting the biggest bully even if the odds were hopeless. He might even do some good on the other side. Tracy's father, if he approved of the match and okayed the papers, would try to get him involved in the police force. They needed more balance there, more officers sympathetic to the plight of mortals, more willing to uphold their rights.

But they couldn't count on that, could they? Because Vachon wouldn't be mortal anymore. He'd be a vampire. And vampires couldn't be trusted.

Not even when they were your partner.

Nick wandered to the side of the building, watching the blues and the coroner's personnel handle the remains of the corpses, trying to ignore the iron tang of the drying blood. The bomb squad would handle the questions of the type, power, and placement of the bomb. His job, at the moment, was to make guesses—who else in the crowd of gawkers might be a suspect, where had the bomb come from, where might the suspects have run. . . .

Footsteps echoed down the alley beside the remains of the club. Drawing his gun, Nick flattened himself against the wall, then peered down the dark alley.

The footsteps had stopped. In the darkness he could see a flash of skin and frightened eyes before the sounds started again. "Freeze! Police!" he called, flattening himself against the wall in case the suspect fired.

There was no response. Nick stepped out from cover and inched his way down the alley wall. Between the tension and the heat, his shirt was soaked through with perspiration, his hands slippery with sweat. But the grip of the gun was firm in his hand. That, at least, hadn't changed.

He nearly jumped when he realized Tracy was beside him, but kept his back against the wall. Only his heart betrayed him, skipping a beat.

"I heard you call," she whispered. "What's up?"

They were back to business.

"One suspect. Male. Teens to early twenties. Caucasian. Mortal." Nick kept his eyes trained on the depths of the alley, knowing that Tracy was doing the same. "I don't think he's armed. Could have come out to see what the fuss was about."

"Or . . . he could be the bomber."

There was a metallic clang in the alley. Before Nick could say "fire escape," Tracy had taken to the air, flying into a darkness for which her eyes were suited. Nick moved down the alley. His back to the wall, he looked upward as he ran. He spotted them just as the moon came out from behind a cloud, the youth screaming as the vampire descended upon him from the air.

Tracy grabbed the fire escape and swung herself onto the suspect. Shouting, "Freeze!" she flipped the suspect onto his stomach. But, instead of taking the cuffs from her pocket, she reared back. Her fangs descended, glinting in the moonlight. From where he stood, Nick could see the ruby-red of her eyes. Tracy had gone too far over the edge. She couldn't control her blood lust.

"Tracy! No!" Standing beneath the fire escape, Nick grabbed the ladder with both hands and rattled it. He had one hand on the lowest rung of the fire escape and one foot on a bar, when there was a high-pitched scream from the mouth of the alley. Even with the brilliance of the moon-light, he could make out only a silhouette. Whoever it was took off at a run.

Dropping back to the ground, Nick glanced up to see that Tracy had come back to herself—she was pulling the cuffs from her belt. There was no time for explanations or recriminations. "I'll get it," Nick called, then turned and headed up the alley.

At the mouth of the alley Nick stopped again, flattening himself against the stone wall, this time on the side opposite the club. He peered around cautiously, but there was no sign of the suspect. Behind him, he could hear the occasional wail of a siren, the firefighters trying to control the blaze, the sounds of the uniformed officers and other detectives as they went over the rest of the scene with a fine-tooth comb.

He glanced over his shoulder, now certain that only he had seen the other suspect. And after the little problem he'd just had with Tracy, he figured he'd be better off on his own.

The building beside the club was an abandoned apartment house. Wooden planks had been nailed over the doorway, but part of a board had been pulled away, leaving barely enough room to fit through. Nick hesitated only a moment before slipping inside. It was a tight fit for him, but probably hadn't been a problem for the small shadow he'd seen at the alley mouth.

He waited just inside the opening, letting his eyes adjust to the moonlight that filtered through broken glass windows and spaces between the boards on the doorway. A stairway went upward to his right, perhaps as high as five or six stories. It was an awful lot to search on a hunch.

A light shower of dust drifting down the open center of the stairway turned silver in the moonlight, accompanied by the creak of old wood. He moved to one side of that center section and looked up, seeing a shadow against the wall. There *was* someone up there.

Procedure required that he cordon off the building and get help. Procedure, however, didn't take into account some thirty to forty uniformed vampires with blood lust in their hearts and the law behind them, not to mention a blood-thirsty crowd on the verge of riot. Daring to err on the side of humanity, Nick started up the staircase, his back to the wall. He took the steps a few at a time, stopping to listen every so often. Shaking his head, he tapped his ear with his hand, wondering why his hearing was off—he should be able to hear the slightest whisper. But then . . . *why* would he? He was a mortal, not a vampire.

The second floor was clear, as were the third and fourth. It was when he reached the fifth floor—the highest level— that he saw the disturbance in the dust on the handrail and the footprints leading to a closed door. Slowly, Nick approached the door. He stood to the far side, gun held to his chest. "Police!" he shouted. "Open up!"

When the door didn't open, he slammed his shoulder against it, jumped back and flattened himself against the wall, waiting for a hail of bullets . . . *any* resistance.

Nothing.

He counted to ten, then ran into the room, gun held out and ready to fire. Swinging in an arc, he'd covered most of the room by the time he reached the center of the floor. There was a figure huddled against the wall just inside the door—a dark-skinned child, her hair corn-rowed. She was sobbing quietly, fist in her mouth to muffle the sound.

Holstering his gun, Nick approached her. "It's all right," he whispered. "I won't hurt you." Then he froze, as the moon again pulled itself from behind a cloud, light shining through the broken windows and into the empty room. "Lindy?"

Her eyes were wide and for a moment he thought she'd gone into shock because she hadn't responded to him. Then, as she stared at him, she seemed to realize who he was. Taking a deep breath, she whispered, "I saw my daddy. He was there! And I saw a monster!"

Nick knew exactly what she'd seen—Reese walking the perimeter of the crime scene, eyes gold. And Tracy, fangs bared and eyes red, ready to sink her fangs into the suspect's throat. He reached out, rubbing the skin on her upper arm. "Lindy, honey, that wasn't—"

"I saw my daddy," she repeated, still staring with blank eyes. "I saw him." A sob broke through and her tears started again, leaving wet trails in the grime on her face. She threw herself into his arms. "Oh, Nick," she cried, between sobs, "I *saw* him."

Nick held her tightly, uncertain of what to do or say other than make comforting noises to quiet her. How could he help her reconcile the monster she'd just seen with the man who'd read her stories, told her to turn down her music, and tucked her in at night? How could anyone?

That could wait. He had to get her out of here, away from the crime scene. "Lindy, what are you doing here? You should be in bed."

She pulled her face away from his collar, enough to meet his eyes. The mild scolding got through to her. "I talked to LaCroix. He told me if I came here with him, I'd see Daddy."

LaCroix was using Lindy against her father, hoping Reese would find her. They'd have words about this when he returned to the apartment at dawn. It wasn't the first time LaCroix had used one of the refugees as a pawn.

"Nick?" Lindy frowned, then shivered in his grasp. "I saw him, Nick. He was a *monster*. He—"

"Nick? You in here?"

He froze as he recognized Tracy's voice in the lower hall, then looked around quickly. There was no place to hide from heightened vampire senses. And after the conversation he'd had with Reese at the station, he didn't dare let any vampire on the force see the captain's daughter. Only disaster could come of that.

Holding Lindy close, he whispered, "Do exactly what I say. Don't make a sound. All right?" He looked down and saw understanding in her terrified eyes.

Rising, Nick almost lifted Lindy from the floor, setting her on her feet. He hurried to the doorway and positioned her with her back against the wall, just to his left and hidden from view. Placing his hand on her shoulder, he willed her to stay calm and quiet, hoping that keeping her that close would help mask their two heartbeats—with luck, Tracy would pick up only one.

"Nick?" came the call again.

"Here," he answered, standing in the doorway.

Tracy appeared at the center of the stairwell, rising

119

straight up in the air. She hovered there, just above the level of the railing. "Have you found anything?"

"No. Nothing." He tightened his grip on Lindy's shoulder, feeling her shudder beneath his fingers. "You?"

"Just the one outside. The blues are taking him in." Tracy met his gaze across the distance—Nick felt like his soul was being inspected. She knew something was up.

"Should you be doing that?" asked Nick, gesturing toward the hovering Tracy with his free hand. "You've gotta last the night, after all."

"Yeah." Tracy settled on the upper landing, not more than ten yards from him. "You're right. It's gonna be a long night." Her eyes narrowed as Lindy made a small sound. "You sure there's nothing—"

Nick forced himself not to look at Lindy, prayed that his voice could keep from cracking. "Nothing," he repeated. "Trust me."

Tracy's eyes never moved from his. "Trust you," she repeated softly. "Yeah. Okay." Nodding slightly, she turned, facing the staircase. "The witnesses are on their way to the station and the crowd's starting to disperse."

"Good."

She turned, took a step toward him, but then stopped herself. "Vachon—"

"Not now, Trace," he said wearily. Leaning against the door, he gave her a wan smile. "It's been a rough night."

"Okay." Tracy nodded once, her hand resting on the banister of the staircase. She lifted her hands, glanced at the dust patterns on the banister, then met his eyes again. "Okay. Later. I guess you've got enough on your mind, what with the captain giving you papers." She grinned. "I saw the names on that list. No matter who you choose to bring you across, the rest are going to be jealous. You're going to be one very unpopular vampire with the women in the 96th Precinct, Detective Knight."

Lindy shifted beneath his hand, but Nick held her in

place. "Yeah," he said, in what he hoped was a sheepish tone. "I was hoping you might help deflect some of the fallout."

"I'll cover for you," promised Tracy, as she headed downstairs. "That's what partners are supposed to do, right? Cover for each other?"

"That's right . . . partner."

He waited—one heartbeat, then two, then ten—until Tracy's footsteps were gone, before he knelt beside Lindy. She'd shoved her fist in her mouth, as if afraid to make a sound. Dark eyes wide, she stared at him.

"It's okay now," he said softly.

She placed her hands on his shoulders. "You can't be one of them, Nick. I saw Daddy. They'll make you a monster, like him."

"I'm not going to turn," he promised. Carefully, he removed her hands from his shoulders, holding them in his own. "You have to listen to me. Stay here until dawn. Hide in the closet if you have to, but stay here until you can see the sun. Then go straight home. When you get there, you find LaCroix. And you tell him I want to see him as soon as I come back."

Lindy stared at him. He shook her, lightly, and her eyes focused on him again, this time with some understanding. "I'm not going to let them bring me across," he repeated. "And I need you to deliver that message for me. Can you do that?"

"Yes," she answered, in a small voice.

"Now, go," he told her. "Hide in a closet. There's an empty one over there. And don't come out until sunrise."

Lindy hesitated, one hand on his shoulder. "You won't turn?"

"No."

"Promise?"

"Promise," he repeated, crossing his heart with a quick movement of his fingers.

She hugged him tightly, a shy smile on her lips, which he matched with a grin. Glancing back at him, she ran to the closet. Lindy stepped inside, then peered out.

"Not a peep," he told her, rising to his feet. "And you give that message to LaCroix. I'm counting on you."

"I can do it."

"Good." He closed his eyes for a moment, wishing that he could stay, or find some other way to get her out of there. Had it been any other mortal child, there wouldn't have been a problem, but with Reese around. . . .

Sighing, Nick opened his eyes and walked out into the hallway, then down the stairs. Outside, he found Tracy and more uniformed officers. "This one's clean," Nick told them, gesturing toward the building behind him. "You'll want to concentrate on anything with a fire escape or door on that alley or the one behind."

"You heard the man," said Tracy, making a shooing motion with her hands. "This one's clean."

The vampire police officers hesitated, glancing at one another and muttering among themselves, then moved off to search the buildings. Nick looked down at the ground, knowing how much authority he had with them— practically none. And now that word was getting out that he'd been offered a chance to turn after six months . . . it was going to be a rough couple of days, which would only get rougher when he announced that he had no intention of giving up his life for the law.

"You should get out of here," said Tracy softly. "It's not safe." Reaching into her jacket pocket, she withdrew the keys and dangled them. "I'll stay here and log bodies for a while. Why don't you take my car back to the station?"

"The captain said the same thing." Nick looked over his shoulder at the uniformed officers who'd just left them. "Tracy, I've gotta pull my weight."

"You can pull it better when you've got vampire strength."

When he met Tracy's eyes, she smiled faintly. "I'll keep an eye out for more witnesses . . . or suspects."

"But your car—"

"I'll fly." Tracy flipped the keys into the air and Nick caught them. "We cover each other, okay?"

"Okay." He started toward the car, then turned. "I don't think my insurance—"

"Mine does." Tracy waved at him. "And it's paid. At least, I think I paid it last month."

Nick opened the car door, then paused before he got in, his eyes going to the building where Lindy was hiding. He didn't doubt the uniforms would ignore it, now that Tracy had given it the okay.

Much as he was tempted to drive back to his apartment and face LaCroix and Vachon, he knew he was needed at the station. With open hostility against mortals exhibited by many of the uniformed officers, his presence during the questioning of the witnesses might save their lives. In fact, he'd ask Reese about Tracy's idea—holding them in custody until after sunrise. Given a chance, he'd handpick the officers, make certain Bettes was nowhere near them, and accompany some of the witnesses home himself.

That is, if he managed to stay awake that long.

With a yawn, Nick slid behind the wheel of the car, turned his head—then drew back quickly as something soft struck him between the eyes. There was a gold and blue tassel from a graduation cap hanging from the rearview mirror.

He hadn't noticed it before. Running the strands through his fingers, he smiled at the small medal attached to it. This had been part of her mortal life, the life that included having children, growing up, and growing old that she said she'd traded for her career and her car. Tracy regretted that trade—he could see it in her eyes when she saw a woman with a baby, had heard it in her voice earlier that evening. He'd never met her when she'd been mortal, but in his mind's eye he could imagine her as she might have been,

123

full of life and energy, determined to make a career for herself, but free of the desperate longing that accompanied the choice she'd made, to become a vampire and leave the mortal world behind.

The memory of the look in Natalie's eyes haunted him—she knew he was right, that it was crazy for him to join her in a life she detested, but she'd still asked. Did Tracy feel the same way about Vachon? Did they think that love might make their existence bearable, that misery shared was halved instead of doubled?

And were they wrong?

Setting the tassel swinging, Nick placed the key in the ignition. He didn't know.

Natalie was a vampire, but she was his friend . . . and more. Tracy was a vampire, but she was still his partner. Reese was a vampire, but he was also a father who had lost his family. He cared about them, all of them, but then he'd remember the eyes of the other vampires glittering when the wind had carried the scent of fresh blood, how their fangs had gleamed against the red of their lips, and a shiver ran through him.

Nick leaned his forehead against the steering wheel and closed his eyes, wondering what he was going to do, what he *could* do about Natalie, about the situation between Tracy and Vachon, about LaCroix and the resistance movement, about Reese and his family, about providing justice for the mortals *and* the vampires in Toronto. He came to the conclusion that he couldn't save them all, no matter how hard he tried.

He wasn't even certain he could save himself.

7

THE TAPPING WAS INSISTENT, LIKE THE BANGING OF A LOOSE shutter in the wind.

Nick opened his eyes and stared at the fogged interior of the windshield, then leaned back in his seat. The car engine was running and the heater was making a humming sound. For a moment he couldn't remember where he was. He forced himself to take a deep breath, then one more, but a dull ache lingered behind his eyes. He was exhausted, and he knew why.

He'd been dreaming again, about being a mortal in a world of vampires.

There was another rap on the fogged, driver's side window. He ran his hand over the glass and saw Vachon standing outside the car, looking anything but pleased. Turning off the engine and leaving the keys in the ignition, Nick took another deep breath. He wanted to talk to Vachon about—

Tracy. About seeing Tracy. Vampires and mortals didn't mix.

It was cold. Nick opened the door, was hit with a blast of frigid air, and seriously thought for a moment about inviting Vachon inside the Caddie. But he braved it, closing the door

125

behind him and stepping carefully onto the ice-covered street. Rubbing his hands together to warm them, Nick approached Vachon, who was leaning on the hood of the Caddie.

"I got your message." Vachon stared across the street, at the entrance to the Raven, his tone indicating his lack of interest. "What's up?"

Nick hesitated and placed his bare hand on the hood of the car, then withdrew it quickly—the metal was so cold that it stung his skin. He stared at his hand for a moment, wondering at the sensation, then glanced back at Vachon. He wanted this done as quickly as possible. "Tracy. It's over."

"Is it?" Vachon pursed his lips, glanced at Nick, then returned to staring at the entrance to the Raven. "I'd like to hear that from Tracy."

"You will."

"What did you say to her?" Vachon asked, a hint of suspicion in his voice.

"That it's not a good idea to get too close to her snitches. That I don't think she should be seeing you. That you're from two different worlds."

"Can't argue with the last one." Vachon took a deep breath, as if mustering his defiance. "This is between us, okay? Tracy and me. You don't tell me what I do and who I see."

"I don't care what you do or who you see," countered Nick sharply. "Just so long as Tracy's out of it." The wind picked up and he shivered, tucking his hands in his pockets to keep them warm. He thought about moving the conversation somewhere else, but that would mean the Raven . . . and he didn't feel like running into LaCroix again.

A pair of mortals left the club as he watched; they were oblivious to the hungry look on the face of the man watching the door. He imagined Tracy on her few ventures into the Raven and wondered if she had noticed the bouncer, had known what that predatory smile meant. "She doesn't know what she's getting into," he said aloud.

"You sure about that?"

His eyes and his attention remained on the mortal couple—the man's arm around the woman, holding her close as they walked together. That's what it should be like, at least for him. That's what he wanted. He could imagine himself with Natalie, going out to a club, spending an evening having drinks and conversation, watching the crowd. And afterward, going back to the car, or even walking home, his arm around her. They'd stop beneath a street light and he'd look at her—her eyes shining, strands of her brown hair whipped to one side by the wind. And then he'd kiss her, with no beast inside him to awaken at the nearness of her warmth, the promise of her blood. That's what it should be like.

That's what he'd never have.

"What?" he asked, suddenly realizing that Vachon had asked him a question.

"Are you sure she doesn't know what she's getting into? "Tracy's been taking it slow, but she's been asking questions. Lots of questions."

He was right, he'd let this go on too long. "Then it's got to stop."

"Why?"

"Because she's mortal. Because she's my partner."

"Wrong answer—both times." Vachon looked at him from beneath lowered lids. "She's got a right to her own life, Nick. She's spent most of it trying to please her father, and just when she starts crawling out of the hole he's stuck her in, you come along and tie her up with a whole new set of rules. Maybe it's time for Tracy to do something because Tracy wants to, instead of trying to please her dad or impress her partner."

"She doesn't have to impress me."

"But she's trying. I don't know why, but she thinks you

know what you're doing. With the police stuff, maybe she's right." He shrugged, then eyed Nick thoughtfully. "But with everything else—Nick, you've got your own problems, okay? But some of us *like* being vampires."

Nick took a threatening step toward Vachon. "This isn't about me. It's about Tracy. It's about letting mortals live their lives without our interference."

"What if this particular mortal *wants* to be interfered with?" asked Vachon. He rubbed the back of one partially gloved hand into his other palm, still watching Nick. "Hey, if she tells me to walk, I'm history. But it's gotta be because she wants it that way, not because she's trying to make points with you."

"I'm telling you to leave her alone."

"And you're gonna stop me?"

When Vachon started to walk away, Nick reached forward to grab his shoulder. Without warning, Vachon shoved Nick, hard.

He shouldn't have felt a thing. In fact, he raised his hand, prepared to push back and take Vachon on for real, if he had to. Instead, he fell back against the Caddie's side mirror, then the heels of his boots lost purchase on the ice and he fell. Nick pushed up from the ground, but his palm was wet and cold, covered with bits of ice and gravel. He wiped it on his trousers, placed his hand on the ground again, and felt a wave of dizziness wash over him.

The world tilted. He closed his eyes, not certain which way was up.

He felt a shoulder placed just below his, supporting him before he could pitch forward. Nick opened his eyes and stared at Vachon. "What—?"

"What's wrong with you, man? Here, hang on—" Nick held tightly to Vachon's shoulder as he was helped to his feet, then leaned back against the Caddie for support. "You've gotta lay off the hard stuff." Vachon ducked his head, trying to meet Nick's eyes. "Or maybe you haven't had *enough* of the hard stuff. Have you fed recently?"

Nick rubbed his palms together to shake off the dirt from the street, then wiped his hands down his face, his skin feeling almost warm compared with the cold of his fingers. "When I get back to the loft. When I—" He stared hard at Vachon for a moment, seeing a double image—Vachon not as a vampire but as mortal, with tanned skin and his long black hair tied back in a ponytail. "I had a dream," he whispered. "I keep having the same dream. Not the same, but the same place, the same people. . . ." He glanced at the hand on his shoulder, then his eyes moved back to meet Vachon's. "She wants to bring you across."

"Bring me—?" Lifting his hand very carefully from Nick's shoulder, Vachon backed into the middle of the street, as if unnerved. "Look, go home, okay? And let me and Tracy handle our own lives."

There was a light breeze and Vachon was gone, lifting into the air. Nick stood there for a long moment, staring at the door to the Raven, his eyes focusing again. The weakness was passing. He'd never felt like this before, even when he'd had the fever, the only illness to which vampires had ever been susceptible.

The click of heels caught his attention. Urs had left the shadow of the club doorway and was standing on the sidewalk. She waited while a car passed, then hurried over to him, her pace slowing only as she made her way over the patches of ice that covered the street. "I saw what happened," she said. "Are you hurt?"

Her hand cupped his chin and she stared into his eyes, searching. Then Urs reached down to hold his hands in her own. Nick tried to pull away, but she touched his hands to her lips and frowned. "Your skin is warm. You're flushed."

"I'm fine. The ice—" To show her, Nick brought his heel down sharply on a patch of ice, which cracked and shattered. "I slipped on the ice."

"Sometimes Vachon doesn't know his own strength." Urs backed away a step and drew a black shawl close around her shoulders, her expression concerned. "Come inside. You can rest on the couch in the back. Once you've fed—"

"I'm fine." He smiled to reassure her, the concern touching his heart. He realized that if he was cold, she must be freezing, wearing nothing but a sleeveless top, a mini-skirt, and tights. "Go back inside—you'll get frostbite."

It was Urs's turn to smile, that knowing, confident look that vampires got when they prided themselves on being beyond the reach of earthly, mortal ills. "I'm fine," she echoed. Taking a step closer, she ran her fingers down his cheek, her touch cool against his face. "If you won't go inside, then come home with me."

Her offer touched his heart as much as her concern had. He met her eyes for a moment and realized just how short a time he'd known her—months, when many of the vampires he'd known had been his friends or acquaintances for centuries. There was nothing between them but friendship. And since both of their hearts were occupied elsewhere, friendship was all there could be between them.

"I don't think so." With as much care as his frozen fingers could muster, Nick took hold of her hand, squeezed it gently in gratitude for the offer, then released it. "Thanks, but no."

Over the centuries he'd had women slap him after far more gallant offers or refusals. Urs merely turned her head and nodded in understanding, her smile still in place although it was tinged with disappointment. And, as always, that lingering sadness.

Nick opened the car door and sat behind the wheel—the keys were still in the ignition. Urs leaned in the open door, her fingers on the frame loosing a brief shower of ice and frozen snow. "Then let me drive you home," she offered, in a tone that let him know that was all she was offering.

"Believe me, I'll find it." He paused, searching her eyes,

wondering if her offer to leave was more for himself or for her. "Do you need a lift somewhere?"

Urs glanced over her shoulder, toward the Raven, as if she'd been called. "No. He needs—*they* need me inside." She turned her attention back to Nick, still smiling sadly. "Be careful. Vachon . . . he'll come around."

"I know."

She pointed past him, toward the passenger seat. "Oh— what's that?"

Nick glanced down and saw what had caught her eye— the dream doll. Picking it up, he barely managed to hold it in his fingers as a shiver ran through him.

An arm was now bent inward, in addition to the two legs.

Before he could move, Urs took it from his hand. "Mexican, isn't it?" she asked, examining it. "Or South American?" Turning it over, she frowned for a moment, then tapped it on the back with a manicured fingernail. "Definitely South American. Old, too."

Surprised at the accuracy of her guess, Nick gaped at her—having knowledge like that wasn't something he would have guessed of Urs. Seeing his expression, she grinned, eyes twinkling. "Hey, after a century or so a girl gets around. Especially with Vachon."

When Vachon's name was spoken, the smile disappeared. Urs concentrated on the doll again. "Too bad it's broken. It's really kind of cute. Where'd you get it?"

"It's sort of a good luck charm," he said, after a moment's hesitation. Leaning wearily against the headrest, he added, "But it hasn't done me any good."

"Can I keep it? I could put it on a necklace or something."

Nick lifted his hand to take the doll from her, but clenched his fist and stopped himself. Now that he'd suffered through a third dream, he knew he had to rid himself of the doll. Giving it to Urs would be relatively safe—it wouldn't hurt her. And if she dreamed, he hoped her dreams might be more pleasant.

"All right," he said, feeling pleased with himself as he saw her eyes shining with childlike delight. When her fist clenched possessively over her prize, hiding it from sight, a sense of relief settled in his chest. He smiled at her and added, "You'd better go back inside before you catch cold."

"Worrywart!" Leaning forward, she planted a kiss gently on his forehead, her hand lingering on his cheek as she met his eyes. "Go home, okay? And drive safely."

Nick rested a hand over hers for a moment. "I will."

Urs drew away. She glanced down both sides of the street, then hurried to the sidewalk.

Closing his door, Nick turned the key in the ignition. The driver's side window was fogging again, and he wiped his hand across it. Through the blurry glass he could see Urs standing on the curb in front of the Raven, watching him. She raised her hand in farewell.

Nick held up his hand in answer, then pulled the car out onto the street, the tires crunching noisily over the ice built up along the line of parked cars. After a block, he had second thoughts about leaving the doll with Urs, but knew that his concern was unnecessary—she wouldn't come to any harm. It was just a toy. She'd probably get bored with it, or throw it away. Just as well that she'd never know how much that trinket had cost him, both in dollars and in lost sleep.

The drive back to the loft was uneventful. The streets seemed awfully deserted; it seemed wrong that so few people were out this close to midnight. Didn't they know the sun would be rising in four hours—no . . . six?

Nick leaned against the wall of the elevator and closed his eyes. Just thinking about a good eight to ten hours of uninterrupted sleep set him at ease. He'd have a drink first—the hunger for blood was gnawing at his insides— then shower and hit the sack. He might even skip the shower . . . although his skin felt itchy, like he was covered with sweat and grime.

Yawning as the elevator doors opened, he walked into the loft. Nick decided that even the itch of his skin wouldn't keep him from falling asleep the second he stopped moving. He headed for the refrigerator, opened the door, grabbed the first bottle that came to his hand, pulled out the cork with his teeth, and spit it out. He started to touch the bottle to his lips when the smell assaulted him—

Blood.

A tremor ran through his body and his stomach heaved unmercifully. His fingers trembled and the bottle slipped. Only the fact that he jumped back so quickly kept him from being covered by the thick liquid as the bottle smashed on the floor, sending spatters of red and shards of glass everywhere.

Nick stared at the mess, his hand going to the refrigerator for support as the tremors continued to race through him. The smell had gotten stronger, if anything. He took a few steps away and leaned on the wall beside the refrigerator, trying not to gag.

The feeling passed after a moment; even the heavy scent of the spilled blood seemed to lessen. And his hunger returned, burning hot and bright in his chest. Nick rested his hand over his heart, closed his eyes, and took a deep breath, willing himself to relax. Nothing like this had ever happened before. He accepted the hunger as a good sign and turned back to the refrigerator.

Ignoring the spilled cow blood, and avoiding the edges of the spill where possible, he opened the refrigerator door and reached for another bottle. But he hesitated, his fingers inches from the glass. The smell of blood assaulted him again, and he shut the refrigerator quickly, leaning heavily against the door.

Nick closed his eyes again, but the smell wouldn't go away this time. It nauseated him, sending his stomach heaving and causing such a lump in his throat that he could barely swallow. Opening his eyes, he stumbled into the

133

living room, not caring that he left a trail of bloody footprints.

His fingers closed around the edge of the black leather couch and he threw himself onto it, fighting back the revulsion. It took longer this time, but the nauseous feeling slipped away again. Only the hunger still burned within him.

But he didn't care. The weight of all that lost sleep pressed down upon him until he felt as if he were being smothered. He closed his eyes, cheek resting against the familiar surface of the couch, and let sleep overtake him. It was easier now, knowing that the doll was gone and rest would finally be his.

8

A RAY OF AFTERNOON SUNSHINE SLIPPED AROUND THE CORNER OF the shade on the window, piercing the darkness of the bedroom. Nick opened his eyes to the blinding glare, then shut them just as quickly. He felt exhausted, troubled by the strange dreams that continued to haunt him—a winter world where he walked in darkness and drank blood as a matter of course. Even in his dreams, he didn't want to be a vampire. Shading his eyes with his hand, he started to move, then looked at the bed beside him.

Urs was curled against him, her head resting in the crook of his arm, her blonde curls falling on either side of her face. She seemed so young when she slept, so innocent and carefree. He contented himself with watching her for a moment, the gentle movement of the sheet that covered them both as she breathed, dreaming of . . . what? The time before the world had changed, when vampires existed only in myth? Of how Vachon had found her, rescuing her from a vampire's private blood harem, where her life was leeched away, a few drops at a time?

Her sleepy smile was too soft for such dark thoughts. Leaning over to kiss her forehead, he had a sudden flash of memory—that sun-bronzed face turned white, eyes gold

135

and dangerous, red lips redder still with blood. He stared down at her, wondering where the image had come from. Not memory—Urs wore makeup only when disguised, though she wore that well enough. Could it be from his dream, a companion to all of the other disquieting images that swam through his brain?

Carefully, so as not to disturb her, Nick left the bed and dressed for work, although he had an hour before he had to leave for his shift. He was anything but graceful at the best of times, and now everything he touched seemed to slip through his fingers—his watch, his shoes, and his badge all ended up on the floor at one point or another—but Urs's reaction was nothing more than a sigh as she shifted her position in the bed. His eyes kept returning to her as he buttoned his shirt and knotted his tie.

When he'd returned from shift, he'd found her in his apartment—LaCroix was busy elsewhere. She'd promised him that Lindy was fine, agreed that LaCroix should never have done such a thing, and admitted that Lindy had told her about his authorization to turn, as well as the promise he'd made to refuse the summons to darkness.

He'd had to make that promise again, to Urs. And his attempts to comfort her fears for Vachon and himself had gone further than he'd intended, further than they'd ever gone before. Although there was something in Urs's manner and eyes that had never failed to touch him, he had always known that her heart belonged to Vachon. And had thought, until this past evening, that Vachon had felt the same. They'd worked together, played together, been part of one another's lives publicly and privately—or in as much privacy as resistance fighters could find, hiding from the vampires and the darkness in such crowded, squalid conditions.

He'd been happy that Vachon had found a kindred spirit, for at that time he'd had Janette with him. He used to watch her sleep in just this fashion, wondering where her thoughts wandered in her dreams. She'd spoken little of her other life, the time before her wealthy family had become vampires, then cast her out when she'd refused to be brought across and surrender her light to darkness.

Too many had died the day she'd first crossed his path, when he'd found himself alone and fighting for his survival in the lawless streets. Her smooth skin and sweet smile helped erase the bloody memories that had threatened to haunt his dreams that night and for many nights after. It was she who had brought him to LaCroix. And it was at least a year or so before he'd realized that she'd been ordered to ensnare him, to bring him to the man who orchestrated the attacks of a mortal refugee resistance force with all the skill and care he'd once applied to one of his concert performances.

But he'd forgiven her that. For although Janette had been under orders and slept with whomever LaCroix wished, assuming whatever role was necessary, she'd always returned to Nick. The word "love" was never mentioned. Love was a dangerous indulgence in a world where death walked the night and human blood was a commodity. They'd given each other comfort, pleasure, and a little of the joy that had managed to survive in their hearts, until they'd found themselves living in two different worlds—she fighting with the resistance and working with the refugees, while he spent his days and then his nights mingling with the vampires and those who worked for them. When he'd been transferred to the night shift as a detective, he'd found himself thinking more often of Natalie Lambert. And Janette had slipped further away, until one day she'd disappeared entirely . . . without a trace.

Slipping his badge into the inner pocket of his suit coat, Nick turned to look at Urs one more time. If his plans succeeded, he'd never see her again. He couldn't take her from this place—too much of her belonged to LaCroix. He suspected that they'd been lovers upon occasion, but doubted that was what held her to the master musician turned resistance leader. Nick knew too well how the power of LaCroix's magnetism ensnared the soul, fired the imagination. He'd grown to believe in LaCroix's cause of freeing mortality from the rule of the vampires and had done all he'd been asked—fought and killed, lied and cheated, waited and watched . . . even joined the police force.

The last had been LaCroix's undoing. Nick took his oaths seriously. And when he'd sworn his police oath—to protect and to serve—something in him had changed, moved beyond the reach of LaCroix and his plotting, or the vampires and their attempt to stabilize their brave new world.

On an impulse, he walked back to the bed and sat down beside Urs. Nick kissed her on the forehead, fearing that she would wake and fearing that she would not. Once more she sighed, still unable to shake off her slumber, her lips twisted in an innocent smile, her hand outstretched to where he'd slept beside her. Brushing her fingers once with his own, he left her and walked into the living room.

His heart almost stopped when he saw LaCroix on the window seat. The blinds had been opened and the light rained down upon him, burnishing his tan skin and making his hair seem the color of bronze. He held his left hand in his right, massaging it, as was his habit when he was lost in thought. Two of the fingers had healed but were twisted awkwardly.

"Is it bothering you today?"

LaCroix started, dispelling some of Nick's anger—LaCroix was next to impossible to surprise. He settled back against the window and stared out again. "I'm sorry—I didn't think you'd risen yet. No. Old habits, I suppose. They wouldn't make that mistake now, you know . . . leaving me alive. They'd turn me or kill me."

"You've taught them how dangerous mercy can be."

A twisted smile crossed LaCroix's lips. "I should be

thankful I had some fans among their hierarchy. And I *have* taught them a thing or two since then. I suppose it was my saving grace that they loved their music."

An image flashed before Nick's eyes—LaCroix, in medieval garb, playing some sort of stringed instrument. He shook his head to clear it.

"What?" asked LaCroix, curiously.

"Nothing. A dream I had." He blinked, and another image filled his vision—fangs and blood. *His* fangs . . . and human blood. "I was a vampire. And you—you were the one who brought me across."

LaCroix laughed and rubbed his neck ruefully. "Such fancies from you, Nicholas. And I thought officers of the law were supposed to be an unimaginative bunch." Then his eyes became hooded. "Lindy said you wanted to speak with me."

"Yes, about taking her with you on that bombing raid last night. After I'd talked to her, gotten her to trust you." Nick reached behind him, intent on closing the bedroom door so that they wouldn't disturb Urs . . . but he hesitated, taking a long look before quietly pulling the door shut. When he turned back to LaCroix, he felt his anger rise again. He'd been furious the night before when he'd discovered that LaCroix was nowhere to be found and had left Urs to calm him. "You could have faced me yourself."

"Ah, but you had more fun with her." LaCroix's jaunty attitude and smile suddenly became grim. "I was busy elsewhere. Urs came to you of her own volition this morning—I had nothing to do with it. Although you probably won't believe that."

"Does it matter what I believe?"

"I don't suppose it does." Sighing, LaCroix drew up his leg, resting his foot on the edge of the table. "If it's any consolation, it *was* a heavy-handed move and ill considered. I was wrong. But that doesn't mean that I'm not prepared to sacrifice any one of us. Even you."

"For the cause." Something in Nick was chilled by the determination he saw in LaCroix's eyes. "They offered me my papers last night."

"So I was told."

"You want me to accept their offer—to become a vampire."

"Yes." LaCroix turned his head, looking out the window again, into the daylight world. "We need someone on the inside, who has access to information we can't get any other way. You'll be perfect."

"Even if it kills me? Makes me what you hate the most?"

"We all make sacrifices."

Nick flopped onto the couch, the noise catching LaCroix's attention, even if his words couldn't. "You saved me," he pressed. "You taught me. You brought me to the police—"

"And lost you to them." LaCroix's short laugh was bitter. "You see, I do make mistakes. But it was what you were meant to do. I was meant to play symphonies and overtures, while you were meant to . . . what is it? Protect and serve? What better than to serve humanity?"

"At the cost of losing my own?" Nick leaned forward. "You're asking me to give up everything."

"Except survival. No matter what happens, you'll be protected. They do protect their own, I'll give them that."

Something was missing from LaCroix's customary manner—his arrogant optimism. And this talk of surviving, should all else fail. . . . "What are you not telling me?"

"The artificial blood plant goes on-line tonight."

Their attempts at sabotaging the plant had slowed construction, but Nick hadn't realized it was that close to completion. "You're not ready."

"I know."

"You can't attack." Nick meant the comment as a statement, not a question. LaCroix simply didn't have the numbers or the weaponry.

LaCroix merely looked back to the window.

Horrified, Nick jumped to his feet, his voice rising. "You'll be slaughtered!"

"Tonight. Or tomorrow. Or tomorrow night . . . what does it matter? We're going to die eventually. That's what mortality means—death. To die. And if we're going to die, we should make it count for something, make a stand. The vampire elite will be at the opening, as well as the people who planned and built the damned thing. To get even a few of them might cripple the operation for years, perhaps a decade."

"If you and the others are captured, they'll use you as donors. You'll disappear."

"But if we live," countered LaCroix, gesturing with his mangled hand, "we fight another day. Until we win. Or die."

Nick stared hard at the man he'd admired, followed, fought for and beside—there was no gleam of insanity, but hard, cold ruthlessness shone like a light from his eyes. "You're a fanatic."

"Pragmatic," corrected LaCroix, with a smile. "Even prey have the right to be predators now and again, if they've got the stomach for it."

The eyes told the story—there was nothing he could say that would sway LaCroix from his decision. And those who'd followed him would continue on the path they'd chosen, even when it led them to the jaws of hell itself.

Nick turned his back and walked to the table beside the door, picking up the papers he'd been given the night before, needing to hold them for a moment. And this was what this madman wanted him to do? To obey without question? To throw his life away on one futile expression of defiance?

"I'm on duty tonight," he said, after a moment's pause. "They'll assign me to security detail at the plant."

"I know."

He closed his eyes and leaned on the table, pressing his palms flat against the wood. There was no way he could

141

stop this plan, but if he were part of it, if he could manage to save even a few of the mortals who'd so blindly placed their faith in LaCroix. . . . "What do you want me to do?"

"Buy us time. Get as many out as you can. That's all."

"That's enough." Opening his eyes, Nick turned his head. "I'll try—on two conditions. The first is that Lindy and the other children stay here tonight."

LaCroix smiled and held out his palms, accepting that much. "I wouldn't have it any other way."

"I'm leaving in the morning."

The smile vanished, replaced by a blank stare. "To go . . . where?"

"Anywhere." Taking a deep breath, Nick stared at the wall, at the door, at anything but LaCroix. "I won't be able to stay after I refuse to be turned."

He heard LaCroix move from the window. "You're going to reject the promotion?"

"Yes."

"Why?"

"Because I want to live." Nick turned again and faced LaCroix. "Because that's all I have left." He paused, licking his lips. "And I'm taking Denise and her daughters with me. Reese is going to start looking for his family soon—they'll be safe only if they leave. That's the second condition."

LaCroix raised a finger to his lips, considering. His gaze fell on the closed bedroom door, which he indicated with a flick of his wrist.

Nick stared at him with hard eyes. "You'll tell Urs. After we're gone."

LaCroix's eyes widened slightly—Nick had scored a second point, surprising him again. "You're not taking her with you?"

"No. In your own way, you've turned her. She belongs to you, now. They all do." Shaking his head, Nick took a step toward LaCroix, his fingers clenched into a fist. "They're no longer refugees—they're an army. Your army."

"They're fighting for their humanity—"

"They're fighting for you." For a moment, Nick was angry enough to strike LaCroix . . . but in that pause he regained enough self-control to let his hand drop to his side. Walking to the table, he picked up his car keys. "You tried to do the same thing with Lindy. Where Lindy goes, Mrs. Reese and Sarah follow. I won't let you do that to them. They've suffered enough. And I don't trust you to keep them safe."

Nick didn't know what reaction he expected . . . or wanted. After another pause, LaCroix said, "Fair enough. Will you tell your coroner friend that you're leaving? Does she rate more of a good-bye than Urs?"

The words stung him. He turned quickly, his cheeks burning, although whether at the thought that LaCroix knew what feelings he had for Natalie or the fact that he'd put off thinking about her, he wasn't certain.

"I'd advise against it," said LaCroix sincerely, his tone devoid of sarcasm. "She's one of them."

There was no answer to that. Dropping the keys in his coat pocket, Nick cleared his throat. "I'll be leaving for my shift in a few minutes."

"Then we part here. I won't see you before you leave, but I'll have Denise and her children ready for the trip."

"Thank you." They stared at one another for a second, then Nick extended his hand. "Good luck with your war. I hope you survive it."

LaCroix shook his hand, then pulled him into a quick hug. When Nick drew back, he said, "I hope you find the safe place you're looking for. For your sake, as well as the others'. And if you find it . . . let us know."

Nick nodded, suddenly unable to speak. LaCroix tapped him on the shoulder, then headed for the door. Before he left, he added, "Walk in the light, Nicholas."

"And you," Nick managed, finding his voice again. But the door had closed before the words left his lips.

143

He realized then that neither he nor LaCroix had mentioned Vachon. Nick took a step toward the door but stopped himself, his hand falling back to his side as he reconsidered telling LaCroix about Vachon's involvement with Tracy . . . and the possibility that he'd let her bring him across. LaCroix knew—he *must* know this, as he seemed to know everything. He'd consider Vachon a traitor to the cause. There was a good possibility that after he became a vampire, Vachon would become a victim of one of their daylight raids.

Unless Vachon took the place LaCroix had intended for him, becoming their contact on the other side. . . .

Nick could do nothing about that. He would save himself, Denise Reese, and her children. That was all he could manage. The others were on their own. He couldn't save them all.

Opening the closet, he withdrew a backpack and started to gather the things they'd need on their journey and the few mementos that he couldn't leave behind. It didn't take long, and as he worked, he found himself stopping every now and again, flashing on images of himself, Urs, Vachon, and LaCroix as vampires and, wonder of wonders, Tracy and Natalie as mortals.

It was the latter that held his attention the longest . . . and explained why he'd had such strange thoughts last evening. Was it just a dream? Or was it possible that Natalie's work would eventually bear fruit and she'd become mortal again? That there might be a future for them?

If he left, he'd never know.

Slinging one strap of the backpack over his shoulder, Nick took a last look around the apartment. His gaze rested on the bedroom door, but he fought the urge to go back and wake Urs—he'd made his decision. He could live with it.

Avoiding the others on the way to his car was a little difficult, but he managed that, too. The backpack was hidden in the trunk of his car, beneath the first aid and various evidence kits his job required him to carry to crime scenes. They'd come in handy when he, Mrs. Reese, and the children were on the road.

Nick drove to the police station, reviewing possible destinations for their trip, then discarding them just as quickly. South wasn't an option—the United States was in a worse position than Canada, and the further south one went, the more dangerous things became. He'd heard tales of roving vampire bands traveling north from Central America, bringing across or murdering all who strayed into their path. If anything, west would be better . . . somewhere in the backcountry. They'd find a small, isolated town untouched by this madness. And he'd carve a niche in that wilderness, using his knowledge to set up defenses until the dust settled and humans or vampires ruled. There had to be a place like that left. If not . . . he'd build one from scratch.

The sun hadn't yet disappeared below the horizon, so traffic was still light. He made the station in record time and clocked in early—it wouldn't do to be late two days in a row. If he was going to make his break in the morning, it had to be clean. Leaving on good terms would gain him some traveling time and distance. Distance might mean survival.

Not surprisingly, Tracy wasn't in yet. He nodded to the members of the departing shift, stopping to speak a word to one or another of the mortals. But they'd all heard the news—that he'd been offered a chance to turn. From some he got curious stares. The gazes of others held hostility, veiled or open. Still, he smiled and pretended nothing had changed. Nothing could be out of the ordinary tonight.

However, nothing about this night would be normal. Nick's thoughts kept returning to the supplies in the trunk of his car—there was always one more thing to add. He'd noticed that the scratch on his arm was almost healed, as was the wound on his head. Whatever Urs had used on the wounds would come in handy on their forced flight, but he wasn't about to call and ask her for a supply. He doubted he could come up with a plausible excuse on such short notice. If he saw her again, he might be tempted to tell her about Vachon . . . or to stay.

Nick headed for his desk, a sense of duty still driving him. If there was any chance to leave his cases in order for Tracy, he'd take it. He owed his partner that much. It was while he sat there, filling in the missing details on last night's bombing, that he realized two of the vampire uniformed officers were watching him. Not too openly, but enough to get his attention.

Pretending not to notice, he went on with his business, trying to place them. They were both patrolmen. One had failed the detective exam just about the time Nick had been switched from day to night shift, and the other was Bettes.

They were speaking to one another, one's back half turned toward him, but both glanced at him throughout their conversation. Pretending to rub his eyes, Nick stared across the dimly lit room. His lip-reading capabilities were acceptable but not advanced, and the lack of light in the station defeated any chance he might have to pick out more than one or two words in ten.

Then words began to drift in his direction, the whispers clearer and more audible, as if amplified.

"Don't know how reliable it is," said the first one, shaking his head. "The captain finds out we raided the fast track's place with nothing more than the word of one half-dead snitch—"

"Who isn't even around to spill his guts? I told you to take him in."

The first cop snarled, "I was hungry!"

"Yeah, well, they're not donuts." Bettes frowned and looked toward Nick, who glanced away. "I think he knows something. But the brass'll want him down at the opening tonight, so he won't have a chance to do anything about it."

Someone passed by and the two men parted, then moved into the next room. Nick looked up and tapped his pen against his lips thoughtfully. He'd heard every word, almost as if he'd had the selective and sensitized hearing of a vampire. But . . . how? He was as mortal as mortal could get.

And then the words sank in—these two had it in their heads to raid his apartment building. The place LaCroix had stashed at least fifty of his refugees!

Nick reached for the phone and began dialing, then jumped as a hand clamped on his shoulder. Swallowing, he turned his head and looked up, certain that the officers had discovered his eavesdropping.

It was Natalie. She seated herself on the desk edge, her expression wary. "Rough night last night."

"Yeah." Nick tapped the open file folder on his desk—the bombing report. "What's the casualty total? Do we know?"

"Ten mortals. Anywhere between fifty and seventy vampires." At his questioning look, she shrugged, then turned her head, her attention on the wall opposite. "The fire doesn't leave much. When we burn, we're reduced to ash. We've been using anything we can to identify victims— jewelry, wristwatches, remains of wallets."

"And how many floaters this morning?"

"At least there wasn't a riot. It could have been so much worse—"

"How many?" he asked again, taking her hand.

Natalie looked down at her hand in his. "I haven't gotten a full count yet, but there could be as many as forty."

Nick could see the guilt in her eyes and squeezed her hand. "It's not your fault."

"But I'm part of the problem, aren't I? Just another bloodsucker?" She raised her gaze to meet his, then looked away again quickly. "It's going to get worse, Nick. It's going to get a lot worse on both sides. Every evening I go in to ID the bodies, I'm terrified you're going to be one of them."

"I won't be, I promise you. Nat?" He reached up to turn her face toward him, his fingers resting on her cheek for a moment. "They won't touch me—I'm a cop. I'm protected."

"Not if you turn down your papers, if you tell them you don't want to be brought across. We both know what that means—you're off the force. No more protection. You're just another warm body on the streets."

"So that's what you think of me." Clasping his hands around hers, he pressed her fingers to his lips.

"Stop it!" Natalie drew her hands back and dropped them to her lap, frowning. "Nick, I'm serious. You have to accept the offer—you have to let me bring you across. And if not me, somebody else." With a sigh, Natalie looked away again. "It doesn't matter. The only way you'll be safe is if you become a vampire."

"If I was planning on being brought across, I wouldn't want anyone but you to do it," he told her, leaning over to plant a light kiss on her cheek.

He'd hoped for a smile. She still wouldn't look at him, but he would have sworn that he saw a bit of red glistening at the corner of her eye. "So you're not going to do it, then?"

The lie was out before he could stop it. "I haven't decided."

By the time the sun rose, he planned on being well on his way out of the city. But he couldn't tell her that. Not now. He'd have to leave her a note and hope that she got it. After they were settled, he'd try to keep in contact with LaCroix, see if he could keep tabs on her. If Natalie found a way to return to her mortality, he wanted to know as soon as it happened. He'd cross the continent to find her and take her back with him. And if it didn't happen—

At least she wouldn't worry about walking into her lab

some evening and finding his corpse. Better that she know he was safe and far away.

But his plans toppled around him when she looked back at him, hope in her eyes. "Then there's still a chance?"

"Yes." Now that the lie had been spoken, he had to stick with it. Let her have the hope tonight, at least. By tomorrow evening, it wouldn't matter any more.

"I wasn't going to tell you, if you'd made up your mind not to go through with it—" Natalie paused, then placed her hands flat on the desk. "I found Janette's name on the donor rolls."

His heart turned to a lump of lead in his chest. "She's dead."

"No. She was brought across." Natalie dared a glance at him, then looked back down at the desk. "They picked her up as a vagrant and were going to process her when she caught somebody's eye. She was offered a choice of being brought across or staying with the donor group."

Nick took a long, slow breath, only barely aware that Natalie had moved closer to him. "Then she's a vampire."

Janette knew as much as he did about the resistance and how they operated, but she'd never betray them. She could rejoin her family now—their only objection to her was that she wouldn't become a vampire. Now she'd return to her life of privilege. He might even catch a glimpse of her tonight at the gala to celebrate the blood plant opening. He didn't doubt that all of Toronto's leading vampire citizens would be there.

He hoped she wouldn't. He didn't want to know how stunning she'd look in the moonlight. Imagining what the change would do to her was enough. No matter how exquisite she'd become, there would be something missing; some bit of her soul would be gone. It would hurt too much to see her like that.

"I thought you should know," said Natalie. Leaning her

chin on his shoulder, she wrapped her left arm around him, holding him close. "I thought it might make a difference."

He closed his eyes, holding her, knowing that it would be for the last time. He could mourn for the loss of what Janette had been later. Right now, he would mourn for himself, for his inability to stay with this woman.

Because he was tempted. He was very tempted. Nick leaned his head against hers and smelled her perfume, the skin of her cheek cool against his own. All he had to do was agree and she'd be his. LaCroix would be pleased, he might see Janette again, and he would have Natalie.

All it would cost was his life . . . and his soul.

A fragment of dream returned to him—the memory of a rabid, overpowering thirst for blood, a need and desire to kill.

Slowly, he pushed her away and forced a smile. "I've gotta get back to work. Tracy'll be in any minute, and—"

"I'm already here." Tracy was standing at her desk, grinning. "Don't let me interrupt."

"Sorry, you've ruined the mood." Natalie grinned at Tracy, then brushed her palm against Nick's cheek. "You'll call me when you've decided?"

Taking her fingers, he kissed the center of her palm, then released her hand, not trusting himself to do anything more than nod. No more lies. The ones he'd told already were breaking his heart.

Natalie beamed, then bent forward on impulse and planted a kiss on his cheek. She waved to Tracy. "Later."

"Yeah, later." Still grinning, Tracy leaned over her desk. "It's set, right? I told you, you're good for each other. Nick, I'm so happy for you. You won't regret it—"

"Tracy, look—" Realizing that she was too involved in her own version of reality to hear him, Nick waved her away as he picked up the phone. "I've gotta make a call, okay? Then we can hit the road."

Reese chose that moment to step out of his office,

frowning. "You still here?" he asked, hurrying over. "I want you two down at that plant opening now. We've got priority security on this. You'll get area assignments when you arrive."

Nick hesitated, then dropped the phone back into its cradle. Time was passing, and there was no sign of Bettes and his friend—the refugees were in danger. "Just one call—"

"Now!" repeated Reese. He pointed toward the door. "I'm heading out myself. You'd better hope I don't beat you down there."

"On our way, Captain," said Tracy.

Nick closed the folder on the desk and rose, knowing that he had to find some way to warn LaCroix and the others without endangering himself. He had to leave tomorrow morning—he had no choice now. He followed Tracy, but Reese caught his arm as he passed, stopping him, then waved Tracy on. She continued out the door while Nick turned his attention to Reese.

"Nick . . . about our conversation yesterday—have you given any more thought to that promotion?"

Another image from his dream flashed before him— fangs and crimson eyes—and he felt his heart skip a beat. "Yeah," he admitted nervously. "I have. But . . . nothing's been written in concrete yet."

"It's your choice. Remember, the wrong move will get you tossed off the force." Reese patted him on the shoulder. "I can't afford to lose a good detective."

"Captain, I—I've got to go." Slipping away from Reese, Nick all but sprinted for the door, not daring to delay his exit any longer.

Tracy was already in her car, the engine running. He hopped in, casting a longing glance at the Caddie as she steered her car out of the police parking lot.

"So when's the big night?"

Ignoring the question, he closed the door behind him,

151

reached into the glove compartment and pulled the alarm light onto the dashboard.

"Are we in a hurry?" asked Tracy, as Nick set the light flashing.

"I need to stop at my apartment before we head uptown—I left my badge on the table."

"Reese will *not* be happy if we're late."

"So we won't be late," said Nick quickly. He winced as the Ferrari drifted perilously close to a large truck, then swerved into another lane, a chorus of car horns following them. "Geez, Tracy, ease back on the throttle. You might be immortal, but I'm not."

"That'll change soon enough. And the secretarial pool is going to want all the details—"

Ignoring Tracy's comments, Nick concentrated on the traffic and kept glancing at his watch. Too slow, they were moving too slowly. If the uniforms had timed their raid properly, he'd have only minutes to warn LaCroix. And he didn't dare stop and phone because he might not get through—public phone service had fallen by the wayside, along with reliable electricity, water, and sewer.

"Nick, about Vachon?" Tracy shot him a glance, then looked back to the road. "I'm sorry that happened last night. Did you see him, talk to him—?"

"No." Nick took a breath, then stared out the window as they whizzed past the other cars in the darkness. "Tracy . . . it's okay."

"Is it?"

"If that's what he wants." Nick forced himself to swallow, then glanced at her. "If he's *sure* that's what he wants. Just—I don't want anything to happen to him. Keep him safe."

"We've only started talking about it. And we'd have to get the papers approved—if he wants out, all he has to do is say no." Then she smiled and took her hand off the wheel just long enough to punch his shoulder lightly. "But it'll be okay. 'Cause you'll be brought across way before him. You'll still be his big brother."

Nick closed his eyes and leaned back in the seat, reminding himself that he couldn't save them all.

He couldn't. And trying would only get him killed.

Finally, the car pulled up in front of his building. Nick opened the door and leaped from the seat, leaning in the open car window long enough to say, "Wait here. I'll be right down." He ran up the steps, taking several at a time.

"Reese'll skin me alive if we're—"

The rest of Tracy's sentence was cut off as the apartment building's doors closed behind him. Nick paused inside the foyer. There was no light in the entryway, which was a bad sign—a signal from downstairs that something was wrong. LaCroix's instructions were explicit—when the light was out, get the hell out and to the next safe house.

Was he too late? Had they all been captured?

He was grabbed from behind, arms wrapping around his neck and pulling him back, off balance. One of the two uniformed police officers was suddenly before him, fangs bared and eyes gold. "Nothing here, is there, Knight?" he hissed. "You warned 'em, didn't you? But you weren't smart enough to stay away yourself. They won't okay my family turning, but you—a guy with a lot to hide—they let turn in six months!"

"Maybe we should bring him across, Art," breathed Bettes, who pinned Nick's arms behind him. "Might do our careers good, having a detective under our thumb."

Art's fangs retracted slightly as he smiled. "Yeah. Might not be a bad idea, at that."

Nick kicked up and backward, not enough to disable Bettes behind him, but he managed to free his right arm. He took a shot at Art. Expecting a mortal-strength blow, the cop stood his ground.

And flew backward, hitting the far wall when Nick's fist connected with his jaw.

If anything, Nick was more surprised than Art. Rubbing his fist, he wondered where the sudden burst of strength had come from. And if he'd be able to count on it again.

He was struck heavily in the small of the back by what felt like a freight train but was probably a piece of furniture. The force of the blow sent him careening headfirst into the wall Art had dented. He slid down the wall, feeling blood trickle down his forehead. His eyes wouldn't focus properly, and it seemed that every church bell left in the city was clanging simultaneously inside his head.

The last thing Nick felt was a pair of strong hands around his throat, the collar of his shirt digging into his skin, and the fetid breath of Officer Bettes on his neck.

Nick's eyes shot open, and he bit back a cry of alarm and surprise. His lungs heaved, trying to capture air that he didn't need and failing miserably at the task. He shot from the couch and fell to his knees in front of the coffee table.

There, almost at eye level, was the dream doll. It seemed to mock him with its little painted face, legs and arms now curled tightly in rigor mortis.

With a cry, Nick pushed against the couch, terrified out of his wits. The couch slid backward, so that he landed on the floor with a thump. In a split second he was back on his knees again, staring at the doll. He'd given it to Urs—how had it gotten here? How?

"Nick? What's—?"

It was Natalie. Couldn't that woman take no for an answer?

He dug his fingers into the couch, talons ripping through the leather as he pulled himself to his feet. "Leave me alone!" he snarled at her, fangs bared.

Natalie's eyes went wide, her mouth opening and forming a terrified "o." She backed away from him, shouting, "Oh, no, you don't!"

The dream fell away. The shout, her eyes, and the sound

of her steps brought Nick to his senses. He was at the elevator before she could reach it, ashamed and horrified, and still more than a little weak in the knees.

But he'd miscalculated—her plans hadn't included escape. Grabbing a small table for defense, Natalie held it in front of her, legs out. "Stay back!"

"I'm sorry—" Nick took a deep breath and a step forward, his hand outstretched toward her. Then his legs gave way and he crashed to the floor.

He hurt. He'd managed to catch most of his weight on his hands as he'd fallen, which had saved him from cracking his head on the floor. The muscle and sinew and bone throughout his body ached or throbbed, letting him know in no uncertain terms that the pain was there, and what the hell was he going to do about it?

For the moment, he was content to rest there, his head cradled in his arms, hoping against hope that Natalie would leap over his sprawled body, get into the elevator and run for her life.

Instead, she dropped the table—the crash sending a splitting pain through his skull—and fell to her knees beside him. "Nick, what the hell is going on? What just happened? Are you—?"

The cacophony of messages from his muscles suddenly quieted. He waited another moment and, when nothing more happened, rolled onto his side and looked at her. "I'm going mad," he answered, in a quiet voice. "At least, that's the only explanation I can come up with."

Natalie's brow furrowed. "You seem lucid. Maybe you should just stay there."

But he was already climbing to his feet. When she reached to help him, he waved her away, certain that his knees wouldn't give out on him again. Stalking to the couch, then past it, he stared down at the doll. "I left that with Urs. Now it's here. I think it's following me."

A chuckle from Natalie caused him to turn his head.

Clearing her throat quickly, she held her hand over her mouth. But it didn't hide the edges of her smile. "I saw it on Tracy's desk."

"You went to the station?"

"Well, I knew you were rattled after last night. You never answered my message, so I dropped by the station on my way home and Tracy said you'd gone home sick. Then I saw that on her desk."

Urs had gone back into the Raven, maybe had given it to Vachon—as far as she knew, it was a good luck charm. Vachon had probably given it to Tracy.

Which meant that Vachon had gone to the station to see Tracy.

With mixed feelings of relief and annoyance, Nick fell back to the couch. "And you brought it here?"

Natalie walked over to the coffee table, glancing first at the doll, then at him. "Yeah. You don't really want Tracy touching something like that, do you?"

"If I'd been in my right mind, I would have thrown it in the trash." Smiling at her, he added, "Thanks."

"Don't thank me too quickly," said Natalie, reaching for the doll. "I think I broke it. The other arm wasn't bent like that when I—"

"Don't!" His fingers wrapped around her wrist before she could blink, her hand only inches from the doll. Then he saw the fear in her eyes, mirroring his own. "Don't touch it," he added, trying to control his voice. "Just don't touch it."

Natalie placed her hand over the one he'd wrapped around her wrist, wincing. "Nick—"

He released her, then turned away guiltily, knowing she'd have a bruise there tomorrow. "Sorry."

There was a moment of silence between them, the only sound that of Natalie rubbing her wrist, flesh against flesh. "I saw the bottle on the kitchen floor when I came in," she said.

156

Nick turned to stare at her. Then he glanced over his shoulder toward the kitchen. He'd forgotten about that.

"I cleaned it up," said Natalie evenly. "I tried to be quiet. I was afraid I'd wake you."

"It would have been better if you had," he answered. Leaning forward, he clasped his hands together. "But I think you could have shot off a cannon in here and I wouldn't have heard a thing."

She frowned, eyeing him thoughtfully. "You look like hell."

He winced, hearing her echo of Tracy's and Reese's comments. "Is that a diagnosis?"

"The diagnosis is that you're suffering from sleep deprivation." Sitting down beside him on the couch, she reached to touch his eyelid, but he flinched. "You need sleep."

Lightly he brushed her hand away. "I haven't had any."

"Why?"

"Because of that." He pointed to the dream doll, then rested his elbows on his knees and regarded it with a baleful glare.

Natalie moved her hand toward it, but stopped when she saw his eyes follow the movement. "What did you call it?" she asked, slowly drawing back her hand. "A . . . dream doll?"

"I've got a confession to make. I've been living two lives."

"Tell me something I don't know."

"Not like that," he said, shaking his head. Sighing again, he leaned back against the couch. "Here . . . I'm me. When I fall asleep, I wake up somewhere else."

"And you're . . . somebody else?"

He couldn't quite hide his wan smile. "Some*thing* else," he corrected. "Mortal."

Up to this point, he'd sensed a willingness in Natalie to go along with his train of thought, but his last sentence derailed her completely. She met his eyes with a guarded gaze.

"LaCroix, Urs, and Vachon are there—they're mortals, too."

"You haven't watched the *Wizard of Oz* lately, have you?"

Nick pushed himself up from the couch. "No. That would be too easy." Turning, he placed his hands in his pants pockets and stared at the doll. "It's like being awake twenty-four hours a day."

"Don't take this the wrong way, but it sounds like we're straying into psychology. That's not my field." When he looked at her, she sighed. "And you're not about to walk into an office and say, 'Hi, I'm a vampire, and I've got a sleep disorder. Do you work nights?'"

He couldn't help the weary smile. "That's about the size of it. I'm afraid you're all I've got."

"Thanks for the vote of confidence." Frowning, she raised a finger to her lips. "Okay, so when did this start? Exactly."

"When I took *that* home with me."

Natalie shifted her position on the couch, moving away from the doll as he pointed at it. "That's a start. So, what do you know about it?"

He scratched the back of his head thoughtfully and took a few steps away. "I saw a reference to it in a book on South American dream quests and put out some feelers until somebody came across one. It's supposed to lead you to your heart's desire."

"How?"

The question stopped him in his tracks. He shrugged and gave her a blank stare. "Beats me."

"Nick! I thought we talked about this. If you're going to trust me with trying to bring you back across, you can't keep playing with this—this—voodoo nonsense. Especially if you don't know what it does."

He returned to the couch and sat down beside her. Taking

158

her hand in his, he said, "You're absolutely right. And I wouldn't blame you if you lectured me nonstop for a week. But can we get this little problem solved first?"

Slipping her hand from between his, Natalie smiled. "Okay—no lectures. Tell me what happens when you try to sleep."

"I . . . fall asleep. And I wake up somewhere else. I'm mortal." He touched his forehead gingerly, the memory of a throbbing pain returning briefly. "I live another life. And when I go to sleep there, I wake up here, exhausted." He shook his head, trying to remember more of the details of his dream, but they seemed to slip away as fast as he chased after them. "The real problem is that I can't eat—the smell of blood makes me nauseous."

"So . . . there's a good side to this?" She seemed pleased at the prospect of cutting back his blood intake, which she still seemed to think was a major obstacle to his returning to mortality.

"Unless I starve." He pointed at the doll. "And a part of that bends every time I dream."

Natalie was staring at him. "You're kidding."

"You saw it in the lab," he said evenly. "It was straight as an arrow, right?"

She looked down at the doll, then back at him. "Okay, yeah. You're right. So it's been broken." Then she shook her head and stood. "This is crazy. It's just a doll."

"It's a *dream* doll." When she gave him a hesitant look, he held out his hand and ticked off his fingers. "Look, dream talismans are taken seriously in a number of cultures— South American, African, Indian, Asian—"

"Voodoo."

Nick frowned. "No. That has nothing to do with . . . this."

"And the woman you got it from?"

He'd been waiting for that question. Leaning back against the couch, he met her inquisitive stare with an even gaze.

159

"We won't be able to reach her unless she wants to be reached."

"What?"

"Trust me on this." When she raised an eyebrow, he added, "Natalie, you met her. You tell me."

Sitting on the arm of the couch, she looked off into space for a moment, then shivered. "Yeah. Maybe you're right." Turning, her gaze fell on the doll. "Get rid of it."

"I can't get rid of it. I've tried. It keeps coming back." Nick reached forward and, after a glance at Natalie, picked up the doll. "I think it's going to kill me."

Natalie snorted. "Nick, that's silly."

"What's my heart's desire?"

She met his eyes. "To live as a mortal."

"Which I'm doing in the dream. And what's mortality but . . . death?"

It sounded right, the words making sense when he spoke them aloud. Natalie slid down the arm of the couch, onto the seat beside him, and touched his shoulder. "Nick, you can't be serious. It's not real."

"And this is?" He stood up and walked away from her, running his hand through his hair. "I can't go on like this for much longer. I can't eat. I can't sleep—"

"Maybe I can do something about that."

He whirled, a small spark of hope igniting in his chest. But then he asked suspiciously, "Drugs? Because we've tried others—"

"And they haven't worked. But"—Natalie smiled ruefully—"we've never tried to put you to sleep before, have we?"

"I wish you hadn't put it quite in those terms." Then Nick looked down at the doll again. "But I'm willing to try just about anything. Those dreams are . . . weird. The world is different. The same but different. They continue, dream-to-dream, night-to-day, day-to-night."

"I suppose a psychologist is out of the question?"

He nodded. "On such short notice, yes."

"Then I'm off to the lab." Natalie stood, then headed for the elevator, picking up her coat and scarf on the way. Nick took her mittens from a chair and met her at the elevator door. She paused and fixed him with a curious look. "You're in the dream. And Urs. And Vachon. And you're all mortals?"

An image from the dream flashed before Nick's eyes—Urs's tanned skin, those soft lips. . . . "Uh . . . yeah."

"Am I there?"

Nick met her eyes, and suddenly another image filled his vision. Her eyes had been harder and darker, her skin paler. "Yes."

"And?"

He looked away, unable to tell the difference between reality and illusion anymore. "You're a vampire. And you want to turn me, bring me across." Nick dared a glance at her.

Natalie's eyes had widened slightly, her lips pursed. "I think," she said, after a pause, "that we definitely have to put a stop to this." Then she smiled and took her mittens from his hands. "I'll be back as soon as I can. Stay awake. Play music or . . . something. But stay *awake*."

"I'll try."

"Good."

Neither of them knew what more to do. Nick stared at her, wanting to thank her for trying, for caring, for not running away. He wanted desperately to apologize for scaring her, for scaring himself. But he didn't have the words.

Natalie seemed uncertain as well, meeting his eyes and then glancing away. It was an awkward moment, saved by the opening of the elevator door. Natalie darted inside, waved, then was hidden from view by the closing door.

Nick walked back to the living room, drawn to the doll on the table. He picked it up, placed it in his palm, and then gently poked it with his finger. Both arms and both legs had

bent; he'd had four dreams. Only the head and the torso were left. If each part bent when he had a dream, it meant he had two dreams remaining. Two more dreams, until . . .
    What?

9

"I'LL WAIT. THANKS."

Nick sighed and seated himself on the couch, the cellular phone at his ear. Looking at the canvas he'd been working on all day, he grimaced. It was nothing . . . less than nothing. Color had been layered over color, forming great muddy rainbows, but there was no form to the work, no art to the message. It had been something to do during the daylight as Natalie continued to phone every few hours with messages of hope, but nothing concrete to alleviate his condition. Painting had helped to keep him awake, if not lucid.

Rising, he walked over to the stereo and turned down the thunderous music he'd been playing all day, suddenly realizing why the secretary at the police station kept asking him to repeat himself. She probably thought he was in a bar, calling in sick because he'd overindulged or had a big night planned. Then again, did he care what she thought?

Nick leaned his head back, massaging the muscles in his neck with his free hand. For a moment his attention was caught by the dust clustered on his ceiling lights—he'd have to take care of that when he got a chance. Then he shook his head and returned to the couch, trying to concentrate on the phone call. His attention kept slipping from one thing to the next, focus eluding him.

"Detective Knight?" asked the secretary. "I'm sorry to have kept you waiting."

"Yes?"

"The captain's on another call. I'll pass along the message. I hope it's nothing too serious."

He wasn't certain whether the comment was a pleasantry or a sarcastic barb. "I'll check in tomorrow with an update," he promised.

"Just get plenty of sleep. And chicken soup. You know, if you don't have any on hand, I get off shift in an hour. I'll be happy to run some—"

"Thanks, Lauren, but I'm fine." He paused, stopping himself from mentioning that Natalie was looking after him—what would the secretarial pool make of that slip? "Good night."

Quickly he ended off the call, then tossed the phone onto the coffee table. After nearly attacking Natalie this afternoon, he couldn't trust himself around mortals. All he needed was a well-meaning coworker trying to force-feed him chicken soup.

His stomach rumbled at the thought, but he wasn't about to repeat the disaster of last night and waste another bottle of cow blood. Picking up the remote, he opened the shutters to let in the moonlight, then walked back to the stereo and turned the music up as high as it would go.

The sudden blare of sound caught him unawares, and he reached for the dial, dulling the noise to a low roar. After choosing a paint brush, he drew it through a color on his palette at random and made a broad stroke across his canvas. Distraction, that was the answer. Keep busy. Don't think, just do.

But images kept flashing through his mind: Urs laughing in the sunshine, LaCroix picking up a rucksack from the ground, his skin bronze and streaked with dirt. It was disconcerting. He'd never known them as mortals; he'd met Vachon and Urs only recently, and LaCroix had been a vampire for over a millennium before they'd encountered one another.

He moved the brush, choosing another color. Then his hand stilled as he pictured Tracy paused over the suspect's throat, eyes red-gold and fangs extended, snarling in blood lust.

Nick put aside the palette, carefully placing it on the table, and moved to a coffee can that held a selection of brushes. He tested the stiffness of the bristles against his hand and suddenly remembered holding Lindy against his chest, his hand stroking her hair in an attempt to comfort her. Opening his eyes, he whirled, sensing another presence in the room, feeling hot breath on his throat as fangs descended.

He threw the brush in his hand like a dagger . . . but no one was there. The brush hit the wall and clattered to the floor, trailing streaks of green paint against the plaster. Enraged, he tipped the canvas from the easel. It seemed to have grown heavier, and he had to struggle with it; then it turned and ripped as the frame splintered.

The sound brought momentary satisfaction. Then Nick looked around the mess of his apartment and knew that he had to get out into the night. There had to be someplace he could go where he wouldn't be a danger to others, where he could distract himself with sound and motion. Where he could be watched. Where he could be kept from dreaming.

Deciding that it was the lack of sleep that had kept so obvious an answer from him, Nick lurched back to the couch. He picked up the phone and dialed the coroner's office number, then fell back against the sofa as he listened to the ring. "Hello, Grace? Is Natalie busy? It's Nick."

"Nick? We heard you called in sick. Hope it's nothing serious."

He started, staring at the far wall. "I called the station only ten minutes ago—"

"A combination of woman's intuition, Natalie's attitude, and the best damn intelligence network ever developed— interoffice gossip. Believe me, honey, if you sneeze, we know about it before you can blow your nose."

Grace's easy manner made him smile. "I'll remember that next time I need a lead on a case. About Natalie—"

"She just started cutting a priority from downtown. If you want, I'll stick my head in—"

"No." Nick sat up on the couch, his eyes falling on the dream doll, which was still on the coffee table. "Just give her a message. Tell her . . . tell her I'm going to see a friend about a black bird."

"A friend? About a bird? Nick, if you're sick, you shouldn't be running around doing favors for peop—"

It was the best he could come up with. If he told Grace that he was going to the Raven, he had a feeling that half the law enforcement agencies on the continent would have the information by morning. "I know, but I promised. Just give her the message, Grace."

"You're too sweet for your own good, Nick. I'll pass it along as soon as she's out of her scrubs."

"Thanks. See you tomorrow night." He pressed the disconnect button on the phone, adding, "I hope," beneath his breath.

Having decided upon a course of action, he jumped to his feet and headed for the elevator door, grabbing his leather jacket from a chair as he ran. But when he reached the elevator, he stopped and turned.

The doll was still on the coffee table. He didn't particularly want to keep it with him . . . but could he safely leave it behind? What if Natalie dropped by, found the doll, and got rid of it, deciding that his affliction was a mental malady? And what might it do, if left to its own devices, with a defenseless human to prey upon?

Slowly, Nick walked back to the coffee table, his feet feeling like they were weighted with lead. He picked up the doll with two fingers and glared at it, but the painted dots that formed a perpetual expression of astonishment never changed.

"I guess we're in this together."

The doll stared back, seemingly uninterested.

Nick tucked the wicker doll into his jacket pocket, then once again made his way to the door, each step measured. On the ride down in the elevator, he tucked his hands in his jacket pockets. When his fingers brushed against the doll, he clutched it tightly, not shying away.

He couldn't hope to escape now—it was too late for that. Whatever was happening was going to continue happening, until it came to its own end. Nothing he could do would change the inevitable.

Downstairs in the garage, he considered flying, but the cold night air sent a shiver through him. Nick ran his hand along the metal hood of the Caddie as he walked to the driver's side, opened the door, and slipped behind the wheel. After pressing the automatic garage door opener, he reached for the switch to turn on the interior heat, then stopped himself. This was an odd habit he'd started—he never used the heater when he was alone in the car. The cold didn't bother him.

But another shiver decided him. Nick turned on the heater and then the blower, after the engine warmed the chilled air. His fingers tightened around the steering wheel until he felt the textured covering making an impression on his skin. He backed the car into the street, forcing himself to concentrate on everything—his speed, the traffic around him, lights, and stop signs.

It was the longest trip he'd ever taken . . . or so it seemed. But he got there in one piece and without having endangered the life and limb of any mortal motorist or pedestrian. It was a victory of sorts. He'd needed a victory.

He was locking the Caddie when he heard familiar footsteps on the pavement. Nick paused and looked around, then finally spotted Tracy. She was walking toward the Raven.

For a moment he didn't know what to do—approach her or simply leave—especially since he hadn't fed in almost forty-eight hours. Even being around the mortals in the Raven might prove dangerous. But the thought that she might be meeting Vachon at the club both annoyed and frightened him. He was in no condition to confront Vachon, which meant that if he was going to ensure her safety, he had to convince her to end the relationship now.

"Tracy?"

She started guiltily when he called her name, recognizing his voice but taking a few seconds to spot him as he crossed the street. Her smile was anything but welcoming, very hesitant and unsure. "Nick? I thought you were home sick."

"I am." He shrugged, positioning himself so that he blocked her from the Raven. "I *was*. I decided to take a drive, get some air."

"And a drink, maybe?" Tracy indicated the club, not a half block away. "You'd better watch that—especially if you're taking any medication. You *are* taking something, aren't you?" She frowned and stepped closer. "You still look like hell."

"Thanks for the compliment."

"I mean it, you should see a doctor."

Nick leaned against the brick wall and grinned. "So now you're my partner *and* my mother?" But he held up his hand when she started to protest, "Yes, I've seen a doctor. And, yes, I'm waiting for her to come up with something for me."

It wasn't a complete lie—as far as he was concerned, Natalie was his choice for a primary-, secondary-, and tertiary-care physician . . . and he would have said so on the health care forms he'd had to fill out for work if she hadn't warned him that listing a forensic pathologist as his family doctor would probably raise a few eyebrows.

Tracy backed off, smiling slightly. "Good. So go home and get some rest. I'm up to my eyeballs in files. I think we spend more time writing about chasing people than catching murderers."

"Sorry I left you with that file to clean up."

"That's okay. It was a challenge. How many ways can you say 'We chased the guy, he fired, we fired, he ran into a blind alley, and we caught him'?" She shrugged and added, "What are partners for, right?"

"Right." Nick stared down at the sidewalk and kicked the toe of his boot against the cement. "You down here following a lead?"

"I—uh, was in the neighborhood. Thought I might get something on—"

Nick met her eyes. "And how'd it go with Vachon?"

"I haven't really, uh, *seen* him." Her eyes widened as Nick pulled the dream doll from his pocket and tossed it from hand to hand. Frowning, she said, "Okay, so I've seen him. He came by the station last night before shift ended. We really didn't get a chance to talk. Satisfied? And where did you get *that*?"

Her hand shot forward to take the doll from him, but he was able to evade her. Holding the doll to one side, just beyond her reach, he said, "You wouldn't believe me if I told you." He tucked the doll back into his pocket and met her eyes again. "Now, what about Vachon?"

"I told you—we didn't really get a chance to talk." Flushing slightly, Tracy took a few steps past him, then returned, as if she were pacing on a short leash. "Don't do this to me, Nick. You're my partner. I know you're worried about me, but I *can* take care of myself. I have my own apartment. I have a car. I pay my bills. I'm an adult. And I'm a Homicide detective. I *think* I can handle my own relationships. Okay?"

Her speech ended with a glare in his direction. Tracy pushed a lock of her hair out of her eyes and waited, her hands on her hips.

"Okay. I give up." Nick held up his hands in surrender, then smiled. "And not bad. How long did you rehearse that one?"

He saw her hesitation; for a moment she was caught between being absolutely furious and just giving in. Sighing, Tracy chose the second option, folding her arms across her chest and throwing her back against the wall so that she stood beside him. "It shows, huh?" she asked unhappily.

"Only because I've done that myself, once or twice." He winced, thinking of a number of times he'd rehearsed similar speeches for LaCroix's benefit. "Mine never worked."

Tracy placed her gloved hand on his arm. "Nick, what you said about Vachon being dangerous—you're right. He is. I don't want you to get mixed up in this. He might take it the wrong way."

He placed his hand over hers. "I can take care of Vachon."

"I know you can." As she walked away from him, Nick almost smiled at the tone of her voice —she was trying to protect *him* from Vachon! "But you've gotta leave this to me. He won't hurt me. Even if I tell him that it's over." She turned to face Nick, her gaze darting toward the Raven. "That's why I came here—I was hoping to find him. I'm going to tell him that I'm not going to see him anymore."

Nick almost sighed in relief, but there was something in her expression that gave him pause—a wistfulness she couldn't quite hide. "If he's that dangerous—"

"Oh, I know, I know. 'It's for the best.' And it is. It really is." She folded her arms again, still looking in the direction of the Raven. He realized that she was waiting for a glimpse of Vachon, hoping to see him. Tracy rubbed her gloved hands up and down her arms, as if trying to reassure herself. "It's not like it's serious or anything. We haven't really *dated.* Just . . . talked. He's fascinating, you know? He's seen so much, been so many places. And where have I been?" Her smile was self-deprecating. "But you're right, we're from two different worlds. It's not like we *could* get serious. There's no future. . . ."

His certitude crumbled as he heard Tracy talk. She was trying to believe her own words, trying to convince herself . . . trying to kill the hope before it could even be born.

She'd only get hurt if this relationship continued; he couldn't deny that. Better that she say her good-byes now, before it *did* get serious. By then, it might be too hard to leave.

He knew too well how it could begin with friendship, growing into something deeper until the borders between their two worlds were reached all too soon. Then came the frustration of wanting to dare, to push the envelope that little bit, but being so afraid that the next small intimacy might be one step too far over the line. It would mean heartbreak and frustration, not only for her but for Vachon as well.

Unless, of course, they took that step. Unless Tracy decided that she wanted to be brought across. . . .

Nick closed his eyes and found himself faced with a strange vision of Tracy, pale and eyes bright, describing how she'd given up her life, the possibility of motherhood, and growing old. The sadness in her voice clawed at his heart— mortality lost could never be regained.

He couldn't let that happen to her.

"Nick?"

Opening his eyes, he forced a smile as Tracy shook his arm. "Sorry," he said, his voice hoarse. He cleared his throat, then added, "Just tired."

"You should be home," she scolded. "Not standing outside, freezing your—"

The beep of her cellular phone cut off her sentence. Unzipping her coat slightly, Tracy reached into her inner pocket and pulled out her phone. She flipped it open and turned away. "Vetter."

Nick could have listened to her conversation. Instead, he tucked his hands in his pockets and concentrated on being cold and miserable for the moment . . . and on the snatches of conversation he could hear from the Raven. Vachon's voice wasn't among the cacophony, but that didn't mean anything. Vachon didn't talk all that much. He might still be inside. The sooner Tracy ended this, the better.

She slapped the phone closed and tucked it away, then turned back to him. "They found a body in a rest room at Eaton Centre."

"Gunshot?"

"Sounds like an overdose. Nobody heard anything."

Nick smiled grimly. "Nobody ever does."

"Yeah." Tracy stepped toward him, frowning in concern. "Your place is on the way. Do you want me to drop you home?"

"No, my car's here." He took his hand from his pocket to gesture toward the Caddie, then quickly tucked it back into his pocket—it was getting colder. "I'll go inside for a couple of minutes and get warm."

"Have a cup of coffee, soup, or something if they've got it. And just—" She bit her lip, eyeing him warily. "If you see Vachon, don't say anything. Let me talk to him. Don't—don't even go near him. Okay?"

Nick didn't bother hiding his smile. "I told you—I can handle Vachon."

"I believe you." Tracy glanced down, then up at him from beneath her lashes—he wondered if it was a holdover from her childhood, a glance meant to charm and cajole. "But . . . just do it for me, okay?"

"Okay," agreed Nick. Then, when her gaze turned suspicious, he pulled his hands out of his pockets and held them up at chest level in mock surrender. "Okay, okay! I won't go near Vachon."

"Thanks." Her smile was almost solemn. "I'll catch up with him sometime tonight."

The sadness he'd heard in her voice was lying dormant in her eyes—she wasn't looking forward to that conversation, and he couldn't blame her. "Tracy—"

"No, it's okay. You're right—I can't get involved with him. I mean, he's a snitch, right?" She shrugged, as if it meant nothing to her, then she met Nick's eyes. "If it comes down to seeing him or having you as my partner . . . there's no contest." Ducking her head in embarrassment, Tracy backed away, her hand resting over the spot in her jacket where she'd tucked her phone. "Gotta go. Go home and get some rest. I'm leaving half the paperwork for you."

Not trusting himself to answer, he managed a halfhearted wave as she dashed down the street to her Honda. Nick watched her pull away, a lump in his throat. The amount of trust his mortal friends had in him never ceased to amaze him.

It had been the same way with Schanke, his last partner. In their line of work, if you didn't trust your partner, you usually ended up dead, but there was nothing that said trust had to be accompanied by friendship. He'd been lucky in finding himself surrounded by people who really cared about him . . . or the man they thought he was. Often he'd smile at a joke, watch the others laugh, and wonder what they'd really think if they knew that he was a vampire, a monster who'd murdered countless people over the centuries because he fed on human blood.

Natalie knew, of course, but Natalie was different. Natalie was. . . .

The wind kicked up again, and the frigid blast of air woke him from his reverie. Shivering, Nick tucked his hands into the pockets of his jacket and dashed for the door of the Raven. He'd won at least one victory tonight, ensuring Tracy's safety. It was almost enough to give him hope that he'd get through the night without falling asleep and dreaming again.

His confidence somewhat restored, Nick nodded to the bouncer who waited just inside the Raven's doorway and was allowed to pass into the club. The volume of the music stunned his senses as he entered, stopping him for a moment—his eyes were dazzled by the strobe lights and smoke-filled interior. Nick didn't know why, but everything seemed so much more . . . intense. He began to doubt his earlier faith in the Raven as a safe haven—the music would surely drive him mad after an hour or two. He could already feel the beginning of a headache throbbing at his temples.

A hand touched his shoulder and he nearly jumped out of his skin, relaxing slightly when LaCroix walked around him, watching him all the while. "Again? Really, Nicholas, if you continue to keep this schedule, we may have to set aside a room for you in the basement. To what do we owe the pleasure tonight? Still looking for Vachon?"

"I found him." Nick walked past LaCroix and further into the depths of the club, skirting the edge of the dance floor, where bodies writhed to a pounding prerecorded beat.

"Or, rather, he found you?" LaCroix merely nodded when Nick raised an eyebrow in question. "One hears things, after all. And, this being my establishment, I hear more than one normally would."

Nick headed for a table at the rear, equally distant from the stage and the bar, and found one with light enough to dissuade amorous couples in search of privacy. Pulling out a chair near the wall, he seated himself, hoping that LaCroix would grow bored and wander away.

His luck seemed to have changed from bad to worse— LaCroix pulled out a chair opposite and seated himself. "You look like you're in need of a drink. On the house, of course." LaCroix touched his fingers to his lips thoughtfully, then made a slight gesture over his shoulder to catch the attention of one of the waitresses.

"No!" Nick caught LaCroix's wrist to stop him, then met his master's surprised gaze . . . and released his grip. His stomach heaved at the thought of blood, but he reseated himself slowly, aware that he'd now gained LaCroix's unwanted and undivided attention. "No," he repeated, in a quiet voice. "No. Thank you."

"You don't mind if I indulge?" The waitress appeared, and without waiting for an answer, LaCroix turned to her. No words passed between them, but the woman smiled and nodded, her eyes drifting to meet Nick's.

She was a vampire—her skin was too pale and her eyes too bright, too sharp. Her smile was pleasant and professional as he indicated his lack of interest in ordering with a dismissive wave of his hand.

"She's competent," said LaCroix as Nick watched her walk away. "And Lillian knows enough not to trifle with my private stock." Leaning his arm casually on the back of his chair, LaCroix looked up, pretending a shocked expression. "Why, Nicholas, I do believe you're interested."

"Just familiar." He placed his palm just above the tabletop and stared at the distorted reflection in the surface—another version of reality, different but the same. "I thought for a minute that I'd seen—"

He *had* seen her before. Nick placed his hand on the back of his chair and started to rise, remembering the smoke and the smell of blood, a woman with those features in a waitress's uniform, huddled beneath a blanket. A mortal woman.

In his dream.

"What?" pressed LaCroix, obviously interested.

Sinking back into the chair, Nick met LaCroix's unrelenting gaze, then looked away. "Nothing," he lied. "Someone we brought in for questioning. My mistake."

"Ah, a hazard of your profession, always on the lookout for a criminal profile. Speaking of which—" LaCroix steepled his fingers and leaned his hands on the table in expectation.

A minute passed, then Nick asked, "What?"

"If you're not here to drink or to socialize, I assume you're here on a police matter. Information? Or are you here to inspect my licenses? I assure you, the sprinkler system was installed only. . . ."

He wasn't in the mood. Nick looked toward the empty bandstand, anywhere but at LaCroix. "I need a place to unwind for a while."

Leaning forward, LaCroix gently touched Nick's chin with his fingers and turned it to the right and the left, as if evaluating him. Nick pulled away from his touch, and LaCroix drew his hand back slowly. "You *do* look more than a little shopworn. There's a couch in the back. No one will disturb you."

"I don't want to sleep."

"You don't want to *dream*," corrected LaCroix. Narrowing his eyes, he stared at Nick. "It's the doll, isn't it? I told you to get rid of it."

"I did. At least, I tried." When LaCroix's eyes widened in curiosity, Nick reached into his pocket and pulled out the doll. He sat it on the table. "It came back to me."

"Then I'll—"

"No." He grabbed LaCroix's wrist before his fingers could touch the doll, and this time he didn't let go. Staring at LaCroix, he picked up the doll with his other hand and placed it in the relative safety of his jacket pocket. "I'd feel safer keeping it with me. I don't want to know what'll happen if I lose it. It's gone too far."

"I warned you—"

"Yes, you did." Nick released his grip on LaCroix's wrist, then folded his hands and stared down at them, intertwining his fingers and letting them rest on the table. "I just need a place to think, all right? I'd rather be left alone."

When he looked up, LaCroix was glaring at him, blue-gray eyes flecked with specks of gold. "Please?" Nick added, almost as an afterthought.

Prepared to take Nick's words before that as a challenge, LaCroix reacted to that final word as if he'd been struck. He looked away quickly, perhaps giving the request serious consideration. "I'll see that you're not disturbed." Pushing back his chair, LaCroix rose to his feet, then hesitated, his fingertips resting on the table and his attention elsewhere, as if his thoughts were occupied by more weighty matters. "If Vachon should return and there's any disagreement, you're to take it outside."

"Of course. Thank you." Nick found himself staring at LaCroix, smiling slightly at the memory of that patrician profile with sun-tanned skin, the perfect fingers gnarled and twisted, but made to be of use through an act of will.

"You find something amusing in this?" asked LaCroix sharply, glancing over his shoulder as if looking for the waitress.

"I was trying to imagine what you'd looked like as a mortal."

LaCroix glanced back at him, staring for a moment. "That . . . was a long time ago. Don't waste your time with such meaningless trivialities."

A moment later Nick was alone, LaCroix having stalked across the floor, the dancers parting before him without a murmur, then closing ranks in his wake.

The club suddenly seemed warm and stuffy. Nick peeled off his leather jacket, throwing it over the back of the chair beside him. Relatively certain that not even the dead could rest in the motion-filled atmosphere of the club, he tipped his chair back against the wall and watched the dancers.

The light played off their skins, turning colors as it strobed in rhythmic patterns that matched the music. He found it soothing, after a bit. Even the music seemed to drop away, as the light played across his eyes and his mind drifted. . . .

177

10

THE STING OF A SLAP ACROSS HIS FACE BROUGHT HIM BACK TO
awareness. Raising a hand, Nick deflected a second blow
before it landed and scrambled back against the wall. His
vision blurred, he found himself surrounded by swirling
blobs of gray and white and yellow.

"Easy," said Tracy's voice, from somewhere to his left.
"It's okay—they're gone."

Nick wiped a hand across his eyes, cleaning away the trail
of blood that still trickled from his forehead. The world
became solid again as shadows connected to objects. Faint
rays of light illuminated the darkness, seeping into the foyer
through the curtained windows on either side of the door.

The lightbulb overhead was broken. He should have been
blind in the near darkness, but he could see—well enough
to make out the cracks in the plaster near the join between
the ceiling and the wall opposite.

Nick pushed himself up from the floor. Leaning heavily
on his hands for a moment, he took a deep breath, thankful
that the pain in his head was lessening. "They double-
teamed me." Rising to his feet, he ignored both his aching
muscles and Tracy's halfhearted attempts to stop him. "I
didn't see them until it was too late."

"We're lucky they didn't see me until it was too late for *them*."

Wincing, Nick held his hand to his forehead, then glanced down at the dark stickiness on his palm. The blood wasn't all that fresh, yet he'd been hit only a moment ago. In fact—he touched the wound gingerly—it had stopped bleeding.

"Maybe you should take it easy," offered Tracy, concerned. She paced just out of reach, her arms folded across her yellow blazer. Frowning, her eyes still a deep and angry gold, she kept shooting quick glances at him as she walked past. "You could call in, tell them what happened—"

"And let those bozos win?" Her behavior bothered Nick for a moment, then he realized that he was spattered with blood from his head wound—the smell of it must be driving her crazy. That reminded him that heading into a vampire-intensive area looking like a walking advertisement for their favorite blood allotment supplier wouldn't be a smart move. He took a tentative step toward the staircase and, when he didn't fall, continued across the foyer. "Just give me a minute to wash up and change my shirt."

"You're not going to the plant opening after this?"

Nick paused, his hand on the banister, already several steps up the staircase. "Why not?" Turning, he managed a grimace. "I'm a cop, aren't I? That's my assignment."

It was the truth, after all. Not that he dared tell Tracy the other reason he needed to be there—to provide an escape route for LaCroix's people.

Tracy hesitated, obviously not completely happy with his decision. "I'll wait here in case those jerks come back. Cops against cops! You can't count on anything anymore."

"Sure you can—partner." He gave her a "thumbs up," then headed up the stairs as quickly as the throbbing in his skull and his unsteady legs would allow.

Nick hesitated at the top of the stairs; the door to his apartment was open, barely hanging from its hinges. Drawing his gun, he stood to one side of the door, then peered in cautiously.

The whole place had been tossed, and none too professionally. Holstering his gun, he sighed and started through the wreckage, guessing that the rogue vampires had caused the damage. A quick mental inventory, however, told him that things had not only been moved but removed—it looked like LaCroix and his people had scavenged everything they could before they'd left.

The bedroom was, if anything, worse. Nick tried not to notice the destruction, concentrating only on stripping off his bloody jacket, then his torn shirt and his holster, tossing them to one side. Even if the two patrolmen hadn't attacked him, LaCroix and the refugees would have moved on. They couldn't take the chance that he'd disappear early, or that there'd be any suspicion over his not having immediately accepted the promotion. When the police decided to look for him, they'd come here first.

His decision to leave had affected the others in ways he hadn't even considered. Nick stalked into the bathroom, furious at his own lack of foresight. Why hadn't LaCroix reminded him that his choice would mean moving the refugees immediately? His actions had meant uprooting the poor and the young, the aged and the dispossessed, from the only stable environment some of them had found in weeks, or months, or even years. He'd been so caught up with the thought of finding a way of escape that he'd turned his back on the people he'd tried to serve, both as a mortal police officer serving among vampires and as an individual taking the fight to the streets when the courts and the law failed.

The bowl of the sink was unbroken and he turned the tap, passing his hands under the stream of barely warm water, a sick feeling lingering in his chest at the thought of what he'd done. Splashing the water on his face, he vowed that if he'd failed the refugees by forcing them to leave, he wouldn't fail

LaCroix's people tonight. No matter what it cost, he'd get them out safely.

Fortunately, they'd left towels in the bathroom. Barely glancing at the shattered mirror over the sink, Nick wet one of the towels and held it against his forehead. He sat down on the ledge of the bathtub and dabbed gently at the wound. The water stung at first, but the pain had abated to little more than a dull ache.

Curious, Nick moved back to the sink and tried to find enough unbroken mirror to examine the wound. He tilted his head this way and that, finally finding a section of mirror that offered a reflection of his battered forehead. Where he'd expected to find a gash needing several stitches, there was only a cut. It healed as he watched, the thin red line fading to white, then disappearing altogether.

He almost dropped the towel in the sink, stunned at what he saw in the mirror. He forced his attention away from the image, wet the cloth again, and dabbed at the trail of drying blood that ran down his neck.

The skin of his throat was unbroken—he hadn't been bitten. There was, however, a decidedly unhealthy pallor to his flesh and his eyes seemed abnormally bright. Were his lips redder? If he ran his tongue along his teeth, would he find fangs?

Swallowing, Nick rested his hands on the sides of the sink and bowed his head. This wasn't happening. It was a hallucination, brought on by stress—in the last twenty-four hours he'd only begun to understand the meaning of the word. Taking a deep breath, he stared down at the faintly rust-colored water that lingered in the basin. That's all it was, a reaction to simple, human, *mortal* stress.

When he looked in the mirror again, there was no sign that he'd ever been struck in the head, or that his skin had been anything lighter than a bronze tan in weeks. No matter how long and hard he looked, he appeared to be a perfectly ordinary mortal. The fact that there was no sign of a wound on his forehead gave him pause, but it seemed to make sense as he continued to wipe the dried blood from his skin. Head wounds were like that; nothing seemed to bleed more severely than a scrape along the scalp. That's where the blood had come from, just a scrape.

That's what he told himself as he picked up a towel and slung it across his shoulders. Using the end to pat his face dry, he walked into the jumble of overturned and broken furniture that had been his bedroom and bent to pick up his jacket and his holster.

There wasn't a lot he could do about his jacket, but he remembered from his quick packing earlier in the evening that he'd left at least one clean shirt behind. Draping the jacket over the head of the bed, which had been bent and twisted to one side, he leaned over the frame and pried open one of the dresser drawers. He almost tumbled backward when it came loose in his hands, spilling its contents onto the floor. Picking up a neatly folded shirt, he shook it open and tried to ignore the other bits of his life that were lying around his feet.

Nick was shrugging into the clean shirt when his gaze fell to the mattress, which was lying half on the floor, sheets torn and shredded. He could swear he still smelled of Urs's perfume. She'd escaped with the others—they'd all gotten away, relocated to another safe house. He was certain of it.

He had to be certain of it, or he'd never make it through the night.

The prolonged blast of a car horn startled him. Tracy. Fighting the sense of urgency in the sound, Nick shrugged into his holster and picked up his jacket from the bed. As an afterthought, he checked the pocket for his keys and found something else.

He pulled out a small wicker doll that sported a brightly colored scrap of cloth as a dress. For an instant he held his breath, a chill running down his spine as he stared at it, wondering how it had gotten there.

Finally recognizing it, he smiled and relaxed. Lindy had said that a woman in a green dress had given it to her to pass along to him. He hadn't given it any real thought, but he still had no idea which of the refugees that might be—the description of the woman didn't ring any bells, and he'd met hundreds of people in the past few months.

Holding the doll in the palm of his hand, he flipped it over. The doll must have broken when he'd taken his keys in and out of his pocket—it was twisted and bent in upon itself, the arms, legs, and head folded so that it almost formed a ball. He considered throwing it away as he started to slip into his jacket but returned it to his pocket—it reminded him of Lindy. Maybe it would serve as a good luck charm. He'd need all the luck he could get tonight.

Nick headed for the living room, tucking in the tails of his shirt. He kept his eyes fixed on the door, then the hallway, not wanting to see any more of the damage to the rooms that had been so much a part of his life. He almost made it out of the apartment for what he knew would be the last time when he heard the crunch of glass beneath his shoes and looked down.

It was a black-and-white photograph that had been framed on the wall—someone had taken the photo of him and Janette when they'd gone to Montreal to help another resistance group smuggle a dozen refugees out of the city. They'd been standing at the railing of a boat when the photo had been taken, his arm around Janette, her dark hair drifting behind her in the wind. The day had gone well—the refugees had been relocated without any problem, and they'd had time to relax and celebrate.

Bending, Nick picked up the photograph, taking care not to cut himself on the shattered glass. He had no other pictures of Janette as she'd been—the life they'd led was made safer by limiting the number of records they left behind, and photographs were as dangerous as old licenses and identification papers. That Janette would be so different

184

now nearly broke his heart. He tried to console himself with the thought that at least she was safe. Better not to think about how that safety had parted them forever.

He wouldn't become a vampire. He couldn't. If he survived tonight, if he managed to get LaCroix's people out and escaped himself, he'd leave tomorrow as planned. All of his debts were being paid, and what he owed to LaCroix and the people he'd tried to protect would be the last of it. It wasn't being selfish. It was surviving, just as Janette had chosen to survive, in her own fashion.

Nick stretched his arm, preparing to toss the photograph to the floor, but something stopped him. A lump rose in his throat as he studied it again, then he folded it and slipped it inside his jacket. His memories, at least, would always belong to him. No matter what happened tonight, no one could take those away.

He headed out the door and down the stairs at a run; his aches and pains were almost gone by the time he hit the lower landing. Nick opened the passenger side door of the car and slipped onto the front seat beside Tracy. "I'm ready, let's roll."

"Finally!" She gestured toward the car's police radio. "We've gotten three calls—there's probably steam coming out of Reese's ears. I told them we were caught in traffic."

"It'll do." He slid his arm completely into his jacket as the car started rolling, then fastened his seat belt, pulling the car door closed as Tracy steered into the street. "As far as the cops that attacked me, not a word, all right?"

"About what happened?" Frowning, Tracy kept her eyes on the road. "Nick, those guys have to be stopped."

An immediate Internal Affairs investigation would place LaCroix and the refugees in an even more dangerous position, not to mention making his own disappearance a matter of utmost priority. "No. Not right now." Sneaking a glance at his partner, Nick suddenly realized that Tracy's knowing about the attack might help him if he was caught in the next few days—it gave him an excuse for running. "I'm on thin ice as it is, with the promotion," he added. "You know the brass. Something like this could go on for months before it's settled."

"Yeah. I guess." Her tone of voice indicated that it wasn't much of an excuse, and he should expect the subject to be brought up again in the not-too-distant future. Then she shot him a sly smile. "I suppose I don't blame you. You don't want anything to interrupt your hot date with Natalie, huh?"

Nick looked out the car window and into the darkness, not bothering to answer. His reflection stared back at him, and he saw her image in his mind's eye—that softer, mortal Natalie, just within reach yet forever forbidden. Shaking his head, he tried to concentrate on the traffic, on the road ahead, on anything but the dreams that had plagued him and his sudden near turning at the hands of the rogue cops.

Despite Tracy's unorthodox driving patterns, they were still bogged down in traffic. A glance at his watch told him that they'd arrive ten minutes before the opening address, if that. There was going to be hell to pay when they finally logged in.

His estimate wasn't too far off. The light and siren gained them entry to a side street lined with marked and unmarked police cars. After parking the Ferrari, he and Tracy sprinted for the operations center, which was located to the left and behind the makeshift stage and the main speaker's podium.

Tracy outpaced him easily, using her strength to push her way to the police staging area. Nick struggled to keep up as he passed through the crowd that had gathered for the official opening of the artificial blood production plant. He was further slowed because he kept looking for familiar faces, any of LaCroix's people—he had no idea where they were going to be or what type of operation they'd planned. A hard lump started forming in the pit of his stomach when his not-so-casual glances gave him a better idea of the mix of the crowd.

The vampire hierarchy, the engineers, and the builders were all in place, but so were a lot of mortals. Some wore uniforms—obviously plant personnel—and the obvious protesters in the crowd carried placards, but there were also hundreds of others who had come to see what this "new step forward in vampire–mortal relations" would mean for them.

How many of them would die this night because of LaCroix's "cause"? His badge felt like a weight in his jacket, cold and hard against his heart. By all rights he should stick to the oath he had sworn, to protect and to serve all citizens, mortal or vampire, but he couldn't betray LaCroix. Too many mortal lives depended upon him.

He knew then that the lives lost this night—vampire, mortal, and police—would weigh heavily on his soul for the rest of his natural days.

Nick finally broke through the thick of the crowd and into the operations area. He almost fell forward as he escaped the crush of people around him. Dazed, he stumbled into a clear but well-trafficked area marked by police tape, sawhorses, and dozens of traffic cones. It was as much a madhouse as the public area.

Catching sight of Tracy's raised hand, Nick ran to join her. As he passed the edge of the dais, he received a fierce gaze from Reese. He had a feeling that if Reese hadn't been otherwise occupied—talking into a police band microphone—he would have been reamed for his late arrival.

Tracy's eyes widened as Nick approached, a gesture of her hand indicating that she'd seen the look from Reese. "We're going to be burned to a crisp when this is over."

"I'm surprised the beams from his eyes didn't fry me on the spot." Nick turned his back to Reese, but it didn't help—he still felt an uncomfortable itch right between his shoulder blades. "What'd we miss?"

"It seems that the high and mighty want to meet you after the festivities. They wanted to meet you earlier. . . ."

Nick winced. "So now we have to tell them about my run-in with our friends from the force?"

"Reese covered. Officially, you were on 'special assignment.' Unofficially . . . we don't have any choice. Telling him the truth is the only thing that might save our careers." Tracy bit her lip, then shrugged. "Sorry, Nick, but it's not worth covering for those jerks. I've given up too much to be transferred to traffic or flying a beat. It would make me sick if this thing holds up your promotion. Maybe I can get my dad to—"

"Tracy, it's all right. It'll work out." He forced a smile, groaning inwardly—the *last* person he wanted involved was Police Commissioner Richard Vetter. A quiet escape from Toronto was looking less and less likely as the evening wore on.

"Knight! Vetter!" called the duty officer. She stalked over to them, her eyes narrowing as she studied them. "Took your time showing up."

"You know the traffic—," began Tracy, but the duty officer cut her off quickly.

"West side of the plant, we've got three entrance doors. The roof's covered on that side by two uniforms and we've got the outer doors tagged, but there's a loading bay with an alley entrance."

Tracy stared, obviously astonished and disappointed—this was, after all, one of the major events of the year, a chance to see and been seen by the police brass, particularly her father. "We've got door duty?"

"Hey, after showing up this late, you're lucky you've still got badges."

Tracy glanced around, as if looking for someone in authority. Not finding anyone, grabbed Nick's arm, pulling him closer to the duty officer. "Do you know who this is?"

"Yeah, I heard you got your papers, Knight. Congratulations. If they let you keep them—after this stunt—and you need a sponsor. . . ." The duty officer gave him a wink, then moved on, her voice raised in someone else's direction.

"Door duty?" echoed Tracy. She stared at Nick, then glanced after the duty officer and gestured toward the woman. "About your papers, I don't suppose you'd be willing to—"

"No."

With a sigh, Tracy dropped her hand to her side. "You're right. But you'd better tell them Natalie's got the job, and soon, or there's gonna be blood and fistfuls of hair on the floor in the locker room."

Nick's only answer was a grunt as he headed in the direction the duty officer had indicated, trusting Tracy to keep up. There were a lot of unfamiliar faces in uniform, which meant that several precincts were covering security for this event. He knew LaCroix would have taken the additional security into account, but he couldn't help wondering if this would end up being the disaster he feared . . . or far worse. Blood would run in the streets tonight, but what would happen to the innocent mortals afterward?

He cursed beneath his breath, hating himself for not stopping LaCroix from pursuing this madness, for not finding some way to prevent it. But it was too late for self-recrimination. He was here, and that was what mattered.

They fought their way past the barricades and onto the street again, threading through the lines of parked police cars and ambulances. An emergency aid station had been set up to handle the mortals suffering from heat exhaustion, and Nick spotted a number of uniformed personnel among the civilians. Even though the sun had set, the temperature was still hovering in the high nineties—the warmest summer Toronto had ever experienced.

He didn't need a police academy textbook to tell him that these were the perfect conditions for a riot. The scene at the club bombing the other night had been small and controllable, but it felt like half the city was here to see the opening of the blood plant. With enough mortal officers out of commission, the vampires would have free rein. Too many of the vampires on the force were young and unable to control the lust for blood that at times was barely masked by a mortal facade. All it would take would be one incident, a spark, a second where blood was spilled. . . .

The growl of his stomach brought him back to himself as they passed a hot dog vendor. He'd eaten that morning when he'd returned to his apartment, then forced himself to choke down a burger on the way to work. The smell of the cooked meat had turned his stomach, and he'd thrown most of it in the trash. Even the scent of the brewed coffee at the station—which he'd sworn had gotten him through the first three months after his change from day to night shift—had failed to interest him. Nick took the return of his appetite as a good sign, albeit inconvenient.

The artificial blood plant covered two city blocks. Nick occasionally gazed up at the solid concrete walls as they walked around the building to the loading dock entrance they were supposed to guard. The walls were an innocuous beige and blank, except for the graffiti that hadn't yet been removed or covered. Spray paint had been labeled a controlled substance a month ago because of the continuing attacks on the plant exterior. No matter how well patrolled the site had become, how far into the street the barricades and field of containment had been placed, the slogans kept appearing. The content had run the gamut from literate, polite statements to several suggestions that were nothing short of obscene.

"Is that what you think of us?" asked Tracy, nodding toward the wall when he glanced at her.

Nick grinned. "You in particular—no."

"But some of the others? Like the two who attacked you?" When he stared at the ground, she added, "Not that I'd blame you."

"They were jerks when they were mortals. Now they're

190

dangerous." Glancing at the graffiti again, Nick noticed antivampire phrases in places that a mortal obviously couldn't reach. "Looks like somebody's crossing the line."

"Well, we should, shouldn't we?" When Nick stared at her, she added, "They're going about this whole thing the wrong way—it doesn't have to be vampires *or* mortals. We should be working together. Like you and me."

Nick thought for a moment of all the secrets he'd kept from her, was *keeping* from her, his partner. She deserved better than this, better than the lies. What would she think of him tomorrow evening, when she found out that he'd run away?

"Sometimes it isn't possible," he answered in as neutral a tone as he could manage. "We're fighting for our survival, Tracy."

"Don't get me wrong, I'm not saying I support the vigilantes. Just that, well, maybe they've been pushed too far. What you said in Reese's office about justice not becoming 'just us'—you were right."

"Don't let your father hear you say that."

"Oh, no—he'd *flip*," she agreed. "He's hard-line all the way. But they've gone too far. Like forcing you to turn or lose your job—it's not right. Somebody's got to put a stop to it."

"How?" asked Nick, with a harsh laugh. "You just said it—your father's hard-line, and he's police commissioner. The government and the courts are run by vampires. Who cares if mortals get a fair hearing?"

"Some of us do," she protested defensively. "I've even heard—" Tracy hesitated, glancing at Nick, then away again. "I've heard there are vampires trying to work with the mortal vigilantes."

Nick remained silent. Although the organized resistance was entirely mortal, there were rumors of groups of vampires in the city who were sympathetic to their cause. LaCroix wanted nothing to do with them. Any resistance

191

members who'd been approached by sympathetic vampires were sent away for their own sake, as well as for the safety of the movement in Toronto. As far as LaCroix was concerned, the only trustworthy vampire was a dead vampire.

Yet he'd expected Nick to allow himself to be brought across when the opportunity presented itself.

"Don't you think that could make a difference?" Tracy asked, as they neared the area that led to the loading dock. "If we took a stand?"

With a sigh, Nick pulled out his badge and approached the two uniformed officers at the entrance to the alley. "I think it's too little, too late." He showed his badge, then realized that both of the officers were mortal. "What's your precinct?" he asked, knowing that his own precinct had few mortal night-shift patrolmen.

"Twenty-third." The officer nodded at Nick's badge, then met his gaze. "We've been waiting for you. You're late."

"It's a long walk," complained Tracy. She followed the same procedure, holding up her badge case. "Guess they're calling in day-shift. They should have given us more warning on something like this."

"Yeah—and given equal warning to everyone who wants this place leveled?" At her disbelieving stare, Nick smiled. "Come on, Trace—I was the only one in that station who didn't know my papers were coming through. The place is worse than a sieve." He headed into the loading alley, shaking his head.

Exterior lighting for the loading dock was almost nonexistent—three safety lamps with amber bulbs covered the entire area. At the top of the concrete walls three stories above them, Nick could barely make out the brackets where the rest of the lighting was supposed to be installed. He gathered they'd taken some short cuts to get the plant operational, after the months of delays from the damage the resistance had been able to inflict.

He had no idea where LaCroix and his people would strike or what damage they'd planned, but he had a suspicion that this attack would go far beyond any of their previous assaults. He eyed the layout as they walked the length of the loading bay, getting a feel for the place, needing to know where the exits and entrances might be.

At the far end, in deepest shadow, were heavy metal doors that were shuttered and locked. A concrete catwalk ran the length of the right side of the alley, at least six feet from the ground and railed. Steps led down at the front of the alley and midsection, and it connected to the loading ramp at the rear. There were a half dozen doors set in the wall along that catwalk, and the resistance could appear from any or none of them.

"I'm sorry," said Tracy, trudging beside him as they walked the length of the alley.

Nick glanced at her, startled. "For what?"

"For suggesting that you and the duty officer might. . . ." She ducked her head and shrugged. "If you'd said something like that to me, I'd have smacked you. I was out of line."

"It was a joke."

"It wasn't. At least, I don't think it was."

"Let it go. It doesn't matter."

"It's just that this is all I've got now . . . my career. Between my father and my uncles, I've spent my life surrounded by cops. I know how it works. Getting stuck on door duty means getting ignored the next time transfers and promotions hit."

He took a breath, caught her arm, and drew her to one side for a moment. Her eyes were pale blue and anxious. "Is that what this job means to you?"

"Yes—no." Tracy stared past him and clasped her hands together. "Since you got your papers, I've been thinking, remembering what it was like . . . being mortal. Then I started thinking about Vachon, about bringing him across."

She met his eyes. "I don't think I can do it. Not that I *can't*, but that I don't want to." With a sigh, she smiled sadly. "I guess I'm not making any sense, huh?"

"You're making a lot of sense." He squeezed her shoulder, then held it for a moment, pushing her forward. "You just don't know it yet."

They'd traveled the length of the loading bay, turned, and headed back toward the street. At midpoint, they stopped, looking around.

"Want to take the front or the back?" asked Tracy.

"Back."

"Okay—be antisocial. But don't think about dozing off—I can hear you snoring even from way back there."

"I don't doubt it."

Tracy put her hand into her blazer pocket and pulled out a packet of gum. When Nick raised an eyebrow, she explained, "Blood breath."

She tore the wrapper off a stick, and the packet fell from her hand. When Nick bent down to retrieve it, just a shade too slow to beat Tracy, he saw the figure in the shadows behind her.

There was no time to warn her. The silhouette slammed into Tracy, knocking her to the ground and pulling the gun from her holster.

Nick pulled his own gun, shouting, "Police! Freeze!" But as the figure half rose, gun still pointed at Tracy, the glare of one of the safety lights fell across its face.

LaCroix.

"Drop it," said LaCroix, staring into Nick's eyes, the gun pointed at Tracy. "Or I shoot."

Tracy had half turned on the ground, but she was in a bad position—the muzzle was too close to her heart. One of the wood-shrapnel bullets would end her night life . . . permanently.

Fanning the fingers on his free hand and holding the grip with two fingers, Nick very carefully put his gun on

194

the ground. When he released it and backed away, one of the access doors on the concrete catwalk opened outward. The standoff was perfect—no one in the police department knew of his connection to the resistance. LaCroix's people were assured safe passage because Nick was there, and Nick would be cleared of negligence or wrongdoing by any police inquiry board, mortal or vampire . . . if he hung around long enough to be held accountable.

At least ten figures escaped into the shadows of the alley. Blinded by the glare of the safety light above the door, Nick could make out nothing more than silhouettes as they slipped away. Tracy, of course, with her vampire eyesight, would hold the memory of their faces clear and cold until she could identify them from mug shots, then a lineup.

That's when Nick realized that LaCroix had no intention of leaving Tracy whatever vestiges of life she had left.

The others were gone, having moved into the street and away, perhaps blending into the crowds that surrounded the plant. The uniformed mortals at the alley mouth must have been LaCroix's people. There would be no witnesses, if LaCroix had his way.

Nick wasn't about to allow that. Stepping forward, he picked up his gun from the warm tar and nodded toward the mouth of the alley. "Go."

In the half-light, he saw LaCroix's eyes narrow. "Don't be a fool, Nicholas," he hissed. "It's perfect. One less of them, and you come out a hero."

As if testing the balance of the weapon, Nick lifted the gun . . . and pointed it at LaCroix. "She's my partner. I won't let you kill her."

"You'll be killing yourself, then. She's seen them, for heaven's sake." He spat on the ground, near Tracy, who was watching the discussion with wide eyes. "How long before they track us down? But you won't be here for that, will you?"

Before Nick could blink, Tracy moved. She was nothing

more than a blur of motion, a leg scissoring out to knock LaCroix off balance. When LaCroix went down, Tracy scrambled to her feet. Her gun hit the ground, skittering across the tar and into the darkness.

Having fallen on his hands, LaCroix flattened himself to the ground and rolled, evading Tracy's grasp. Nick knew he couldn't let his partner get her hands on LaCroix—the vampire's strength alone could crush him. He fired in her direction, trusting Tracy's vampire reflexes to save her from harm.

The bullet came close enough to get Tracy's attention. His partner froze in place, then turned her head to look at Nick, eyes glowing gold. "Nick?"

"Let him go." Taking a step forward, he nodded toward the alley mouth again. "Get out!" he shouted at LaCroix.

Neither of them moved. "Don't do this," whispered Tracy, meeting his gaze. "Nick, don't throw it all away for one of them."

"One of us," LaCroix corrected, his voice triumphant. "He's one of mine, bloodsucker. He's flesh and blood and living. And he's finally figured out it's us against you."

Tracy shifted position, but Nick was suddenly able to match the vampire's speed. His next shot went through the flap of Tracy's blazer as she started to move toward him, embedding itself in the concrete wall behind her. She stopped instantly, confused and more than a little surprised. He almost couldn't bear the oh-so-human look in his partner's eyes before they hardened to something like steel. "It's not 'them or us,'" said Nick softly. "It's you . . . or him. Don't make me decide, Tracy."

LaCroix had started up the alley, his hand outstretched. "Nicholas, come on! There's no time—"

But Nick stood his ground. If he moved, Tracy would move, and LaCroix would be dead. "Go!" he shouted, letting the rage fill his voice, so that his own ears were deafened with the roar. "Go!"

That's when Tracy moved.

The gun went off, the sound of the explosion echoing in the enclosed alley. Whatever had given Nick his earlier reaction time and heightened eyesight, it had left him. Distantly, he heard the simultaneous sound of LaCroix's footsteps as he ran from the alley and the brush of cloth and flesh against concrete, then tar. Time slowed as Tracy spun into the wall from the impact of the bullet, then hit the ground.

When he holstered the gun, the movement was automatic—his hands knew the drill and followed it to the letter. His feet feeling like lead, Nick walked over to his partner's corpse. He reached down to turn over her body.

Tracy's left arm shot upward, her fingers grabbing his throat and holding him there. He could see the bloody stain seeping through her shirt and blazer, just above her heart.

"Next time, aim lower . . . partner," hissed Tracy. She scrambled to her feet, never relinquishing her grip on Nick's throat.

The flash of light behind them was blinding, followed less than a second later by the sound of an explosion that could have presaged the destruction of the world. Tongues of fire rose into the sky, singeing the clouds. Brick, stone, and metal fragments flew through the air like wounded birds, arcing and falling around them. The sudden wind from the blast was hot, carrying the stench of heat, blood, and death.

Like some great timpani, the peals of man-made thunder followed one upon another. There was none that seemed so loud or lasted so long before another sounded behind it, filling the world with a burst after burst of angry sound.

The force of an explosion hurled Nick out the mouth of the alley, across the street, and into the facade of a facing building. For a moment he was aware only of an empty silence, there being no air to breathe, and a pressure trying to push him flat against the stone wall. Then the pressure eased with the passing of the blast and sound returned, accompanied by the crackle of flame and the fall of debris.

A sharp pain in his ear led him to guess that one of his eardrums had probably been punctured. His hands searched and found mortar cracks in the stone wall as his fingers fought for purchase during his slow slide to the ground. Eventually he lost that battle, falling and striking the sidewalk, leaving a trail of blood on the pale stone from the scratches on his face. Eyes open, he stared up at the white and black plumes of smoke obscuring the night sky and wondered if he was dying, his lungs desperate for air but still unable to breathe.

The air returned. After a few labored breaths, Nick managed to turn over and closed his eyes, resting gratefully. He'd only had the breath knocked out of him—a frightening experience but hardly fatal.

That's when the brief silence after the explosion ended and sound returned to the world around him. Prolonged screams cut through the darkness, both the unearthly howls of the vampires and the weak and pathetic cries of wounded mortals. Sirens and lights and shouted orders, obeyed by . . . whom? Shadows darted through the smoke-filled streets. Behind it all the artificial blood plant burned, adding an angry red backdrop and the smell of charred blood to the hot and dangerous night.

Nick rose to his feet, leaning heavily against the wall. The ache in his ear was already starting to fade, and he could almost feel the scratches on his face knitting together, the blood absorbed into his skin. How this could be, he didn't know, nor did he care. He was only glad to be alive, with the remnants of his shirt and jacket clinging to his back.

What was left of the alley was engulfed in a sheet of flame. The sudden surge of joy at finding himself alive left him as he stared through the smoke at the inferno across the street. His steps were slow, but he could go only so far before the fire drove him back. There was no sign of Tracy. If she hadn't been blown free. . . .

Nick stared at the fire, then turned his head, unable to look at the flames, his eyes tearing. LaCroix would have said it was the smoke that was making his eyes water, that he couldn't care for one of those soulless legions of the damned. She'd been a vampire, she'd lived on mortal blood. LaCroix had determined that she was the enemy.

LaCroix, he decided, could go to hell.

He stood there, stunned, for what seemed like an eternity, staring at the flames as they soared higher and higher into the sky, fueled by smaller explosions that rumbled and burst every so often. It was beautiful in its own way and was a far better send-off for Tracy's spirit than any police funeral.

When he came to himself, Nick started walking aimlessly, not quite knowing where to turn. There had been few victims where he'd found himself and just as little debris—the speeches had no doubt started, and only the officers guarding the rear of the building would have been in the area. Reaching the corner, he stopped and stared, then ran directly into the maelstrom that lay ahead of him.

The area at the front of the plant—where the police had gathered behind the podium, where the vampire leaders had waited for their chance for popular immortality, where the crowds had jostled and pushed to be closer to the stage—looked like a war zone. If the club bombing had been a massacre, the street before him looked like the floor of a charnel house. This time there were mortal and vampire survivors trapped amid the wreckage, and they wouldn't last long if they didn't get immediate help.

Blocking out the sights and sounds, Nick forced his way back to Tracy's car through the tide of stunned survivors and rescuers. He was lucky—the rear end had been dented by a large chunk of concrete, which had fallen to the ground after bouncing off the painted metal surface. With a slap of the flat of his hand in the right place, the trunk flew open. He grabbed whatever first-aid gear came to hand, not bothering to close the trunk behind him.

As he ran to the thick of the disaster area, Nick dropped first-aid supplies to whatever Good Samaritans he passed on the periphery, hoping against hope that other police were doing the same. The sirens he'd been hearing signaled the arrival of emergency personnel and EMTs, but the ambulances and paramedics would be overwhelmed by the casualties.

A scream to his right caught his attention—two mortals were trying to lift a boulder-sized chunk of concrete from a uniformed officer. He joined them, lending his strength to the task. The three of them were able to push it far enough off the woman to pull her out.

It was a vampire—the duty officer, her hair darkened and matted with blood. Her eyes were barely open, but they glowed gold and her fangs were extended. The mortals stepped back in horror, but Nick merely glanced at her. She'd heal in time. She needed blood, but not desperately.

Dismissing her case as less urgent, he rose to his feet and turned, only to face a mortal who held a long piece of wood, his intention obvious. Nick grabbed both ends of the wood and positioned himself in front of the officer, trying to protect her. "Are you insane?" he cried, pushing against the other man's strength. "For God's sake, go help someone. There are people dying here."

"Stinking vampire lover," the man spat, putting his weight behind the wood.

"Stinking *cop*," Nick corrected. Pushing the man back, he reached automatically for his holster and found that, somehow, his gun had remained with him and hadn't discharged. Drawing the weapon, he waved the man away. "Get out of here."

The man hesitated only a moment before turning and running into the smoke. Nick holstered the weapon and turned to one of the rescuers. "Could you watch her?"

"Uh, sure," answered the man. His eyes were glazed, as if he were still stunned, but he nodded, looking down at the vampire nervously. "She needs blood, right?"

"Yeah, but don't donate any. Wait for the medics." Passing close to the man, he added quietly, "And for God's sake, don't get too close to her. She's in pain and she's hungry."

The man blanched, but nodded again. As an afterthought, Nick paused and handed him his gun. "For them," he said, gesturing toward the place where the attacker had disappeared. Then he looked away. "Or her, if she starts for you."

He didn't wait to hear the man's reaction to that one. Nor did he stop moving. It didn't matter whether they were vampire or mortal . . . he needed to save as many of them as he could. At first he worked alone, then beside other mortals—he chased away the vampires who offered to help, stressing the need to look after their own and the danger they posed to themselves and the victims by being so close to mortal blood. The club bombing had taught him that much.

Most had agreed, staring at him with gold or red eyes and moving off to do what they could. There were vampire scavengers, of course, feeding from whatever half-dead mortal victims they could find, but he let the other vampires take care of them. This was a place for saving lives, not taking them. Both vampires and mortals had to join together for those few hours, working against the clock and the elements and their own despair. He knew that despite their combined efforts, many would be lost, but he never stopped trying.

Holding the palm of his hand against the stump of a woman's arm that had been severed at the elbow, Nick met the eyes of the EMT who was working on her. The man shook his head after a second, then leaned forward and motioned him to remove the pressure from the wound. After a brief spurt of blood, there was nothing. The heart had stopped pumping. The woman was dead.

"She's gone," said the man softly. Pulling a white cloth from his case, he ripped it in two and placed a piece across the woman's face, marking her so that the other emergency personnel wouldn't waste their time. He gave the other half to Nick, then slipped the strap of his emergency bag over his arm and moved on.

Nick took the cloth and wiped the blood from his hands. She was no one he knew. No one he'd ever met. Just another mortal. Just another dead woman.

Rage and sorrow battled in his heart. He wanted to throw back his head and scream, as so many others were doing in that place, but there would be time for that later. He had failed to protect them. All he could do now was serve, save those he could and mourn those who had passed beyond any mortal help.

Nick looked up as a hand rested lightly on his shoulder. He scrambled to his feet when Natalie threw her arms around his neck. To him, she was the epitome of an angel of mercy, despite the fact that she was wearing a suit jacket, skirt, and blouse rather than a long, flowing gown and wings. Her strength helped to lift him from the ground, and if his hug lacked some of the strength of hers, it matched the passion. At some point their lips met and continued to meet in frantic, desperate kisses.

He was breathless when they parted, content just to hold her.

"Thank God I found you," she whispered, kissing his cheek, then his ear. "When we got the call, all I could think was that they'd killed you, that you were dead—"

"I'm safe." He grinned and ran his hand down her cheek and into her hair, overjoyed at the sight of her. "It'll take more than a couple of bomb blasts to finish me off."

Natalie pulled back, her eyes widening. "There's blood all over you. And—" She released him and touched a tear in his jacket, as if realizing the possible extent of his injuries. "Sit down and let me take a look at you."

"I'm fine. Just banged up." Nick drew her into his arms again, but as he held her, he heard the cries of the wounded and dying around them. Kissing her gently, he let his fingers rest in the softness of her hair, knowing that this time they shared was stolen.

Reluctantly, he released her and stepped back. He gestured at the body just beyond them, the nameless woman whose face was covered with a white cloth. "Tell me what to do. Tell me how to help you."

Natalie hesitated and shifted the emergency bag slung over her shoulder as she scrutinized him carefully. He seemed to pass muster, because she finally nodded and said, "All right—I could use an extra pair of hands. Follow me."

Hours passed as he trailed behind her, moving from victim to victim, stumbling over rubble from the plant and the grandstand, or over bodies. There always seemed to be one more man or woman or—God help them—child lying crushed or broken or burned or trampled among the wreckage. His mind and his hands grew numb after a time, but he followed Natalie's instructions to the letter, forcing himself to concentrate on her words and ignore his weariness and his hunger.

They were kneeling beside a man who'd broken his leg—the bone, having snapped cleanly, was sticking through the flesh. Natalie had finished setting the leg and was wrapping a bandage around a makeshift splint when Nick's hands were grabbed from behind. He heard the sound of cuffs snapping into place, their presence registering just after the cold metal bound his wrists. With a start he turned, nearly toppling.

Tracy's hand caught his elbow, steadying him. A large gash that ran from her eyebrow down the length of her pale cheek appeared to be healing, and the state of her yellow blazer, charred from her left shoulder to her wrist, spoke volumes about her injuries. Her lips were set in a grim line as she ordered, "Let's go, partner."

Looking up from her patient, Natalie left no doubt that she was angered by the interruption. "What's going on?" Her eyes widened when she saw Tracy, then she met Nick's gaze, the question still lingering on her lips.

Nick ignored her and pulled back from the grip on his elbow. "Tracy, not now. There are people out here who need help. Let me loose. Follow me if you want. When this is over, I'll go anywhere with you, but they need every pair of hands they can get right now."

Tracy's eyes burned gold. "Mortal hands?" she asked, with a snarl. "Or immortal hands?"

Natalie finished bandaging the man's leg, patted his chest as if telling him to stay down, then rose. Grabbing the strap of her medical bag and slinging it over her shoulder, she said, "Tracy, I need him right now—"

"He's under arrest."

"Arrest?" Natalie met Nick's gaze again and he found himself looking away, unable to face her. "On what charge?"

"Conspiracy. Terrorism. Attempted murder of a fellow officer." Tracy swallowed, then glared at Nick again. "That'll be a start."

Natalie frowned, her fist clenching. "But I need him here. *Now.*"

Nick forced himself to meet Natalie's eyes. "It's all right."

"It's *not* all right," she protested. "What's happened?"

"Let's go," ordered Tracy. "Dr. Lambert, I'm going to have to ask you to stay out of this."

When she jerked on his elbow again, Nick nearly fell, but Natalie caught his arm on the other side. She continued to protest, but Tracy simply ignored her, and Nick resigned himself to his fate—there was no way Tracy would listen to common sense. They headed through and over the rubble, back toward the area where they'd left the car. Nick was astonished to find how widespread the devastation was and how far he'd traveled.

He tried to keep his eyes ahead, looking down only to keep from stumbling over debris—he couldn't meet Natalie's gaze. How could he explain to her that he had let this happen or that he had allowed LaCroix's people to escape? Tracy was right—he was guilty of conspiracy, terrorism, and more.

Tracy kept pushing him forward, her shoves occasionally a little harder than they should have been. His partner was uncharacteristically silent . . . and Nick was just as glad he didn't have to make conversation. He'd shot her, tried to kill her.

Despite his capture, there was some part of his soul that was glad he'd missed.

When Tracy stopped short, he nearly stumbled into her. Natalie caught his other shoulder and righted him before he could fall, and Nick turned his head to thank her . . . but then he saw what had stopped Tracy's relentless march toward the last vestiges of authority in the area.

Urs was seated on the ground in front of them, her blonde curls speckled with dust and dirt. Vachon, his eyes closed, had his head cradled against her shoulder. As if suddenly realizing they were there, she looked up at them, face pale and eyes rimmed with red. Her tears left no doubt in his mind—Vachon was dead.

Pushing his way forward, Nick dropped to his knees beside Urs and rested his head against hers. He tried to ask a question, but his voice was nothing more than a croaking sound, sudden sorrow choking him.

Tracy moved around them, slowly lowering herself to the ground on the other side. She reached for Vachon's hand and held it to her cheek, whispering, "There may still be a chance. I could—I could—" Closing her eyes, she shivered.

Nick was faintly aware of Natalie's hands on his shoulders. He leaned his weight against her as she squatted behind him, then turned his head. "Can she—?"

"It's possible," answered Natalie, her attention locked on Tracy. "If there's still blood in the heart, if he hasn't gotten too cold."

"He wanted to be brought across so you wouldn't be alone." Urs sniffed as Nick turned his attention to her, stunned. "He knew they were going to offer it to you. But not this soon. He thought he had time. He thought—he said you wouldn't have anybody to watch your back."

There'd been no parting between him and Vachon—just a rough dismissal last night at the club bombing. There'd been no discussion between them. He'd assumed that Vachon wanted to be brought across because he wanted to save his own life, that he wanted to spend eternity with Tracy. . . .

Tracy opened her eyes and looked hard at him. She'd heard. Of course she'd heard.

"Do it," he told her. "Bring him across. Save him."

She touched Vachon's wrist to her lips sadly, then folded his hand across his chest, releasing her hold on him. "It's too late. He's gone."

Urs began to sob and leaned against Nick's right shoulder, her fingers clutching at his jacket. Natalie's hands tightened on his other shoulder, and he felt her lips press against his cheek in sympathy. Through it all, he couldn't break Tracy's gaze. She continued to stare at him, and he saw sorrow and bewilderment mix in her eyes. Now she'd never know whether Vachon had truly loved her or whether he'd been using her to get what he'd wanted.

Almost idly, she started to clear the rubble from Vachon's body, tossing away the bits of cement and debris that had fallen on him. Nick wanted to tell her what Vachon had been like, that if he'd told her he loved her, he'd meant it, but stopped himself. What difference would it make? There would always be some doubt in her mind.

He'd known he couldn't save them all.

He'd been right.

"It's time to go." Tracy pushed up from the rubble, then dusted herself off. She walked around Vachon's body, then grabbed Nick's elbow again, hauling him to his feet. "Come on." Then she looked down at Urs. "You, too."

"No. Let her go." Nick struggled to maintain his balance and used his body to shield Urs. "She hasn't done anything. You've got me. You don't need her." When Tracy hesitated, he took a step forward, then nodded toward Vachon's body. "Let her go—for his sake."

Tracy met his gaze, her eyes hard and unyielding . . . then softening after a moment, the solid gold fading to blue. She turned her head and nodded, agreeing to leave Urs.

There wasn't any time. Nick shifted his position on the rubble and turned his attention to Natalie. "Take Urs with you—she knows what she's doing. There are still people trapped out here. You might be able to save some of them."

Natalie leaned her forehead against his. "What about you?"

"I'm dead." He kissed her, a brief touch of lips, but then she placed her arms around him, drawing him close, and the kiss deepened. He allowed himself to be lost in it for a moment, savoring the press of her body against him, the scent of her. If this was all they would have, it would have to be enough.

Nick felt a tug on his arm as Tracy grabbed his elbow again. He drew back from Natalie, his gaze falling to Urs, and then to Vachon's body. Closing his eyes, he swallowed, then stumbled as Tracy pulled him forward again. Digging in his heels, he glared at her and raised his gaze to Natalie again. "Before you leave, cover him up."

Dropping the emergency kit to the ground, Natalie started taking off her jacket. As Tracy pulled him away, Nick gave in, but turned his head and continued to watch them over his shoulder. Natalie placed her jacket over Vachon, then

207

grabbed Urs's arm when she realized that he was being led away and tried to follow. He couldn't hear what was said, but Urs stared at him, eyes wide as Natalie spoke to her. When he tried to give her a reassuring smile, she burst into tears and Natalie squatted down beside her, holding her tightly.

Two. He'd saved two. That was in addition to LaCroix and the other members of the resistance, perhaps as many as fourteen. He couldn't save them all. That he'd saved that many had to be enough.

The thought proved to be of little comfort. The ache in his heart didn't lessen, and the void in his soul was as dark and as deep as it could ever be.

During the rest of the trip back to the car, nothing could reach past the numb feeling that had engulfed him. They passed body after body, and he found himself unable to react or even to care any longer. He knew that Tracy said something, said many things . . . but the words and their meaning escaped him. It was only as they reached a patrol car and he leaned against the warm metal that some sense of reality began to return to him.

Tracy glanced at him, past him, speaking with a uniformed officer. "Take him back to the station and have him booked."

The officer stared at Nick, then looked away. "What charge?"

"Attempted murder of a fellow officer." Tracy looked at him again, and for a second, Nick was certain he saw something mortal warring within those hard vampire eyes. But the gold steel fell into place again and Tracy turned away, walking back into the smoke and dust of the still-settling debris.

"Just take him downtown and book him," said the officer's voice. "We don't need any more hassles."

Before Nick could move, a hand grasped the hair on the back of his head. His eyes met those of Art, the vampire who'd attacked him at the apartment building. Nick ducked his head automatically, trying to protect his throat.

The vampire grinned. "Don't worry, pretty boy. I don't turn jailbirds," he snarled.

"Too late," Nick snapped. "You've already turned my stomach."

He realized it was a stupid thing to say just before the vampire slammed his head against the side of the patrol car and the flashing red lights and sirens faded into oblivion.

11

THE THROBBING IN THE BACK OF HIS SKULL WASN'T HELPED BY THE insistent beat of the music. Shaking his head and trying to clear his vision, Nick was startled by the cool feel of the tile floor beneath his hands. He pushed himself up, grabbed hold of the table, and kicked aside the overturned chair as he rose.

Strobe lights cut through the darkness in random patterns. Nick leaned his weight on the top of the table and blinked, staring at the dancers, who were now standing still and staring at him. What had happened?

A fist connected with his jaw—he never saw it coming; the blow was forceful enough to slam him against the wall. Holding his palms out in front of him, Nick managed to deflect two more blows at his face, but another eluded his guard; he doubled over as the fist caught him in the stomach. His assailant grabbed the back of his collar and threw him into the table.

He slid across the floor on his back, then brushed the table leg aside while the coasters and napkins fluttered to the ground. Kicking up with his feet, Nick caught his attacker in the midsection, driving him back against the wall. The move gave him a minute to react, to assess, to figure out what the hell was happening.

The man stalking toward him was a mortal, his features vaguely familiar. Forced to squint in the dim light, Nick finally recognized him as Steve, the dress-for-success mortal he'd gotten ejected from the Raven the night before.

Knowing his opposition made things easier. Steve threw a punch and Nick confidently raised his hand to catch the man's wrist and stop the fist before it could connect.

He missed.

That realization struck him at about the same time as the blow to the jaw. The punch had enough force behind it to knock him against another table. It shifted in place and fell with him, showering him and the patrons seated there with a variety of liquids. Glass crashed to the floor and shattered.

The crowd gathered closer, their cries all but drowning out the music. Nick wasn't surprised to hear that he wasn't the favored winner. Wiping the blood from his lip with his shirtsleeve, he staggered up from the floor and flung himself at the man attacking him.

The enhanced speed and strength that accompanied the blood lust of the vampire within him had disappeared. He struck his opponent as hard as he could, then struck again, landing several punches to the stomach. Steve kicked at Nick's shins, knocking him off his feet.

This time Nick had enough presence of mind to roll with the blow. He might have ended up on his feet if he hadn't slipped in the puddle of ice and alcohol that had spread over the tile.

There was no time to collect his wits. Nick put down his hand and tried to push himself to his feet, then pulled back quickly, cut by a fragment of glass. More cautiously, he made a second effort, but suddenly Steve was standing over him. Grabbing Nick's shirtfront with one hand, Steve landed two hard, sharp punches on the side of Nick's chin, then drew his fist back for a coup de grâce.

The blow was never delivered. When Nick could focus his eyes, he saw LaCroix standing behind Steve, his fingers closed over the mortal's fist. Letting out a cry of pain, Steve loosened his hold on Nick's shirt and grabbed his own wrist as LaCroix slowly forced him to his knees.

"I think that's enough," said LaCroix evenly. Without warning, he released Steve's hand. As the mortal fell, LaCroix placed the heel of his boot against the man's rump, pushing him to the floor. Making a brief motion with his hand over the heads of the crowd, he stepped aside.

The bouncer appeared and all but bodily carried the man from the club. LaCroix squatted beside Nick, taking care not to touch the floor. "I thought you wanted to be left alone."

Groaning, Nick let himself fall back against the floor and closed his eyes. There wasn't a muscle in his body that didn't ache, his head was still throbbing, and the cuts on his palms stung from the alcohol.

"I warned you."

"I don't need a lecture right now." Opening his eyes, Nick noticed the crowd had more or less returned to its interrupted evening out. The tables were being righted and the patrons reseated, with new drinks served. Watching where he rested his hand, Nick carefully pushed himself up from the floor. He winced as he pressed on the glass slivers embedded in his palm.

"You're going to cost me a small fortune in free drinks."

Nick wiped his hands against his jeans, the cuts stinging again. "I'm good for the money."

"It's not the money that concerns me." LaCroix rose and took a step closer, eyes blazing. "You've disregarded my warnings, and look where it's gotten you. You're weak . . . pathetic!"

Nick stared at the floor, suddenly aware that the vampires in the crowd were watching him, laughing at him. He'd just been trashed by a mortal in public, and now his master was giving him a public dressing-down. If he'd actually given a damn, he would have been humiliated.

But he was too tired and sore to care. Turning his head to one side, he took a deep breath. "I'm not—"

"It isn't too late," said LaCroix softly. He took a step closer to Nick and whispered in his ear. "I can still save you. If there's anything left worth saving. . . ."

"Save me?" Wanting nothing more than to sit down somewhere, with lying down a very close second, Nick froze. "Save me from—"

"Your folly." LaCroix stepped back, his expression grim. "You're aware that it will probably destroy you. Or you'll destroy yourself, if you go on in this fashion." Holding out his hand, LaCroix ordered, "Give it to me. Abandon your quest for mortality before you've lost everything."

For a good part of the eight hundred years he'd walked the earth as a vampire, Nick had sought to free himself from LaCroix, fighting him at every turn. Many times in the past he'd been worn beyond endurance or had realized he was in over his head and needed rescue, but seldom had he been so tempted to surrender what little remained of his soul and become the man, the *vampire*, LaCroix wanted him to be.

"If you refuse me now," said LaCroix, "you can see this through on your own. I won't lift a finger to help you." He frowned. "It's your decision, Nicholas. Time is running out."

Nick met his eyes and managed a smile. "We both know mine ran out a long time ago."

Glancing toward the door, LaCroix snapped his fingers. He pointed to Nick, then stalked across the club without a backward glance. Bemused, Nick stared after him, wondering what had just happened.

A hand fell on his shoulder. "Come on, Nick. You're outta here."

It was the bouncer. When Nick didn't move immediately, his grip tightened and he pushed Nick in the direction of the door.

Anger flared inside him. He'd been pushed around by too

many vampires and mortals recently. Needing to strike out, Nick aimed a fist for the bouncer's jaw.

That turned out to be a mistake. The bouncer easily ducked the punch, then landed a fist in Nick's midsection. He flew back, trashing yet another table, but wasn't as quick to rise this time—the wind had been knocked out of him. Gasping, he rested on the floor on his knees and wrapped his arms around his stomach, doubled over. The bouncer hauled Nick to his feet by the back of his shirt and frog-marched him to the door.

He wasn't thrown out of the Raven—strictly speaking—but the force the bouncer used was just enough to send him into a mound of rock-hard snow that had been piled up by the street plow. Bruised, aching, and only half aware of what was going on, Nick slid down the slope of the snow and landed on his tailbone at the bottom. As he was struggling to his feet, his jacket was tossed out the door after him. His keys skidded across the icy concrete walk in front of the club.

Shivering violently, Nick struggled into his coat, zipping and buttoning every flap he could find. Yet the cold still seemed to reach him, and his hands were red and shaking. He stumbled across the ice, nearly sliding again, and retrieved his keys. They fell out of his hands twice before he managed to drop them into his coat pocket. Then he walked across the icy sidewalk to his car. Losing his balance on a slick patch, he fell and slid, slamming his shoulder into the Caddie's door.

For a moment, he simply sat there, frozen and battered beyond comprehension. The chilled air invaded his lungs with every breath, causing him to shiver. Nick tucked his hands into his pockets. One hand clutched the car keys, and the other hand found something small and hard.

He held the wicker doll in his palm. Its features were barely visible in the dim light outside the Raven, but he didn't need to see it to know that the head had folded in on itself.

Leaning against his car and sitting in the snow, he drew his knees to his chest, the doll clutched in his hand. As he shivered, Nick closed his eyes and let his head fall back against the car. Would LaCroix care when he was dead? Would any of them care?

"Self-pity doesn't become you, Detective Knight. But then, it's not very attractive on anyone."

His eyes shot open. At first, he couldn't see anything more than the outline of a figure silhouetted against the dim light. As he stared at her, the features came into focus—an Asian cast to the face, emerald, almond-shaped eyes, and hair as dark and shiny as a raven's wing. She wore a black cloak with a hood that did little to protect her from the cold. And though her dress was sheer—lime and olive and emerald silk that left her midriff bare and nothing to the imagination—she never shivered or showed any acknowledgment of the below-freezing temperature or the chill wind that threatened to cut him like a knife.

He'd never met her, but he knew exactly who she was. Natalie's description, evocative as it had been, hadn't done her justice. "Why are you doing this to me?"

"I've done nothing." The briefest smile traced the outline of her ruby lips. "I only advise. You contacted me, Detective Knight." The smile vanished, and her lips formed a grim line. "You asked for a dream doll. I advised against it, but you asked again . . . demanded, threatened, in fact. I delivered only what you asked."

Another gust of wind swept around the car, and Nick shivered. He tucked his hands into his armpits in an attempt to keep them warm. "But I didn't know. . . ."

"You never do." A sad smile accompanied her words. Stepping forward, she offered him her hand.

Nick took it, using it and the car to regain his footing. While he held her hand, the wind and the cold seemed to avoid him. The fingers that folded over his were long and thin and smooth, the nails hard and lacquered in the same shifting emerald color as her gown.

"One would think you'd have learned by now," she said softly, her gaze falling to the palm of the hand that contained the fragments of glass. "Eight hundred years ago you lost your mortality by not asking questions. Did you think to regain it the same way, stumbling blindly after every glimmer of light?" There was something sharper in her gaze as she met his eyes. "Or was that first merely a 'bad decision'?"

He pulled his hand from her grasp as he heard the words, and stared into the emerald eyes. "You know too much."

"You know too little . . . about yourself." Her smile was frank and even as she met his gaze—she wasn't about to be cowed by threats or mesmerized into submission.

"I know too little about this." Reaching into his pocket, he pulled out the doll. "I have one dream left, don't I? And then . . . ?"

The lacquered fingernails reached out, stroking the doll in the palm of his hand but not taking it from him. "You tell me. They're your dreams."

"Are they really dreams? They're too detailed, too realistic . . . and I know they're not memories."

She clasped her hands together. "One man's memories are another man's dreams."

"A man?" asked Nick sharply, his fingers closing over the doll. "Or . . . a mortal?"

"Oh, let's not play games with words." Shaking her head, she took a step through the snow and seated herself on the hood of his car.

Normally, Nick would wince at such familiarity with his prized auto. Now he simply shrugged and leaned forward, his hands resting on the cold metal. "Why did you come here?"

"To advise you." That amused smile reappeared. "You seemed confused."

He couldn't argue with that. When she didn't seem prepared to say more, he asked, "So, what do you advise?"

She pursed her lips and, for a moment, he thought he saw her legs impatiently kicking back and forth against the car, beneath the silken veils of her dress. "If I tell you, will you listen this time?"

There was the slightest threat in the tone of her voice that got under his skin. But Nick swallowed his pride and nodded. "Yes."

Taking his closed fist in her hands, she met his gaze. "Dream the last dream."

Nick stared at her. "But . . . I'll die."

She released his hand, hopped from the hood of the car, and turned her back to him. "Detective Knight, your arrogance knows no bounds. I can do nothing for you."

"Wait!" He extended the hand that held the doll as if to touch her, but drew it back quickly when she glanced over her shoulder, emerald eyes flashing angrily. "I . . . apologize. I did say I'd take your advice. But at least tell me what's going to happen."

Rolling her eyes, she looked at the night sky, as if beseeching some external power for patience. "First you ignore me. Then you treat me like a common fortune teller." As she shook her head in dismay, she turned disappointed eyes to him. "I told you, *chevalier*, it's your dream. You must live it, not I."

"And then?"

"Then you'll know if you have the strength to pursue your heart's desire. And what that truly is." The hard cast of her lips softened, and she brushed his frozen fingers with her own. "That's all I can tell you."

Nick stared at her, his heart sinking. "It isn't enough."

"It will have to be enough for now." She reached up to touch his face with her hand and smiled sadly. Then she turned and stepped carefully through the snow and onto the icy walkway.

Nick opened his clenched fist and stared down at the dream doll. When he looked up, the woman had disappeared into the darkness. She'd left no footprints in the hard crust of the snow . . . only his own floundering marks could be seen. That, however, was no surprise, given the rock-hard consistency of the previously plowed snow.

His heart heavy, Nick dropped the dream doll back into his pocket and pulled out his keys. The car door resisted him, frozen shut, but it gave after a few tugs, a very small dent, and some swearing. He sat inside with the heater running full blast for ten minutes before he could keep his hands from shaking on the steering wheel.

During the drive back to the loft, he did no better. Nick was tired beyond belief . . . eight centuries of tired. He'd begun to question whether he even wanted to be mortal after the past few days of meaningless deaths. He'd relied upon his vampire abilities of flight and speed, enhanced senses and invulnerability to solve cases and save mortals. Tracy . . . and even Natalie . . . owed their lives to the fact that he was a vampire.

It was simple—if all he wanted to do was save mortal lives, he couldn't be a mortal. Even then, he couldn't save mortals from themselves or each other. He wanted more than a legacy of heroism for himself. But was being mortal worth all the heartache and anguish he'd endured—and would endure—searching for a way back across?

The trip home was only a matter of minutes, but it felt like a lifetime. As he sat in his car for a few minutes before braving the cold of the nearly empty garage, Nick thought he'd never be warm again. From there it was a dash to the elevator—he huddled in one corner during the ride up to the loft.

When the doors opened, he stumbled across the room and fell onto the couch. His hands, his cheeks, his ears, and all of his exposed skin felt like it was being pricked by tiny needles. His body ached from the beating he'd taken at the club and his falls on the ice. He felt thoroughly miserable. If he was going to die, it had better be soon, or he was liable to kill himself just to end the constant aches and pains.

He heard the elevator door open but couldn't be bothered stirring himself, having found some bit of warmth by huddling in a corner of the couch.

"Nick?"

Natalie's voice held a measure of panic. That, and that alone, could move him. He waved a hand and said, "Here."

He sounded pitiful. "I saw you go in and I called—I guess you didn't hear me." Natalie dropped a paper sack onto the coffee table and stared at him. "What happened?" She paused long enough to shrug off her coat, then left it on the floor as she bent over him. She touched the back of her hand to his cheek, then pulled away. "My God, you're frozen!"

"I had another dream," he muttered, hiding his head beneath his arm. "Nat, I think I'm dying. At least, I hope I am."

"You're just cold," she scolded, but there was an uncertainty in her tone that unnerved him. "Come on, get up." Natalie pushed his shoulder, then pulled her hand back and wiped it on her sweat pants. "Your jacket's all wet."

In response to her bullying, Nick sat up, but in concession to how lousy he felt, he draped himself over the arm of the couch. "I got thrown out of the Raven."

"And you've cut your hand—"

"Part of the reason I was thrown out." Meeting her curious gaze for an instant, he shook his head and fell back against the arm of the couch again. "It's a long story."

"It explains why the bartender hung up on me when I called to ask if you were there. Let me see your hand." She took his hand in hers. "Nick, you've still got glass in here. And how . . . ?"

Natalie's voice trailed off. When she remained quiet, he glanced at her. His hand rested in hers, but her other hand loosely held his wrist, her eyes on her wristwatch.

"What?" he asked, trying to pull his hand back.

"Stop." She slapped his wrist. "You've made me lose count. Be quiet."

Frowning, he let his head fall back to the couch and closed his eyes. The least she could offer was a little sympathy. It wasn't every day things like this happened to him. In fact, things like this never happened to him. How was he ever going to live down being thrown out of the Raven? He'd be a laughingstock. The better part of a decade could pass before he'd get up the nerve to go back there.

His lip was still tender, and he touched the spot lightly with his tongue. It wasn't the first time he'd bitten his lip in a fight, but it had always healed quickly before. Why was it so sore?

"I don't believe it," muttered Natalie.

Nick opened his eyes and dared another look at her. She dropped his wrist and held up one finger. "Just one more thing."

"Nat—"

"Bear with me. And stop whining." Kneeling beside the couch, she leaned over and placed her ear against his chest.

"Is this supposed to help?" he asked, then chided himself for protesting. She was warm—he wanted to wrap his arms around her and hold her until he could absorb some of her heat. When he tried to do just that, she pushed his hands away firmly.

"Ssssh!" After a moment, Natalie looked up at him, eyes narrowing. "Take a deep breath and hold it."

"This is silly."

Slapping a hand against his chest, she commanded, "Do it!"

She placed her ear against his chest. At her signal Nick took a deep breath, releasing it as she lowered her hand.

"Again."

After he'd exhaled, she sat back on her heels and stared at him. Nick frowned. "What? Should I wait for the movie?"

Natalie rose to her feet and walked away, shaking her head. "It does make sense, in a weird sort of way. Blood makes you nauseous. You're cold—any idiot knows enough to wear gloves when it's thirty degrees below, never mind the wind chill. Damn lucky you haven't gotten frost-bite. . . ."

"What?" The chill was starting to leave him. Nick sat up on the couch, then rose to his feet when she didn't turn to face him. A shiver ran through him at the thought of what she wasn't saying. "Nat?"

She still wouldn't turn; her voice sounded strange, unsteady. "You don't know, do you?"

Standing behind her, he put his hand on her shoulder. "No, I don't. Unless you tell me."

There were tears in her eyes when Natalie turned to face him. Placing her hands over his, she whispered, "You're almost mortal."

It took a second for the words to register—fear had tightened around his soul when he'd seen her tears, and he was prepared for an entirely different verdict. "No," he answered automatically, believing that his ears were playing tricks on him.

She squeezed his hand, the one he'd cut on the glass. Wincing, Nick pulled it quickly from her shoulder, cradling it protectively against himself.

"Oh, Nick, I'm sorry—" Half laughing, she reached for his hand, but he stepped back.

Nick looked around the loft, but nothing had changed. Nothing . . . except him.

"It can't be true," he whispered, half to himself. "It can't." But he looked down at his hand, which was still bleeding. She was right; he could see two fragments of glass sparkling in the cuts.

"It's true," said Natalie. "That's why you felt the cold—your body temperature is almost a healthy ninety-eight point six. Your pulse is slow but nearly normal, your heartbeat's more regular, and you're breathing." She stood next to him and touched the side of his face with the tips of her fingers, her manner turning clinical. "You're even bruising."

"I fell on the ice," he said absently, still not comprehending what she was saying.

"That's why you've been feeling lousy; your body's getting up to speed. It takes time for the blood to warm, for the heartbeat to speed up. . . ."

"I'm still tired."

"You haven't slept."

"And . . . hungry."

"You haven't eaten." When he turned toward her with a questioning glance, she shrugged. "I don't know how. But it's happening."

"The doll." Reaching into his coat pocket, he withdrew the wicker doll. The arms were still folded tightly, as were the legs, and the head was bent to the chest. Nick stared at it, wondering if she was right.

"No," said Natalie quickly. "That's too . . . weird. Like spells, or magic or—"

"Vampires?" he asked softly.

When he looked at her, she was smiling shyly. "I guess. It's supposed to give you your heart's desire, right?"

His eyes went back to the doll. "That's what she said."

"Who?"

"Your friend from Greenwich Village."

"She's *your* friend." Natalie's tone took on a suspicious cast. "I thought you said you'd never spoken to her."

"I hadn't, before tonight." The doll looked the same. There was no change in the expression. And a light touch against the folded limbs proved they were as immovable as before.

Natalie put a hand on his arm to get his attention, her expression worried. "You saw her? Here?"

"Outside the Raven." He looked at the doll again.

"And she came all the way from New York to see you?"

"She has her own way of traveling." Nick smiled to himself—he didn't quite understand who or what she was, exactly. But sometimes it was better not to question those things. "She gave me some advice."

"Which was?" pressed Natalie.

"Dream the last dream." He moved his hand toward Natalie, and she took a step back when her eyes fell on the doll. "I've had five dreams—there's only one left. I thought she was telling me that I was going to die. Instead . . . I'm alive."

He closed his hand over the doll, feeling the scratchy wicker against his palm. Then he looked at Natalie. "I *am* alive? Mortal?"

"I wouldn't test it with a knife or a noose, but . . . yeah. You're almost there."

The tears still sparkled at the corners of her eyes. Nick opened his hand and the doll dropped to the table, forgotten. He placed his hands on Natalie's shoulders and hugged her tightly, lifting her feet from the ground . . . with the strength of a mortal man. He wouldn't have to worry about crushing her, killing her with an embrace.

Her arms fell around his neck, holding on for dear life. "Nick!"

As he lowered her to the ground, Nick leaned forward, lightly brushing his lips against hers. Natalie's eyes were wide as he pulled back, then she pushed forward, her mouth covering his. The warmth he'd been willing to kill for was in his arms. Cradling her face with his hands, he kissed her eyelids, down along the line of her neck—

And images flashed across the landscape of his mind—of sun-bronzed skin, unblemished and smooth beneath his hands and lips, as they stood on the deck of a boat on a warm afternoon.

He turned away, releasing Natalie, his heart torn asunder by the momentary vision. Nick closed his eyes, willing away the image of that other Janette, but that gave way to an image of a Natalie of darkness, with sharp eyes and an even sharper smile. He started as her hand touched his shoulder.

"Nick?"

"The dreams," he said, around the lump in his throat. "I don't know what's real anymore. I kiss you and I see Janette."

Her hand fell from his shoulder and she frowned. "Tell me if I'm wrong, here, but I think you're really out of practice—"

The annoyance in her tone got through to him. He turned his head, meeting her gaze. "In my *dreams*, Nat. I've told you, I'm someone else there." Running his hand through his hair, he walked away from her. "Janette and I were mortals. We were . . . lovers. But not in love. I loved you—" He stopped in his tracks, then added quickly, "in the *dream*. But you were a vampire. There was no way I was going to cross, even for you. And then Janette disappeared, became a vampire. . . ."

The ache was there, more real than he could bear. He turned to look at Natalie, wanting her to understand but not having the words to explain what he felt. "There seems to be some weird sort of parallel; vampire and mortal, Janette and I, you and I. She became a vampire in the dream, so does that mean you'll become a vampire here? Am I going to kill you, just like I ended up killing her?"

There was a name for the knot in his stomach—fear. Nick could too easily imagine his fangs tearing into Natalie's throat, unable to stop himself, overcome with passion and blood lust. Clenching his fist, he stared down at the floor. "It can't happen. I won't let it happen."

He thought Natalie was going to grab her coat and walk

out the door—her eyes definitely moved in that direction. And some small part of him wished desperately that she would do just that, and take this decision out of his hands.

Instead, she took a step toward him, her lips set in a grim line. "Let's take care of first things first, shall we? Sit."

"But—"

"Sit," she commanded, pointing to the couch. Then, as he sat down, she moved to the kitchen and returned with her medical bag. Sitting beside him, she dropped the bag on the table, her manner completely and utterly professional.

From the bag Natalie withdrew a small zippered pouch, which she unfolded on the table to reveal a number of sharp instruments. She picked up a pair of tweezers, pulled a small antiseptic pad out of a package and wiped off the metal ends, then turned her attention to him again. Her palm held outward, she said, "Hand?"

He hesitated, meeting that professional stare. "It's not that bad—"

Without warning, she grabbed his hand and held it flat, wiping an antiseptic pad across it lightly. "If you're going to be mortal, you're going to have to get used to getting scraped and cut and bloodied and bruised and battered . . . inside and out. Consider this lesson one."

Nick bit his lip as she probed the tweezers into the cuts on his hand, extracting the first, then the second piece of glass. Between the stabs of pain, he peered over her hands, fascinated as small droplets of blood swelled around the cuts.

"Light, please," said Natalie sharply, reaching for another antiseptic pad. He leaned back with a grimace, giving her all the light she needed. The pad stung as it swiped over the open cut. Then she released his hand.

It was still bleeding. Nick absently raised the palm of his hand to his mouth, but Natalie glared at him and grabbed the hand back.

"No backsliding. Don't be such a baby, I'm almost done."

She tore open the wrapping of a small, round adhesive bandage and placed it over the cut. Her sleeve slipped back; he looked away after noticing the bruise on her wrist—he'd held her arm too tightly when he'd tried to stop her from touching the dream doll last night.

"There." Natalie held his hand in hers and he looked at her, then down at her wrist. Following the gaze, she quickly released his hand and tugged her sleeve down over the black and blue mark.

"I'm sorry."

Her eyes met his and she smiled. "Don't be. It can't happen anymore, Nick. You're going to be mortal."

Nick rose from the couch and moved away, looking down at the Band-Aid on his palm. "It's . . . going to take some getting used to."

"And you're going to have to get yourself a real doctor, instead of relying on your friendly local coroner." When he looked back, she was throwing things into her bag. "You're going to need food. And sleep." She looked at him, frowning. "Lots of sleep. I worked out a couple of ideas for sedatives—but they were vampire strength and they'd put a bull elephant into a coma. Right now I think a glass of warm milk would set you up for a good eight hours."

"No. No sleep." He walked to the fireplace, resting his bandaged hand against it, the stone cold against his warming skin. "I still have one dream left." For a moment, he stared at her, matching her against the dream image, the vampire Natalie that his dream self found so compelling . . . and that he found lacking. How could she compare to this Natalie, his Natalie?

She rose to her feet. "I guess I'd better be going."

"Why?" He walked over to her, took her hands in his, favoring his bandaged palm. "Natalie—I'm mortal."

"*Almost* mortal," she corrected quickly. Then she added, at his crestfallen look, "You really should get some sleep."

"I don't want to sleep. I'll only . . . I'll only dream

again." Nick took a deep breath, a small shiver stealing down his spine. Impulsively, he pressed her knuckles to his lips. "I want you to be here if I do. Stay with me. Talk with me."

Natalie pulled her hands away. "Dreams can be good things . . . sometimes. And you don't need me. Not now."

"Of course I need you." He stared in surprise. "You brought me back across. I've got what I wanted. I'm mortal. What's wrong?"

"What's wrong?" Natalie sucked in a breath between her teeth and nodded. "Okay, Nick, I'll tell you what's wrong. You're not completely mortal. Yes, you've made some fantastic, really amazing strides, but we have no idea how it happened—"

"The dream doll—"

"And we have no idea if it's suddenly going to turn around again. One taste of blood, and you could become a vampire like *that*." She snapped her fingers, and he winced at the sound. "If it's the blood. We don't know—*I* don't know." Natalie stepped toward him and placed her hand on his arm. "You've had episodes like this before—when you were shot in the head and didn't remember you were a vampire, you ate chicken soup. I *saw* you."

Nick looked away, not wanting to hear what she was saying. "This is different."

"Is it? Are you sure?" When he moved away from her again, she grabbed hold of his shoulder, stopping him. "This is a big step in the right direction, but that's all it might be . . . a step. This whole thing could be psychosomatic."

A chill ran through him that had nothing to do with the cold outside. Nick stood still. "You mean, I could be deluding myself."

"Yes. It's possible." Then Natalie walked around him. Taking his hand in hers, she led him to the couch, all but pushing him down onto it. "Or . . . we may have a cure.

But I don't want to lie to you. And I definitely don't want you lying to yourself. It's going to take time, tests—"

"What if I don't have that kind of time?" Tugging on her hands, he drew her down onto the couch beside him. "The last dream could still kill me."

Smiling faintly, she pulled her hand from his and brushed it through his hair. "People don't die because of something that happens to them in their dreams."

"LaCroix says they do."

"If LaCroix told you to jump off a bridge, would you—?" She settled herself beside him on the couch. "Forget it." Natalie half turned toward him. "You really do need some sleep."

"Stay with me." Nick slipped his arm around her shoulder and drew her back to him. "Talk to me. Keep me awake until dawn." When she arched an eyebrow, he added, "Just until dawn. If I can stay awake that long, I'll be all right."

Natalie bowed her head for a moment, then glanced at him from the corner of her eye. "Dawn, huh?"

He nodded ever so slightly.

"And then you'll go right to sleep?"

"You can even tuck me in."

"That'd be a thing of beauty and a joy forever." Pursing her lips, she pulled away and eyed him thoughtfully. "If we're gonna keep Mr. Sandman from knocking at my door, I'd better go make some coffee."

She'd barely pushed herself off the couch before Nick asked, "Could you bring me a cup?"

Stunned, Natalie stopped, then turned slowly. "Did you just ask for a cup of coffee?"

"Please?" Nick wondered if that's what he'd forgotten in his initial request.

"That's what I thought." Grinning, she headed into the kitchen, and he turned to watch her. "You know, this whole thing may work out after all. . . ."

Realizing that he was still wearing his jacket, Nick peeled

it off, then threw it onto the chair beside the couch. He leaned forward and picked up the dream doll, tossing it back and forth in his hands. "What should we talk about?"

"I don't know," Natalie answered from the kitchen. "What do we ever talk about? Murder, blood alcohol, bullet wounds, fatality rates?"

"Kind of a grim conversation, isn't it?

"Well, we're both in pretty grim professions."

"I guess so." Again Nick turned the doll over in his hands. It was frustrating to have so many questions and no answers. "If you could go anywhere in the world, where would you like to go?"

"Twenty questions, huh?" Natalie picked up his jacket from the chair when she returned, then carried it over to the coatrack by the elevator door. "Warm destination or cold?"

"Doesn't matter."

When she went to sit down in the chair, Nick pointedly shifted his position on the couch, leaving more than enough room for her. Natalie seated herself beside him without a moment's hesitation. "One of each, then. Cold . . . I guess Switzerland."

"Switzerland?" said Nick in surprise. When she socked him lightly in the shoulder, he raised an eyebrow and asked, "What's in Switzerland?"

"Chocolate. Lots and lots of chocolate." Natalie clasped her hands together and leaned forward. She stared at the fireplace, as if she had a perfect view of her destination. "Skiing. I always wanted to ski."

"You don't know how?"

"No. You do?" When he attempted to shrug modestly, she grinned. "Then you can teach me. I want to swoosh down a slope. All that white, untouched snow, way up in the mountains, where the air is crystal clear, nobody around for miles and miles." She glanced at him and noticed his sour expression. "What?"

"I'm not into cold right now," explained Nick, with a shiver. "Or swooshing. Or snow."

"Warm, then. Hawaii. Flowers. Surf. Sea. Sand. Food. All the comforts of home and no corpses to cut."

He watched her as she talked about her dream vacation, relishing every moment of the conversation—the way her eyes lit up when she talked about things that she'd heard about and wanted to see someday. They talked about dreams and their favorite colors, the rights of the press versus the individual's right to privacy, which westerns they'd liked and which they'd hated . . . a dozen different topics each hour for six hours straight. They argued about art and politics and religion, whether fire engines should be yellow or red, and was there a future for man in space. They talked and drank coffee and talked more, until their arguments were punctuated with yawns and his arm was sore from Natalie's hitting him every time he nodded off.

Nick started awake and realized his arm was numb— Natalie was sleeping on it. Trying not to disturb her, he carefully moved his arm and allowed it to drape over her shoulder. She shifted and her nose twitched, but she remained asleep.

He could feel the rise and fall of her chest with each breath, her body warm against his. Nick watched her sleep for a time, then stared the length of the loft, gazing at the posters and paintings, counting the number of bricks in the wall, anything to keep himself awake. He would have shifted Natalie and paced the length of the room, but he no longer had the energy. He was too tired. The dreams had worn him out. There was nothing left to do but what the woman had said—dream the last dream and have done with it.

Moving carefully, he kissed the top of Natalie's head, his lips resting against her hair. Then he closed his eyes and surrendered himself to the darkness, some part of his heart certain that he would never wake again.

12

Nick opened his eyes to blackness. Staring into the dark that surrounded him, he licked his lips, willing to give his soul for a glass of water.

The straight-backed chair on which he was seated was anything but comfortable. His hands had been cuffed behind him, to the chair. That much told him he was in one of the smaller interrogation rooms. But why he was here, instead of a cell, was beyond him. Unless . . . the police were going to take care of their little "problem" by themselves, without public embarrassment.

He had no idea how long he'd been there, or how long they'd leave him alive. He shook with a sudden chill, cold enveloping his senses. Images from his dreams haunted him—Natalie in his arms, as a mortal woman, her lips touching his without fear of fangs or golden eyes. Leaning his head back, he stared at the ceiling and let the images play across his mind, almost bringing a smile to his lips. Just as well the vampires weren't able to monitor mortal dreams, or his would have been censored.

Then he remembered Vachon, lying still and cold beneath the rubble. His hands jerked violently against the cuffs. It was stupid, useless to resist—handcuffs had been redesigned to withstand the strength of vampire suspects—but he needed to vent his anger and sorrow somehow.

The light flicked on, blinding him for a moment. Nick closed his eyes and turned his head away from the glare. Footsteps echoed on the tile floor as someone entered, then he heard the soft click of the lock as the door closed. After blinking for several seconds, enough of his vision returned to allow him to recognize the room.

It was one of the old interrogation cells, the walls and doors reinforced to hold vampires who failed to turn successfully. There were still splotches of blood on the walls, and even the ceiling, from the last occupant. He'd been here not too long ago, when Natalie drew the short straw and was assigned to wait out the vampire's suffering, declaring it "dead" so that it could be legally terminated.

Identifying the room added a frightening dimension to his captivity, and instinctively he jerked his hands against the cuffs. The room was soundproofed. He was a mortal in custody and a suspected member of the resistance—he had no rights. Anything could happen to him here.

Reese stood at the door, staring at him. He nodded, his manner no different than it had been when Nick had been a detective under his command, sitting on the other side of the captain's desk to receive an assignment. "Knight."

"Captain," he managed, through dry lips.

"Just to get this out of the way—were my wife and daughters there last night? I've been on the phone to every hospital and medic center—"

"They're fine," said Nick, with more certitude than he should have dared. "I don't know where they are—they've been moved by now. But they're safe. And they'll stay safe."

"Thank God."

Walking to the table in the center of the room, Reese reached into his jacket and withdrew several items: Nick's badge, his car keys, his wallet, the photograph of Janette, and the wicker doll . . . everything that had been in his pockets when he'd been arrested. "Your gun?" asked Reese.

"At the scene. I gave it to someone." When Reese raised an eyebrow, Nick added, "The duty officer—I don't know her name—she was wounded. Someone tried to stake her while I was there. A mortal civilian was watching her until help arrived. I gave it to him to protect her . . . and himself."

Reese's immediate reaction was a nod. "There were two of you in the alley when the first bomb went off. Vetter gave me her version. I'd like to hear yours."

Surprised, Nick met the captain's even stare for a moment, then looked away. "Why bother? It's Tracy's version that'll end up in the report."

"Tracy says that you were both jumped in the alley by the bastards who blew up the plant. She said they were mortals. She didn't get a real good look at them because the wall exploded in her face. She says you freaked and shot her—but she blames that on the yahoos who jumped you when you stopped at your place to pick up your badge."

Nick kept his gaze on the wall, trying to comprehend what Reese was saying. Tracy had lied. Tracy had lied about being shot by her own partner!

Unable to help himself, he met Reese's eyes.

"Yeah, I know," said Reese. "Partners cover partners, but this is so full of baloney, I don't know if I can sell it to the brass." Then he shook his head. "I guess you'll get points because those idiots jumped you—they're in a cell down the hall, charged with disorderly conduct and infraction of the turning statute. We'll handle in-house charges later."

"They're dangerous."

Reese's eyes sparkled. "They're idiots. *You're* dangerous." He rubbed his chin thoughtfully. "Right now, you're charged with unlawful discharge of your weapon. Tracy's not pressing charges. In fact, she thinks you should be classed unfit for turning and honorably discharged."

Nick's mouth fell open. Inwardly, he offered thanks to his former partner.

"She won't be by to see you—can't say I blame her." Nick flinched at the captain's words. "She had a message for you, though. She said it doesn't matter, that she still believes in justice. Whatever the hell that means."

"I know what it means." Lowering his gaze to the floor, he thought back on their conversation about vampires wanting to assist the resistance and her reluctance to bring Vachon across. With all that had happened, Tracy's feelings hadn't changed. As a vampire and the daughter of the police commissioner, she might be able to do some good for the mortal cause. He looked up at Reese and smiled. "Thanks. Tell her . . . she was a good partner."

"You might be able to tell her yourself." Reese met Nick's eyes again, with a gaze that almost stripped away the sudden hope he'd had of a reprieve. "The brass took Tracy's recommendation under consideration. They turned it down." He picked up the photograph of Janette from the table and glanced at it. "They think you'll be stable enough as a vampire. But they want you turned, tonight."

Nick straightened in the chair, the cuffs rattling as he clenched his fingers into fists. "Against my will?"

"That'd be illegal." Reese's smile was grim. "And political disaster, after you became one of the battlefield angels of mercy last night. Not wanting to turn would indicate mental instability. If you decline the offer, you get sent for psychological evaluation."

"And become a donor," spat Nick.

"And *disappear*," corrected Reese. "They don't want a martyr. They seem to think you have some sort of standing in the community—that if you're turned, the opinion of some of the mortals might shift in our favor. And if you're not turned. . . ."

Reese's shrug left nothing to the imagination. Nick looked down at the floor. Either decision was a death sentence, but at least he had a choice in the way he was going to die. Donors didn't come back. Lifting his head, he was ready to announce his decision to Reese when the captain held up a hand.

"Not yet." He gestured around the room. "First off, this place is clean, and you know why . . . you know what happens here. The brass don't want too many of our dirty little secrets on tape. There's no way to see in or out, no way to tell what's going on unless that door opens." He gestured toward the door, then, very slightly, indicated the ceiling with a tilt of his head. "This place hasn't been cleaned in a while. So there might be some things lying around. Old stuff. Like paper clips, rubber bands, maybe an old gun from the evidence room with a prechaos bullet in it. Might even be from one of your old cases."

The breath caught in Nick's throat. It took a moment for the captain's words to sink in. Reese was offering him a way out—suicide. But who else would know there was only one bullet in the gun, or that it was harmless to vampires? Maybe he could take a hostage, bluff his way out of the station—

"Those cuffs are coming off only if you give me your word—the gun never leaves this room." Reese's eyes were firm and hard. He placed the photograph back on the table, then leaned forward. "You're a good cop, Knight. At least, I thought so until last night. That's why I'm doing this for you. If you decide to take the promotion and turn, you're being transferred to another station tomorrow. If you decide not to turn . . . should be a man's prerogative to live or die as he wants. You served this force as best you could. I owe you that much."

LaCroix would have given his word, taken the gun and a hostage, and tried to escape.

But he wasn't LaCroix.

"All right," Nick said, nodding slightly. "If I have to take that way out . . . the gun never leaves this room."

Reese's shoulders relaxed. The captain produced a key on a ring from his pocket, then walked over to Nick. He leaned down and turned the key in the cuff locks.

Never forgetting that the man offering him an honorable end was also a vampire, Nick slowly pulled his hands free from the cuffs and rubbed his wrists for a moment, attempting to restore circulation. He rose from the chair, leaned heavily on the back of it, and tested his weight on his legs. His feet tingled, the numbness slowly wearing away.

Reese walked to the door and stood there, watching him. When Nick finally met his eyes, he frowned. "One last thing—somebody wants to see you. You can say no—" As he spoke, the captain opened the door.

Natalie stood in the doorway. Her face was drawn into a tight frown, mirroring the captain's. "Hi, Nick," she said hesitantly.

Instantly, he turned his back to her. The first words in his throat nearly choked him. He wanted to tell Reese to send her away, that he didn't need this temptation. If anything or anyone could make him turn, it would be Natalie.

And Reese knew it.

The words rose to his lips, but they'd never be spoken. Images from his dreams still haunted him. His eyes burned as he thought of what might have been between them in another world, another place. To be fair to himself—to be fair to her—he would have to say good-bye . . . without losing his life or his soul in the process.

"It's all right," he said, after a moment's pause. Then he turned to face Reese. "Could we have a minute alone?"

Reese nodded, sharing a glance with Natalie before he pulled the door closed behind him.

"Nick, I won't let them take you away." She walked toward him slowly, a flash of gold in her eyes. "Please let me do this for you. Let me bring you across."

"I'd rather you killed me."

A small snarl escaped her, and she glared at him. "You're

238

a complete and utter bastard, you know that? You lead me on all this time, then push comes to shove and now I'm not good enough to turn you?"

He raised a hand to his lips, trying to hide his smile. "Natalie, you know that's not true. It isn't you. I don't want to be what you are."

"And what's so bad about what I am?" she demanded.

He had to admit that she had a point. She was perfection in almost every way—with the exception that she couldn't walk beneath the sun and that her diet consisted of blood.

"My soul is my own," replied Nick evenly. "I don't want a master, or a sponsor."

"But it wouldn't be like that with us," protested Natalie, her facade of confidence and anger crumbling. "We'd be equals, partners—"

"Like you were with your sponsor?"

Her lips tightened and she turned away. "Don't."

"If he hadn't been killed by mortals, he'd still be here." Taking a step closer, Nick whispered, "Remember what it was like? That petty bureaucrat had you all under his thumb, at his beck and call, his every whim—"

"That was before you could choose your sponsor," she said defiantly—but most of the spirit was gone from her voice.

"And do you remember what he was like before he turned? A quiet, unassuming little man, or so I'm told. Kind, in his own way. After he was brought across, he became a tyrant." Smiling sadly, he raised a hand to her cheek. "What would I be like, Natalie? I could easily become as loathsome and detestable—"

"Never!" she protested, wrapping her fingers around his.

"And that's only one reason, of a hundred." He raised her hands to his lips and kissed them. "It's why I don't want to see Janette, see what she's like now that she's been brought across."

Natalie looked down, then away. "That's another reason I'm here. Janette——"

His breath caught in his throat, and he felt his heart stop. The thought that Janette might be here both frightened and elated him. He was having a difficult enough time resisting Natalie's persuasive words, but if Janette were here as well——"You've seen her?"

"No." She met his eyes for a second. "She's dead."

Natalie's fingers tried to slip from his, but Nick held them tightly. "How? Tell me how. Was it the resistance? Did they——"

"No, nothing like that. I lied to you about what happened to her." She pulled her hands from his grasp the instant he released them, and turned her back to him.

"She wasn't on the donor rolls?"

Hope rose in his heart, to be crushed almost as quickly by her words. "Her name was there. She was processed for donation."

Nick closed his eyes and sank back against the wall at the news that Janette had been murdered, drained of every drop of blood her mortal body could offer, then cremated. Her ashes would have been mixed with the others, dumped into a disposal pit somewhere.

"I thought that if I told you she was alive, it might make a difference, you might let me bring you across. I know she meant a lot to you, that there'd been something between you. If you wouldn't do it for me, then you might do it for her. . . ."

He could hear the tears in her voice. Opening his eyes, Nick took a deep breath and walked up to her. He stood behind her, placed his arms around her. Her hair was soft against his cheek, her perfume a mix of some sweet scent and chemical disinfectant from the lab. "Not for you. Not even for her. I won't become a vampire, Natalie. I can't."

She turned in his grasp, her mouth opening to protest again . . . then stopped herself and took a step backward.

He saw the surrender in her eyes, the subtle shift of her shoulders. Crossing her arms, she walked away. "Then there's no way out, is there? They'll take you away, bleed you until you're dry, and there'll be nothing left of you but ashes." Shuddering, she whirled, eyes gold. "I can't let them do that, Nick. I won't let them take you."

"You can't stop them."

"But . . . I could give you an easier death." Eyes still shining gold, Natalie stalked toward him, not seeming to notice as he moved around the chair, putting it between them. "At least I could live with that memory, feel like I didn't abandon you—"

"But you'd end up turning me," he warned, meeting her eyes, almost daring her to try to mesmerize him. "I'd never forgive you for that."

She stopped, and she knew that the hardness of his eyes and set of his shoulders spoke nothing but the truth. Helplessly, she held out her hands. "Then, there *is* nothing—"

There was no warning—a sudden coldness shot through his chest, and it felt like someone had torn out his heart. Nick grabbed at the remnants of his torn shirt and jacket, falling to his knees against the chair. He held the back of the seat for support and closed his eyes as pain swept through him. Dimly he was aware that Natalie was on the floor beside him, calling his name, calling for help.

The pounding in his ears lessened and the pain in his heart receded. Certain it was a heart attack, he wasn't surprised by the sudden numbness in his arms and legs. As his heartbeat slowed, he waited for the darkness to come, pleased at least to have Natalie's arms around him in his last moments. But then something snapped away in his hands and the sudden pain was fleeing, leaving only the numbness.

Opening his eyes, Nick raised his hand and found that he'd wrenched the metal back off the chair. He flinched as the faint scent of blood assaulted him, the dried blood on his clothing and skin, then took a deep breath as a hungry fire raced through him. Dropping the chair to the floor, he struggled out of Natalie's arms and climbed to his feet, his senses screaming. The seams in the wall stood out as hard lines as his heightened vision took in every detail of the small room. When his gaze fell on Natalie, he almost gasped, seeing her immortal perfection in every detail. He could even hear the solitary, almost nonexistent beat of her heart.

Which, a second later, he realized was his own.

Natalie rose to her feet but stayed where she was, staring at him. "Your eyes," she whispered. "Nick—it isn't possible. You haven't been turned!"

Nick touched his fingers to his lips in wonder, then stared at his hand. It looked normal enough, but the marks from the handcuffs were fading from his wrists. A touch to his face confirmed that the same was happening to the remnants of the scratches he'd received from the blast. Strength flowed through him; he no longer felt beaten and bruised and weary beyond words. He was whole. He was dead.

He was a vampire.

"This can't happen," repeated Natalie, taking a step toward him.

She was right—this couldn't happen. To become a vampire, you had to be bitten and drink the blood of your maker, your master. There was no precedent for this. Except—

In his dream, his vampire self had gone back across, become mortal. He'd never heard of that happening before, either.

He was standing beside her before his heart could beat again. Catching Natalie's wrist, he held her hand to his chest. "Don't question it," he said softly. "Just accept it. For the moment, accept it."

After a moment's thought, her hazel eyes widened and she nodded hesitantly. "All right. I'll accept it."

"Good. Because it may be my only way out." Releasing

her, he walked past the chair, his eyes drawn to the torn metal. "I've been having these dreams—odd dreams—about being a vampire. I haven't been sleeping, figured it was this business with having to turn and—" He looked at her, suddenly distracted by dream images. "You were there. You were mortal. And I was the vampire."

Natalie looked askance at him, and he saw a flicker of fear in her eyes—she thought he was going mad. Shaking his head, he kept his distance from her. "When I woke up, here, there were times when my body acted like I was a vampire. I healed quickly. And when they attacked me in the hallway, I threw one across the room hard enough to dent the wall. I was mortal, but I had vampire strength." He met her eyes, knowing there was so much to say, but not enough time to say it. "Natalie, this could save me. I can get out of here."

"How?" Her steps were slow, hesitant, as she crossed the room toward him. "Nick, even as a vampire, you couldn't get past all those cops and all those guns. Granted, I'd be a willing hostage, but still—"

"They'll let me go if I turn. Reese promised as much." He smiled. "So let's not and say you did."

"Turn you?" Natalie stared at him as if certain he were mad, then shook her head sharply, dismissing the notion. "No. It's too quick. You wouldn't be up and around yet. It takes too long—"

"What if I played dead?" Without another word, he let himself slump to the floor, motionless. Concentrating on his heartbeat, he slowed it even further.

"Nick!" He heard Natalie drop to her knees beside him; one hand pulled back his eyelid. He tried not to move as light glared into his eyes. When he felt her panic set in, he reached up and grabbed her arm, causing her to let out a short scream of surprise.

She slapped his face, hard, but it stung for only a second. "Bastard! You took ten years off my life with that stunt."

243

"You can spare it." He forced back a grin, sobering almost instantly as he propped himself up on his elbows. "You've seen newly turned. Will it work?"

Natalie stared into space, thoughtfully stroking her lower lip with her finger. "Maybe. It wouldn't bear close inspection, but everybody's queasy about the newly turned. You never know when one can backfire."

"Which is why you'll want to keep an eye on me, take me home," he prompted.

"Yeah, now that you say it." Her smile faded as she nodded again. "It might work. But . . . how long will this last? If it wears off while we're still trying to pass you off as—"

"It's the only chance I've got." Reaching up, he took her hand in his, squeezing it. "I know it puts you in danger. If you can't go through with it—"

Natalie raised his hands to her lips, kissing his knuckles. "Ten minutes ago I was offering to kill you. Believe me, this option I can live with." Dropping his hand, she hissed, "Now be a good Nick and play dead."

Letting his hand fall back to his side, Nick turned his face to the wall, hoping that the bits of shirt and jacket gathered around his neck would hide the lack of a wound. He listened as Natalie crossed the floor, the click of her heels across the tile more than audible to his vampire hearing. He could imagine her standing in the doorway, opening the door.

At first, he heard the noises of police business along the corridor. The room was at the back of the building, near an alley exit—the newly turned who weren't going to make it were quickly hidden away, to pass their few last mad hours in solitary agony. He couldn't have wished for a better place. But even the few noises in the hallway—footsteps, file drawers, and voices in midconversation—stopped instantly when Natalie opened the door.

"It's done," she said, with such a tremor in her voice that

244

he almost smiled, remembering barely in time that he was supposed to be dead.

Reese's footsteps were easily recognized—slow and heavy. "Did you—?"

"Bring him across? Yes." She cleared her throat. "It wasn't entirely his choice."

Reese's voice was meant to be comforting. "You did him a favor, Nat. You'll want to check on him before we—"

"I'm taking him home."

The steel in her tone almost sent a shiver through Nick. Again he was grateful that he hadn't succumbed to the temptation Natalie had offered. Sponsor or master, the word was just a word—they never would have been partners in death. In the end, he would have had to fight her for control of his soul. And he wasn't certain he'd have won.

The tone of her voice seemed to affect Reese, too. Before he could respond, Natalie added, quietly, "He's been traumatized. And this is the first time I've tried this. He has to come across safely, for my sake as well as his own. He needs my help, my attention . . . not some mortal nurse with a ward of fifty newly turned to care for." He barely heard the added whisper, "We don't want to have to bring him back here, do we?"

He could almost feel Reese's stare, hear the captain running over the options in his mind. His shoes squeaked on the tile floor as he shifted his weight. "All right. I'll call for the EMTs. They'll take you back to your place. And I'll be sending a patrol around, to keep an eye—"

"I told you, he's been traumatized—by your cops. You know he was uncertain about turning. If a uniform, any uniform, shows up while he's still in transition . . . well, I won't take responsibility for it. And I'll put that in writing for the report, right now."

He didn't envy Reese. Facing Natalie on the warpath left two choices—you either got out of her way or you got run over. Normally, Reese wasn't a man to step aside, but he heard the hesitation in the captain's voice. "There's something you should know . . . I think he's connected to the mortal resistance. If they heard he turned, they might try to kill him. And they're desperate enough to send you with him."

"They'd have to find him, first. Which is another good reason not to have lights and sirens flashing in my neighborhood. In a couple of days, when he's over the burn-in, maybe we can talk about protective custody."

Again Reese hesitated. Nick would have held his breath if there was any air remaining in his lungs. "If you're sure you can handle him—"

"I'm a big girl, Captain. I'll take care of him."

"You know what you're doing. I'll clear the corridor for you and have someone bring your car around back." He took two steps down the corridor, then paused, steel in his voice this time. "Make sure you bring him back, Dr. Lambert."

"I will. Eventually."

Nick almost couldn't wait until the door closed. The instant it had, he leaped off the floor and landed in front of her. Startled, Natalie crashed into the back of the closed door.

"Don't do that!" she hissed angrily.

"He bought it?"

"Yes." She wiped her fingers across her brow. "Can they stake you for lying to a police captain?"

"And harboring a fugitive? And faking a turning? And—"

"I think I liked you better when you were dead." She held up a warning finger, her smile sharp. "And no additional comments, please." Then her eyes softened. "Are you ready?"

He gathered up his personal items from the table—the wallet, his keys, the wicker doll Lindy had given him . . . but he left his badge on the table. Nick's gaze lingered on the photo of Janette before he folded it and tucked it in his jacket. Then he turned back to Natalie. "As I'll ever be."

Before he could blink, Natalie reached forward and slung him over her shoulder. "Hang limp," she said, shifting his weight.

"That's easy for you to say." He closed his eyes, suddenly dizzy, and realized that he was very lucky none of the escape route involved trying to fly. When he opened his eyes, it was another matter entirely. "The view's not bad."

"I don't think you were this sarcastic as a mortal," she hissed. Then he was jolted slightly as she took a step forward and reached for the door. "Time to play dead, again."

Closing his eyes, he concentrated on slowing his heartbeat to an almost imperceptible level. It was harder to play dead when slung over Natalie's shoulder as she walked through what Reese had promised would be a cleared corridor. But there were offices there, and it wouldn't have taken vampire senses to hear the creak of hinges as doors opened slightly, the occupants of the offices peering at them as they passed. It wasn't his most dignified exit from the station, but it would be his last . . . with luck.

They made it through the heavy metal door that faced the alley, but still he didn't dare open his eyes. Once outside the air conditioning, he was afraid he'd start to sweat, but the heat of the night didn't bother him. His senses screamed that it wasn't far from dawn—vampire survival warnings ringing in his mortal brain.

The car doors seemed to have been left open. Natalie lowered him into the passenger seat, slipping the seat belt over him. He kissed her neck as she leaned over him and she froze, then took great care to slam the passenger door as hard as she could.

His ears echoed with the sound of the slam for several seconds, long enough for her to sit behind the wheel on the driver's side. Nick heard the engine roar, then fell against the belt slightly as the car moved out of the alley. It was then that he noticed the humming in his ears, interrupting the silence that should have been broken only by the sound of the engine. His strength seemed to ebb away, and he slumped back against the seat, exhausted. He wanted to open his eyes, to see Natalie one last time with that exquisite vampire sight, but he didn't dare move, didn't dare take anything more than the shallowest of breaths until she gave the all-clear.

After what seemed like an eternity, she sighed. "All right. I suppose we're safe enough."

Nick opened his eyes, focusing at the street beyond the windshield. It was very close to dawn; he saw the violet of the eastern sky giving way to blues and grays, oranges and reds. There were some cars on the road, the last few vampires racing back to their sanctuaries before the daylight burned them to cinders.

They were about fifteen minutes from the station. "We've come quite a distance."

When he met her eyes, she frowned, her attention returning to the road. "You're back, aren't you? You've gone mortal again."

"Disappointed?"

She pursed her lips. "Does it matter? You wouldn't be able to tell if I were lying."

"There are ways other than counting heartbeats to know someone's giving you a story. I was a cop, a mortal cop, after all."

"Yeah. You were."

Her confirmation of that past tense disturbed him, almost as much as her having avoided answering his question.

"So where do I take you?" asked Natalie, her voice even.

They were on a back street off the Gardiner Expressway. One of LaCroix's many safe houses, the one secondary to his old apartment building, was no more than five blocks away. "You'd better drop me at the corner. It's almost dawn, you should get back—"

"I'll take you where you need to go," said Natalie firmly. "I won't have anybody say I left you to walk the streets."

Nick started to argue, then bit back the words and leaned against the seat. Rubbing his eyes, he realized how tired he was. In some way, he'd disappointed all of the people who'd mattered to him, both vampire and mortal—LaCroix, Tracy, Natalie, Urs, Reese . . . Vachon. Putting his life back together wasn't going to be easy, especially as a fugitive. He needed time to think, but time was a luxury he didn't have. He'd have to come up with a plan to cover Natalie, another to get out of the city. And he'd never been particularly good at plans.

But he knew someone who was. And . . . maybe he didn't have to disappoint all of them. "Turn here. Right. Then right again."

Natalie glanced at him, her eyes filled with curiosity, but she did as he asked and turned the car down a side street. "You've got a plan. I can tell."

"I've got a way to keep you safe."

"For the day."

"Longer than that . . . I hope." As they cruised down the street, he kept his eyes open for the alley. "Turn here. Stop the car and wait until I signal you."

Again she gave him a curious glance, but turned where he asked. Once the car was stopped, she twisted in her seat to look at him. "Are we gonna talk about this?"

"There's no time." After he unbuckled his seat belt, he leaned across to plant a kiss on her cheek. "Trust me, Natalie."

"Oh, yeah, sure. Trust—"

He slammed the passenger door, cutting off her comments. Outside the air-conditioning of the car, the summer heat assaulted him again. He looked up at what he could see of the lightening sky between the buildings and realized the day was going to be another scorcher . . . in more ways than one.

The door was set back into the wall, another basement entrance. Trust LaCroix to maintain the image of rats scurrying behind the walls. Nick walked down the steps, then knocked on the steel door.

The door flew open almost immediately, and one of the mortals relocated from his apartment building stared at him as if he were a ghost. "Christ, Nick, we thought you were dead! After that cop in the alley—"

"Get LaCroix. Now," Nick commanded. "I'm in a hurry. We don't have much time."

The man nodded, then disappeared back inside. Nick knew there'd be arguments among the lower echelons as to whether it was really him, if he was about to betray them to the police, and half a dozen other plots and possible plans. Word would reach LaCroix within minutes. He didn't have much more time than that.

Leaning his forehead against the still-cool brick that formed the cellar entrance, Nick looked down at his hands in the dim light. At least he was well enough to travel, after he'd had a chance to rest up a bit.

The door flew open sooner than he'd expected. He took a step back, raising his hand to signal Natalie, who would be able to see the gesture from where she was sitting.

LaCroix leaned out the door and stared at him for a moment.

"It's only me," said Nick quietly. "And I've brought a friend who needs protection."

"You should be dead."

Nick knew he was being studied for any signs of duplicity or vampirism. The fact that there wasn't a mark on him didn't help. And he knew beyond a shadow of a doubt that LaCroix's other hand, behind the door, held a gun containing bullets that would kill mortals or vampires. "I should be.

Like I said, I had help getting out. I got tired of waiting for you."

At that, LaCroix's lips twisted into a half-smile. He stepped forward as Nick came down the steps—he was right, there was a gun in his hand.

But it wasn't about to be used on him. LaCroix grabbed his hand, then embraced him. When he stepped back, his smile dissolved. "You know about . . . Vachon?"

Nick looked down and away. His brief time as a vampire hadn't healed that hidden wound. "Yes. I saw him." He looked up when LaCroix's hand fell on his shoulder.

"It was his choice to be there," said LaCroix. "I tried to make him stay behind, to protect the children and some of the others. He wouldn't listen to me."

The break in his friend's voice matched the look in his eyes—a wounded, haunted look. LaCroix, who'd spoken of his lost family only in abstract terms, who'd seemed to miss his stolen music more than anything, was mourning for Vachon. It was only a momentary lapse—the eyes hardened quickly—but the fact that it had happened at all gave Nick hope that his spur-of-the-moment plan would succeed.

A shadow fell across them. Instantly, LaCroix tossed the gun into his right hand, placing his back against the metal door. "Is this a trap?"

Nick stepped forward, pulling the muzzle of the gun to his chest, holding LaCroix's arm and aiming at his own heart. "I told you, I brought a friend to meet you."

Natalie hurried down the steps. Seeing the gun, she pulled back slightly and hissed at LaCroix, fangs bared and ready to launch herself at him.

"One of them?" asked LaCroix, angrily.

It was a standoff. If Natalie moved, Nick would be shot. And LaCroix wouldn't be able to shoot Nick before Natalie would get him.

Nick smiled, noting that this combination had definite possibilities. "Dr. Natalie Lambert, this is Lucien LaCroix.

251

LaCroix, you remember my friend, the vampire coroner?" When they continued to glare at one another, he added, "She saved my life, helped me escape from the station when you couldn't." A quick glance from LaCroix told him the idea of a rescue had been entertained, then discarded. "They gave me a choice—turn or die. Natalie got me out of there, intact and mortal."

He felt LaCroix's grip on the gun lessen. After meeting Nick's eyes, LaCroix nodded toward Natalie with that arrogant civility it seemed only he could master. "Then I owe you my thanks, Dr. Lambert."

"I did it for Nick, not for you," she answered sharply.

"And she'll be up on charges if we don't find a way to cover her. Natalie's in charge of turning me. I'm supposed to be back at her place. If I don't show up after a couple of days—"

LaCroix nodded, eyeing Natalie thoughtfully. "Yes, I see. I suppose something could be arranged. A break-in."

"Reese wanted to provide police protection—he thought some of your people might come after Nick if they found out he'd been brought across." Natalie smiled. "So if I had to run out to pick up some supplies, then found a fire and what was left of Nick when I returned. . . ."

Matching her smile, LaCroix turned to Nick. "I like the way her mind works. That would be just the thing. Of course, we'd need some of your clothes. And vampire ashes."

"I'm a coroner," said Natalie smoothly. "Add together a few spoons from some urns and who's going to know the difference?"

"Done." Then, seeing Natalie glance uneasily behind her, Nick added, "She'll need a place inside, for the day."

LaCroix nodded. "Agreed."

"Nick and I can find something." Natalie walked down the rest of the steps as LaCroix lowered the gun. "I don't want to put you out."

"Nick has to disappear."

She stared at LaCroix, then turned flashing eyes to Nick. "No. You can't just bring me here and leave me . . . with him."

He took her hands in his. "I can't stay here, especially after I'm declared dead. That would put you in danger, as well as the others here. If they hunt me down, they'll go through every one of you to find me."

"Others?" Her eyes widened. "What others?"

"Refugees. Mortals, all," explained LaCroix. The lazy smile rose to his lips as he added, "You're our first vampire. Congratulations."

"Now wait a minute—"

Nick raised a hand to her cheek. "You want to be mortal. Think, Natalie, you can't be the only one of your kind who feels like that. Tracy, for sure, and at least half a dozen of the family men on the force. Maybe even Reese, eventually. And how many more outside?" When she looked away, he moved his fingers to her lips, bringing her gaze back to him. "LaCroix can help you get the supplies you need, help you with your research. You can help him get the information he needs to protect his people . . . within reason."

"Reason being dictated by necessity," said LaCroix, smiling slyly.

"Reason being dictated by humanity." Releasing Natalie, Nick took a step toward LaCroix. "She'll be able to temper your violent streak. I tried and failed. Because of that, Vachon died. But maybe you won't be able to sway Natalie as easily. Let her be the judge of what's in the best interest of mortals *and* vampires, of what's right."

At the mention of Vachon, LaCroix looked away. "Perhaps," he relented, after a few seconds of silence. He met Nick's eyes. "Although the memory of what happened to Vachon may do more toward that end than any of her words." He looked up at the sky, then back at Natalie. "Give me a moment with them. If I walk in with you now, we may have some difficulty."

Natalie shivered as she looked at the lightening sky, but acquiesced. "All right."

As LaCroix reached for the door, Nick added, "And I'm still taking Denise and the girls with me. If something happens and they start after me, they'll be looking for a lone man, not a man accompanied by a woman and two children."

There was a slight sound from Natalie, and LaCroix turned to look at Nick. "You're sure? You want that responsibility?"

"I owe that much to Reese, to keep them safe. There's nothing for them here." Then he met Natalie's eyes. "Yet."

"I'll tell them," promised LaCroix. He hesitated a moment longer. "I had them ready for you, as I'd promised, just in case—I was going to send them out with the next group if you didn't return. We have a car for you, licensed and untraceable. Your possessions were removed from the trunk of your car at the police station, the moment we'd heard you'd been arrested."

Nick smiled, knowing that LaCroix couldn't have taken the chance that he'd betray the resistance or might have taken something with him that would lead the police to the refugees. "A car break-in at the precinct parking lot? That should go over well."

"We thought so." LaCroix glanced at Natalie. "Only a moment, doctor." When she answered him with a hesitant nod, he opened the door and disappeared into the basement.

Natalie was quiet for a moment, staring at the closed door. She glanced at him, then turned away. "You seem so sure that I'll go along with this."

Nick placed his arms around her, standing behind her. "I was sure of you."

He felt her fingers run along his arm. "Before, at least, we could see each other. And now . . . you'll be so far away."

"Not in my dreams."

"But you're leaving me."

"For now."

She turned in his arms. When he went to speak, she raised a finger, touching his lips. "I'll find you," she promised. "When things are different here, when I've found a cure, I'll bring you back."

"Ah, but you have the luxury of time," he whispered in her ear. "I don't. I'm mortal."

Natalie pushed him away. Gesturing toward the closed door, she asked, "What about them? What's going to happen to all of those refugees?"

"I'm certain you and LaCroix will work something out."

"Don't they mean anything to you? Don't I mean anything to you?"

Again Nick moved forward to put his arms around her, but she slipped away, her back still toward him. "Yes," he admitted, after a second's pause. "More than you'll ever know." He touched her shoulder, turning her toward him, and grabbed her hand. Placing the palm of her hand against his chest, he said, "But this—warm flesh, a beating heart—means even more to me. I don't know if you'll ever understand—"

"I do," she said, her hand falling away but her eyes locking with his. "I hate you for it, but I understand. You know, by the time I wake up, you'll be long gone. . . ."

When she leaned closer, her lips brushing his, he placed his arms around her shoulders. He could feel the tension in her, knew that she closed her eyes so that he wouldn't see the hazel give way to gold and red, as she fought back the blood passion that doomed any relationship between them. It wasn't a long, breathtaking kiss, but it was sweet. Natalie broke away from him only when the door opened.

LaCroix stepped through. Glancing at her and then at Nick, he nodded and motioned her inside. "We're ready for you now. Well, as ready as we can be."

"Thank you." Slipping her fingers from Nick's hands, maintaining contact as long as possible, she backed toward the door. Then she took LaCroix's hand and walked through the door and into the safe house.

There was no backward glance, and the door closed behind them. Nick stared at it for a moment, wondering if he'd made the right decision. It was too much to ask of her, to be so close and yet not dare the boundaries that signaled danger for them both. If he was to remain mortal, he'd have to leave her behind. Who knew what would happen? One day, between her efforts and LaCroix's, the world might be different. When that day came, he'd return to her. But until then. . . .

Slowly, Nick walked up the basement steps and into the alley to watch the brilliant streaks of dawn segue to blue skies and bright sunshine. It was going to be a beautiful day for traveling.

The brilliant white light shining through the windows of the loft was so bright that it obscured everything else. For a moment, Nick held his breath in fear that he'd gone blind, but when he raised his hand to shade his eyes and blinked, he could still see. The light shone just as strong and as sweet and as pure.

Natalie's head was resting on his chest. She was silent, still sleeping, still dreaming, warm and soft beneath his arm. He touched his lips to her hair and wondered at the brightness of the dawn.

Was he still dreaming as well, or was this real? Had he truly come back across the divide between life and death and become mortal again?

The thought struck him that she was too still and fear lodged in his heart. He brushed aside her hair and raised his hand to her throat and along the edge of her jaw, searching for a pulse. The warmth of her skin alone was enough to convince him, but her mortal heartbeat, hurried even in slumber, confirmed that she was alive.

She stirred, shifting against him, and he lifted his hand from her until she settled comfortably on his chest, then let it rest around her shoulder again. It was impossible, and yet it had happened. He was mortal. His dreams had come true.

Idly, Nick stroked his hand against her hair and let his gaze roam around the loft. Closing the shutters had been the last thing on his mind last night, so they were still wide open, the room bathed in morning sunlight.

He knew the pros and cons of this brave new world. Having lived as a mortal once before, eight hundred years ago, and what he'd experienced for the past few days more than prepared him for the disappointments he knew he'd face. Then again — he kissed Natalie's hair and smiled — the wonderful delights and surprises that awaited him would more than make up for rough patches.

A sense of peace fell over him. The vampire inside him had faded away with the passing of the night. The guilt remained, but was lessened by the thought that he would never have to kill again. He could do such things — wonderful things — with the fortune he'd amassed over the centuries, and perhaps make up for some of the devastation and death he'd caused throughout his long, tortured existence. His arm tightened around Natalie at the thought of the children he might have. He could live and love and be mortal.

Once before, not two years past, he'd stood in the sunlight, thinking they'd found the answer, believing that he'd become mortal. The situation had been temporary, a condition induced by an addictive drug that had nearly destroyed him. The crushing blow of that defeat might have convinced him to follow LaCroix's advice and accept the inevitability of his fate — he was damned to a life of eternal darkness. How grateful he was now that Natalie hadn't let him lose hope after that failure, cajoling and even bullying him, reminding him that the experiment had been something of a success. He had, for a brief time, been mortal.

This time, it was for real.

The call of the light was too compelling. Biting his lip and moving slowly, Nick slipped from beneath Natalie, terrified that she would awaken. When he'd gotten her resettled on the couch without disturbing her, Nick stood and stretched. He felt grimy, still wearing the same clothes as the night before, and exhausted, but none of that mattered. He was mortal.

He shivered at the chill in the room as he headed toward the windows and made a mental note to recarpet the place completely, fix the loft's furnace, and buy himself a pair of slippers. There'd be so many changes to make in his life, among them a change from night to day shift. Maybe not at first, though. Nearing the large windows that composed a wall of his loft, he decided that he wanted to enjoy the daylight for a while.

Nick paused, bathed in the shaft of light shining through the window. He held out his hands, basking in the warmth of it. There was no pain or burning now, just a feeling of ease. Then, intrigued by the patterns of frost melting on the glass, he stepped closer to the window.

The world outside was bright and light, the sun glistening off the drifts. It had snowed again during the night, and he noticed that Natalie's car was half buried in a drift due to the snow and some maniac plow driver. She'd probably appreciate his digging out her car. Then again, he hoped she wouldn't be in such a hurry to leave. Not when they had to make up for so much time. . . .

She was still sleeping on the couch. He walked over and watched the light playing on her face; one hand was tucked beneath her head, the other was curled into a fist and held tightly against her chest. Sitting down beside her, Nick ran a finger lightly along the skin on the back of her hand. He ignored the chill that ran through him and gathered her into his arms, her body warm against his. Natalie murmured in her sleep, and he kissed her eyelids tenderly, drawing back to watch the skin above her nose crinkle in a surprised frown. As her eyelids fluttered, trying to open, he softly pressed his lips to hers.

Natalie's eyes opened immediately. Her hand moved to the flat of his chest, pushing at him in alarm, but Nick kissed her again, his mouth capturing hers. She relaxed against him, falling into the kiss, her arms moving up and around his neck to draw him closer.

His dream had come true; he was mortal and Natalie was in his arms.

She gasped for breath as they parted and Nick trailed kisses along her hairline and her cheek. The chill within him erupted into flame and he tightened his hold on her, knowing that he'd never let her go. She was his now, that was all that mattered. The pain inside him was nothing. The fire was only his passion, a hunger that needed to be fed, that needed to feed from her.

He moved his lips to her neck and kissed down its length to the hollow at the base of her throat. One of his hands moved into her hair, wrapping it around his fingers, playing with it, then grabbing hold. He pulled her hair and she cried out in pain as her head shifted to one side, exposing the line of her throat to him.

Rearing back his head, Nick snarled, fangs bared and eyes gold, anticipating the sweet taste of her blood—

13

With a wordless cry of anguish that arose from the depths of his soul, Nick pushed Natalie from him, then stumbled from the couch and backed away in horror. The world that surrounded him was a vision in red and she was the center of his predatory attention, the blood within her burning hot and bright before him. He watched as she tumbled from the couch, still only half awake. She started to shout something as she fell. The words ended with a loud "crack" as Natalie smacked her head on the coffee table, then rolled to the carpet and lay still.

Nick started toward her, then hissed and drew back when the flesh of his hand began to sizzle and burn in the sunlight, smoke rising from the reddening, then blackening skin. A stab of pain twisted his innards and he doubled over, the hunger for blood unwilling to be denied any longer. He fell to his knees, then forward onto the sun-warmed carpet, crippled by the hunger and denied refuge from the burning light.

Survival instincts took over and he spotted a shadowed haven underneath the staircase. He forced himself to his hands and knees and crawled the length of the loft as quickly as he could, scuttling into the small patch of darkness and pressing his back against the underside of the stairs.

Although the windows were free of shutters and the light poured into the loft, he was safe in his hiding place . . . but "safe" was a relative term. The hunger struck again, the inside of his chest and stomach burning just as his flesh had been seared by the sunlight. Drawing his knees tightly to his chest, Nick closed his eyes and tried to breathe, tried to concentrate past the fire that threatened to consume his mind and body. It burned strong and deep within him, but he knew it would last only so long.

Nick leaned forward, gasping, when the worst of it had passed. Wiping his hand across his forehead, he found it covered with a light sheen of bloody sweat. He had to feed soon, but to reach the refrigerator and his store of bottled cow's blood, he would have to pass directly through the sunlight and he wasn't strong enough to make it. The remote would close the shutters on the windows and plunge the loft into blessed darkness, but it was on the other side of the room, on the table behind the couch, where Natalie. . . .

Natalie.

Closing his eyes, he pictured her tumble from the couch and winced at the sound of her head cracking against the coffee table. She was injured, might even be dead—

Nick clenched his fists and denied his panic. Keeping his eyes shut tight, he forced himself to listen, extending his senses. The hum of the refrigerator motor became a loud and prolonged buzzing in his ears. The clock on the wall ticked quietly, but the precise movement of the second hand sounded like a sequences of blows. And then, beneath the other sounds, he heard the soft, steady "thump-thump" of a human heart.

It was regular, slow but not abnormally slow, as if Natalie were asleep. The sound seemed to grow louder, his own heart answering with a single beat of its own. His mouth watered and he became transfixed by the steady beat, felt it flood his body with the promise of the rich, warm blood that it pumped.

Nick wasn't aware that he opened his eyes—not at first. He found himself peering around the corner of the staircase, searching the loft for the source of the sound. There, just in front of the couch, he saw Natalie's hand. Staring at her fingers, he willed them to move, willed her to consciousness.

There was no response. Her heart continued its maddening, pulsating beat.

Nick licked his lips, still staring at her hand. It was as if he could see the arteries beneath the skin, the blood flowing within them, carrying oxygen throughout her body. His left hand moved forward of its own accord, settling palm flat on the carpet, and was followed by his right. The blood was all that mattered, was all that he saw, as he started to crawl across the carpet.

Almost immediately his fingers moved into a patch of light and began to smoke. Drawing his hand back to his chest, Nick huddled again behind the staircase, shaking. He had to control himself; he couldn't let the beast win.

"Nat?" he called, then waited for a response, any sign of life or motion.

Nothing.

Smelling something other than his burned flesh—he would normally have healed by now, but his body was starved for fresh blood—Nick sniffed at the air. The smell of stale blood, yes, from the bottle he'd spilled the night before in the kitchen, but there was a sharper, keener scent in the air. Fresh blood.

Natalie's fall replayed in his head, that angry "crack" and then . . . a spurt of blood, crimson viewed through a red haze, bright and warm and sweet—

Nick buried his face in his hands and counted to ten slowly, but now that he'd recognized the scent, it clung to him, threatened to smother him. Her heartbeat picked up in volume, drowning out the other quiet sounds that had always been an unnoticed and ever-present part of his life here. Clearing his throat and clenching his fists, he again called, "Nat?," his desperation making his voice hoarse.

No response. Her heart was still beating.

Beating. Beating. Beating.

"Natalie!"

The glass in the windows rattled at his bellow of panic and frustration, the sound echoing from the wall and under the staircase that sheltered him. It buffeted him, and he fell back against the underside of the staircase, cracking his head on the wood.

She wasn't dead, but unconscious. If he left her there until the sun passed beyond the building and the shadows gave him safe passage to the refrigerator, then to her, she might bleed to death. He could try a dash to the refrigerator first—if he drank enough blood, he might be able to dare a few more seconds in the direct sunlight, reach the remote at best and the phone at worst. . . .

The hunger boiled up inside him again and his stomach cramped. Clasping his hands together and holding his knees tightly to his chest, Nick groaned aloud and rode out the wave of pain. The vampire within him didn't care about saving Natalie. The beast needed blood and it needed blood now, so desperate to feed that it had overridden his instinctual fear of sunlight to get what it wanted. The pain was a reminder, this bout lasting longer and burning brighter.

As it passed, Nick fell limply against the staircase and took several slow, deep breaths as he counted to ten, then twenty. If anything was going to be done, it had to be done soon. He'd be able to control the beast only so long, and his will would give out before the shadows were anywhere near long enough to allow him passage to the refrigerator, the phone, Natalie, or the remote control that operated the shutters.

Her sigh was so soft that at first he thought he'd imagined it. His throat dry, Nick turned his head, his cheek resting against the wood, straining to hear. "Nat?"

Another sigh followed, then a groan.

"Nat?" He swallowed. "Nat—if you can hear me, stay where you are. All right? Stay right where you are!"

"Nick?"

Her voice was hesitant, heavy with sleep. Nick forced himself to take another deep breath and stare at the wall directly ahead. He couldn't look at her, couldn't even imagine her. But the sounds of her movement echoed in his mind—the table leg being moved and brushing across the carpet near the fireplace, the leather of the couch cushion giving way beneath her hand as she pushed up from the floor.

"Don't move!" he shouted. "Nat, don't move!"

Another creak, then a pause, the couch cushion giving way beneath her full weight. "Where are you? Oh, my God, the light!"

Hearing her scramble for the remote, he shouted, "No! Don't close the shutters! Nat—" He took another long breath in the silence. "I'm hungry. You're safe in the sunlight. Don't close the shutters. Just leave. Just . . . leave."

The last word ended on a choked sob—he couldn't help it. Another wave of hunger passed through him, and he jerked his head hard against the wood of the staircase when he lost hold of his knees. There was a loud bang.

"Nick? What's happening?"

Through the pain he heard her footsteps crossing the floor. . . .

"No!" he roared, forcing the words out past the pain of the hunger. "Don't—come—near—me!"

The footsteps stopped. The pain crested, then fell away. Nick slipped to the floor and lay on his side, curling into the fetal position until his muscles relaxed. Then, hearing the motorized shutters starting to descend into place, he sat up quickly. "Nat—don't—"

"It's all right," she said firmly. "I'm only closing the shutters on the left side of the room. You'll be able to reach the refrigerator now."

Nick sensed the darkness falling even as she spoke. Before she finished, he scrambled to his feet and was at the refrigerator, nearly tearing the door from its hinges in his eagerness. The door slammed against the wall as he reached inside and grabbed a bottle. He used his teeth to tear out the cork.

The blood was cold and cow, not warm and human, but he didn't care. It was blood. Although it wouldn't satisfy the hungry beast within him, it would appease it and stop the pain. It would be enough to make him heal.

The thick red liquid spilled from his mouth and trickled down his chest, inside his shirt, as he upended the bottle and drank. He barely noticed the mess, finishing that one in a matter of minutes, then grabbing another and drinking again. By the middle of the second bottle, he could feel the charred skin on his hands and the side of his face flaking away, replaced by new, pale flesh. The pain lingered, as it often did, but soon it was gone.

And so was the second bottle.

Nick leaned his hands on the top of the refrigerator door and simply hung there a moment, exhausted.

"How are you?" asked Natalie.

She was still across the room, standing in the sunlight. Taking a long slow breath, Nick pulled another bottle from the refrigerator, then closed the door. "I've been better." He leaned his back against the cool metal surface, then gestured toward his temple. "How's your head?"

"My head?" Natalie lifted her fingers to the right side of her forehead, mimicking his gesture, then stared as they came away wet with blood. She looked at him and he heard her heartbeat quicken. "I fell—"

266

"Against the table." He watched her as she turned and looked at the coffee table behind her. There was no hesitation in her, no fear. She should be afraid. It was the only way she could stay alive.

"I was dreaming." Natalie shook her head slightly, then touched her fingertips to her forehead with a frown. "I had a dream about—" Her cheeks reddened slightly, and the corner of her lip curled into a crooked smile. "You kissed me."

"It wasn't a dream." Pulling the cork from the bottle with his fingernails, Nick took a swallow. He recorked the bottle, then walked to the table behind the couch. "I nearly killed you. You were right—it didn't last." He moved past her on the darkened side of the room, to the fireplace, frustration and anger building within him as he began to realize what had happened. "It was a dream. That's all it's ever been . . . just a dream. Just a dream."

He hurled the bottle of blood into the fireplace. Natalie grabbed his arm and pulled him away as it shattered, a mixture of blood and glass scattering onto the floor.

"Nick!"

She hung onto his arm as he stood there, facing the shutters—he could feel the warmth of her fingers through his shirt, but his heart was cold and dead inside him. "LaCroix was right," he whispered. "My folly."

"Wanting to be mortal again is *not* your folly," said Natalie sharply, tugging at his arm when he didn't look at her. "Don't you fall into that again! This is your life, Nick. *Yours*, not LaCroix's. There aren't going to be any quick fixes. We're going to have a lot of failures. But if you want this—if *you* want this—I'll be here for you."

"Like you were here for me last night. You warned me that it might not be permanent." He placed his hand on the glass of the window, which had grown cold now that the light had been denied it. So close and yet so far. "I didn't listen to you. You were right."

"Yes, I was right," she admitted. When he looked at her, there were tears in the corners of her eyes. "You don't know how sorry I am that I was right."

Nick wrapped his arm around her and held her close. He breathed in the scent of her hair and listened to her heart, which was beating too fast, too anxiously on his behalf. "My heart's desire," he said. "There aren't any happy endings, are there?"

"Sometimes we can come close." Wiping her eyes with the flat of her hand, Natalie pushed back from him and smiled sadly. "This is the closest you've ever come—even if the symptoms were psychosomatic. We know it can be done, Nick." Hitting him lightly in the shoulder with her fist, she added, "And—hey! You didn't die in your dream, huh?"

"No. No, I didn't."

They stood gazing at one another for a moment, an awkward silence between them. "You should go," he suggested softly.

"I'd like to check you over, make sure there's—"

"You *should* go."

His tone was careful, final, and contained a warning. He saw her back straighten as she automatically started to protest. Then she looked away from him, as if recognizing that he might have his limitations.

"Maybe I *should*," she admitted reluctantly.

Nick reached out as if to touch the bloody spot near her temple, then pulled his fingers back quickly and glanced away. "You should get that looked at."

She spit on her fingers, then wiped at the spot. The blood disappeared almost instantly, leaving a small, red scrape. "It's just a scratch. Head wounds always bleed like crazy."

He started at her words, remembering having heard them somewhere . . . in his dream? Nick watched her as she packed up the things she'd brought with her. "You could have a concussion."

"I have a headache—which I'm guessing is due more to the caffeine buzz from all that coffee I drank last night." Natalie closed her bag, picked up her mittens from the table behind the couch and glanced at him, an odd expression on her face. "You drank coffee last night."

"So I did." He smiled as he looked at the empty coffee cup on the table. The smile froze when he spotted the dream doll beside it, curled into a tight ball. Picking it up, he stared at it. "No more dreams."

"You should be glad of that." Natalie walked over to the coatrack and removed her coat from the hook. Slipping her arms into it, she turned toward him. "As your doctor, I suggest that you march upstairs, take a nice, hot shower, then crawl into bed."

As he closed his left hand over the wicker ball, Nick tapped his right temple with his forefinger. "Physician, heal thyself."

"Okay, okay, I'll have someone check it. It's just a bump, that's all." Natalie frowned at him as she pulled on her mittens. "I still have that stuff I brought with me, if you think you won't be able to sleep. . . ."

"Believe me, that won't be a problem."

"Glad to hear it. I think I've got more than enough information right now on the effects of sleep deprivation on vampires." She picked up her bag and hit the button for the elevator.

Nick walked to the coatrack and fished his car keys from his coat pocket. Turning, he grasped her mittened hand and dropped them onto her palm. "Your car's plowed in. Take mine—you should be able to get out of the garage."

"I don't think that's—"

Gently, he folded her fingers over the keys. "I'd feel better. Bring it by tonight, after shift. I should have you dug out by then."

There was a moment of hesitation on her part, then she smiled. "That's an offer I'd be crazy to refuse. You sure I'm not stranding you or—" At his grin, she shook her head and tucked the keys into her pocket. "No, I guess not, huh?"

Nick leaned past her and opened the elevator door. He waited as she entered the elevator, watching her, the memory of a different Natalie lingering in his mind's eye—pale skin, red lips.

That was the only way they could be together. But he would never bring her across, especially not after he'd seen her in the morning light, the sun shining on her face as she curled up on the couch in peaceful slumber.

"What?" she asked suspiciously, as he stood there, studying her.

"Thanks. For staying here last night. For trying to keep me awake." He kissed her forehead, carefully avoiding the wound near her temple, then drew back.

"You're welcome." Natalie returned the kiss, her lips touching his own for a tantalizingly brief second. She smiled softly at him from inside the elevator. "Stay home tonight, all right? And sweet dreams."

"For you, too," he called as the elevator door slid shut.

Nick paused for a moment and looked around his apartment. Half of the room was bathed in brilliant sunlight, the other half fading from gray into darkness. Two different worlds, just like he'd told Tracy, only it applied to himself and Natalie, as well as to Tracy's relationship with Vachon. To follow his own advice would mean to leave Natalie forever, as his other self in the dream had done.

Closing his eyes, Nick rested his head against the wooden frame of the elevator door and sighed. Someday, perhaps, but not yet. To save her, he'd have to leave her. Leaving her would mean tearing apart his heart, losing his hope. Losing his hope would mean abandoning his quest to return to mortality, the only way he could redeem his soul.

To save her life would cost him his soul.

Still clutching the doll tightly in his hand, Nick walked to the refrigerator. Opening the door, he took out a bottle, then

270

closed the door with a push from his elbow. His steps were heavy as he walked to the darkened end of the couch and sat down. He placed the bottle and the doll on the table, then caught the doll as it threatened to roll off the edge.

It was round now, a near-perfect ball. Holding it in his hand, he realized that it wasn't over yet, that he had a few more things to do before he could rest, before he could sleep. He sat there for hours, throwing the ball into the air and catching it, watching the light advance and then retreat across the other side of the room, and wondered if there was any way to save himself.

14

THE BOUNCER POSITIONED HIMSELF IN THE DOORWAY OF THE RAVEN as Nick approached, his eyes dark and forbidding, massive arms folded across his chest. He held out a hand, the palm less than an inch from the center of Nick's unzipped jacket. Although the bouncer was wearing only a sleeveless T-shirt and jeans, he showed no sign of being affected by the below-zero temperatures.

Neither did Nick. He simply stood there, his eyes meeting the gaze of the other vampire, waiting. He could afford to wait, knowing what the answer would be. Despite the spectacular brawl of the other night, he'd be allowed inside. LaCroix wanted to see what might be left of him, what might be salvaged and poured back into the mold that he'd been trying for centuries to make Nick fit.

The stern expression on the bouncer's face never changed, even as he lowered his hand, stepped aside, and held open the door of the club.

Nick walked inside, hands in his pockets. He paused at the railing along the upper landing, hearing the bouncer enter behind him, the door closing softly. It was less than an hour after sunset and the mortals were only beginning to arrive, stopping in for the drink that prefaced the transmutation from their working lives to their home lives. The bar was full, the dance floor all but empty, with the exception of a few vampires who were slow-dancing to a muted, almost hypnotic beat. Several of the tables were occupied, but there was only one that interested him. For some reason, he'd been certain that she'd be here, waiting for him.

She was.

Nick started down the steps, his eyes on her the entire time. She was seated at a table in the back, the table he'd occupied the night before. Her dark hair fell softly around her face, cut shorter and barely reaching her throat, her clothing far less daring than when he'd last seen her—the suit was a forties style, in the colors of nature, ranging from the pale olive of the blouse to the dark forest green of her jacket. A filled wine glass stood before her, red wine, and the faint scent of lavender drifted around her like a cloud, obliterating the usual smells of the club—alcohol, musk, stale sweat, and old blood. As he drew closer, he saw that there were large cards lying on the table in a pattern . . . the tarot.

His shadow fell over her when he reached the table. Only then did she look up at him, emerald eyes shining. With a smile she gestured him to the seat opposite her, then returned her attention to the cards before her. Lifting one, she placed it beside the cross of cards already on the table.

Her casual attitude stirred a sense of anger within him, but Nick clamped down on the emotion and glanced around the club nervously—he was here on sufferance, and any disturbance on his part would get him ejected from this place for a long time, possibly for the duration of his life in Toronto. Seating himself, he pulled the small white box from his pocket—he'd stopped at a jeweler's shop on the way, trying to duplicate the original container as best as he could.

Nick placed it on the table before her. "Why did you do this to me? I never harmed you. Why?"

"It's always the same with you, isn't it?" she said softly. "Must everything be a reward or punishment? Can't things simply happen?"

"It didn't work." With a flick of his finger, he knocked the lid from the box. The doll inside was still curled into a tight, wicker ball. "In case you haven't noticed, I've turned back."

"I never said you wouldn't. Or that you'd change at all. I only said you'd know if you had the strength to pursue your heart's desire." She picked up another card, laying it carefully above the first. "And what that truly was."

"That's supposed to make me happy?"

"No." She looked up, her emerald eyes regarding him thoughtfully. "That was never part of the bargain. All you asked for was the doll. All the doll gave you were dreams."

Fragments of the final dream came back to him—escape and survival, setting up a partnership between vampire and mortal, saying good-bye to Natalie, watching the dawn . . . all of it happened only because his other self had changed from mortal to vampire, however briefly. It was unheard of, impossible—just like a vampire becoming mortal for a time. "Was it real?" he asked, still dazzled by that dream dawn. "Was *he* real? The other me?"

"Who is the dream and who the dreamer? Was he part of your dream, or you part of his?" When he stared at her, she smiled, raising her free hand to her lips. "When you do ask questions, Detective Knight, you never ask easy ones."

Nick stared down at the doll. "He got away," he said aloud, with no small amount of envy as he turned over the images in his mind. "He survived because he took a part of me and I . . . took a part of him."

"It was your dream, *chevalier*." When Nick glared at her, she looked back down at her cards. Picking up another, she placed it atop the other two. "Yes, he survived. Because some part of you, the vampire, became part of him. And, for that time, you were permitted to taste mortality again."

"But it didn't last!"

"It wasn't supposed to. Dreams never do, Detective." She met his eyes evenly, not seeming to notice the anger that flickered there. "Don't blame him—it wasn't his doing."

"You planned this," he accused. "You used me—"

"You asked for the doll. You opened the door to dreams, to heart's desire." She smiled slightly, and shrugged. "I merely made certain that you opened a door that could cause some good. Your brief mortality was your reward, not your due. Accept that and move on, back to what you were."

Nick looked across the club. He'd wasted all that time, the time his body had taken to complete, or nearly complete, the transformation from vampire to mortal. Just as he'd wasted the time he'd been given when he'd thought Natalie had cured him once before. Then it had been because he'd thought he would have a lifetime to live in the light. This time it had been because he'd been too dulled by self-pity, too consumed with attempting to control Tracy's and Vachon's lives. But if he had another chance. . . .

"Give it back to me." His hand reached for the doll.

Mortal though she might be, she was faster. Her long, bronze fingers intertwined with his own, holding his hand effortlessly above the box for a long moment, then releasing it. When he drew it to his chest and stared at her in amazement, she smiled and said sadly, "It can be used only once."

"Get me another."

"Is that what you want, Detective Knight? To live in dreams?"

He swallowed, remembering Natalie sleeping against his chest, the warmth of her body cradled in his arms, the taste of her lips. "If that's the only way."

"To have your heart's desire? But you still don't know what it is, do you?" When he glared at her, she ducked her head, trying to hide her smile. "Mortality? Redemption? Salvation? Do you want to save the world?" When he didn't answer, she looked down at the cards again, lifting yet another and placing it above the other three. "To love . . . and to be loved—that's the heart's desire. No man could wish for more. Or should."

Her hand moved from the card to the box lid. Lifting it, she placed the lid onto the box, then tapped it twice. When she flicked the lid from the box again, the doll had returned to the unbent condition in which he'd received it.

"I live in dreams, Detective Knight." She met his gaze, her eyes dark green, large, and empty. "The heart's desire is the only true light."

"You know what I am." He felt his eyesight sharpen and his vision was tinted with a golden hue, reminding her of his true nature. "You know that love, true love, is denied my kind. Our love is destructive, murderous."

"Not always. Your own experience has taught you that."

Closing his eyes, Nick thought of Janette and how her love for a mortal had led to her becoming mortal . . . but her lover had been killed. And when she was near death, he'd been unable to face the thought of losing her, had made her a vampire again even though she'd wanted to die a true death. How could he risk Natalie's life that way? If something went wrong. . . .

The first thing he saw when he opened his eyes was the shine of the candlelight on the cards she'd spread on the table before her, the colors dancing as they reflected the flame. "That's why you wouldn't read Natalie's tarot when you gave her the box. You knew this would happen."

"The cards might have indicated it, but so much of her future rested with you, continues to rest with you." Her fingers brushed the surface of the final card as she stared into space. She closed her eyes, then shivered, saying, "There are too many choices, decisions yet to be faced and made. . . ." When she opened her eyes, her gaze was harsh. "Her future rests between you. As does your own."

Nick bowed his head. Of course her future rested with

him. The only way he could assure himself of her safety was to abandon her, as his dream self had done. He'd almost done it before, after Schanke and Cohen had been killed in a plane accident, but something had made him stay until she could talk him out of it. This time, he doubted he'd even make it through the preparations, unlike his dream counterpart.

"How could he leave her?"

"In your dream?"

He hadn't realized he'd spoken aloud until she answered him. With a smile, she said, "Perhaps he knew his heart's desire—he valued his mortality over her love. If the choice had been your own, which would you have chosen, your heart's desire or your life?"

Nick started as he was tapped on the shoulder, then turned to find himself facing Lillian, the waitress from the night before. "Somebody wants a word with you," she said, gesturing toward the bar. She moved off to deliver the drinks on her tray.

Looking past her, Nick spotted Vachon sitting on a bar stool. He met Nick's gaze for a moment, his expression somber, then turned his attention back to the drink in his hand.

"Would you deny another what you've fought so hard to attain for yourself—the freedom to make your own choices?" asked his emerald-eyed visitor.

He stared at Vachon's back. "What about the freedom to make your own mistakes?"

"That, too." When he turned, he saw that she'd moved her hands across the table, gathering her cards together. Tapping the deck against the table, she lifted a card and placed it in front of herself, the face hidden from him by the height of the deck. Frowning, she placed a second on top of the first, then she looked up at him, her expression grim. " 'Free will' is a misnomer, *chevalier*—we pay for our mistakes, as well as the mistakes of others. Sometimes dearly."

The tone of her voice sent a chill through him . . . and Vachon was waiting. Nick rose to his feet, but she quickly picked up the cards she'd placed on the table and he was unable to glimpse their faces. "I'll be back in a minute."

"Of course." Again she tapped the deck of cards against the table, her eyes locked on the movement of her hands.

Nick hesitated, waiting for something, but when she said nothing else he headed across the dance floor, to the corner of the bar. He made an effort to ignore the smirks and stares of the vampires he passed—they all knew what had happened here the night before; word of an incident like that swept through the community like fire through a drought-ravaged wheat field.

Vachon didn't immediately acknowledge him as Nick slipped into an empty space at the bar beside him. Feeling a stirring of hunger at the scent of the human blood Vachon was drinking, he raised a finger to catch the bartender's attention.

"Sorry I missed the fun last night," said Vachon, setting his glass on the bar.

"I'll bet." Nick turned his back and leaned his elbows on the bar, staring defiantly across the club, hoping to give anyone at least a moment's pause before trying to approach him. "I wasn't myself."

"So I heard."

There was a sound behind him. The bartender was placing his glass on the bar. Reaching back, he lifted the glass, then sipped at it, wondering how to broach the subject of Tracy and Vachon's relationship. "I was wrong."

"About?"

"Tracy. And you." Half turning, Nick set his glass on the bar and smiled faintly at Vachon's wide-eyed stare. "You were right—what happens between you two is your business. I've got no right to interfere."

Vachon continued to stare at him as if so amazed by his

good fortune, he was certain there was a catch to it. "Okay. Have you talked to Tracy yet? Because as far as she's concerned, I'm right below the plague on her ten most unwanted list."

"I'll call her tonight and apologize. From then on, it's up to her." He lifted his glass and took another sip, noting Vachon's sudden smile. "I'd like you to keep in mind that if you bring her across against her will or she comes to any harm because she knows about us, I'll have to kill you."

Vachon regarded him thoughtfully for a moment, then nodded. "Seems fair to me." Reaching into his pocket, he pulled out two bills and a handful of change, then threw them on the counter. "Guess I've gotta get my hands on those concert tickets after all." He met Nick's gaze with a suspicious look. "You're yourself tonight, right? I'm not gonna get the riot act again next time I run into you?"

"No. No more turnabouts. Let's just say I finally saw the light." With a grimace, Nick took another sip of the cow blood, then looked toward the back of the club. "You got a minute? There's somebody I'd like you to meet."

Vachon had turned, prepared to walk away, but he shrugged and gestured toward the crowd. "Sure. Any friend of yours—"

There were more mortals in the club now. The bar scene was giving way to the dance scene, and Nick couldn't see her table from where they were standing. He crossed the dance floor without hesitation, knowing that Vachon was behind him. When he finally broke through the crowd, however, there was no one at the table.

A faint plume of smoke rose from the extinguished candle. The wine glass was still filled, untouched. The cover had been placed on the white jeweler's box, which was resting exactly where he had left it.

Vachon walked around him, glanced at the scene, then smiled. "Gone?"

"Yes." He picked up the wine glass and held it up to the colored lights strobing across the dance floor. There were no discernible prints that he could see. She'd never touched it.

"Look, I've gotta see a man about some tickets. So if there's no hard feelings—"

"What?" His train of thought broken, Nick stared at Vachon for a moment, puzzled, then smiled and shook his hand. "No hard feelings."

"Good." Vachon headed toward the dance floor at a trot, then turned back, pointing at him. "Make sure you call Tracy. *Tonight!*"

Nick waved, then seated himself in the chair he'd had before. On an impulse, he lifted the glass to his lips, sniffing the alcohol, then tasting it.

It was bitter and vile. Nick picked up a napkin and quickly spit the remaining liquid into it. Then he sensed a presence at his back.

Urs's hand traced the length of his shoulder. She smiled at him, offering the glass of cow blood. "I think this is yours," she announced, seating herself opposite him.

"Thanks." Genuinely grateful, Nick sipped the blood—it was gruesome stuff, but it took the awful taste of the undiluted wine from his mouth.

Picking up the wine glass he'd so hastily abandoned, Urs tilted it slightly, causing the liquid to run along the curve of the bowl. "Vachon seemed to be in a hurry. Is everything all right?"

"I hope so." Nick half turned in his seat, trying to look through the crowd, but there were too many dancers. Vachon was already gone. "I think he had an errand to run."

As Urs twirled the glass stem between her fingers, the wine formed two waves traveling in opposite directions. Smashing together, they obliterated each other. "He doesn't really know what he wants. Maybe when he figures it out, he'll be happy." Urs looked at him, eyes bright, her smile sad. "That's all I want, for him to be happy."

281

Nick reached across the table to cup her cheek, lightly stroking it with his fingers. "With you to look after him? I'm sure he will be."

Sensing LaCroix's presence, he dropped his hand to the table and glanced at his master, who was watching from the edge of the crowd. "I don't plan on causing any trouble for you tonight."

"Good. It was becoming tedious." He stood beside Urs, towering over her, then rested his fingers lightly on the bare flesh of her arm. "Isn't it time for you to enchant the patrons into consuming more alcohol?"

Urs met LaCroix's eyes, then rose as he pulled her chair back for her. She started past Nick, then paused and leaned her hand on his shoulder for a moment. "I hope you're happy someday, too."

He placed his hand over her own, then looked up at LaCroix as her fingers slipped from beneath his own.

LaCroix watched Urs as she walked back to the crowded dance floor. "A goddess, but too sensitive for her own good. If she survives another century, I'd be surprised. Vachon doesn't look after her properly."

"And you would?"

"Don't I?" With a sly smile, LaCroix sank into the chair across from him, then leaned forward and tapped the white jeweler's box with his finger. "What's this, Nicholas? A gift for a special friend?"

Remembering LaCroix's previous reaction to the doll, Nick slid the box across the table so that it sat directly in front of his master. "Open it and see."

LaCroix eyed him, then carefully lifted the top from the box and tipped the contents onto his left palm—a small pile of dust. "Is this a joke?"

Nick stared at the dust—the doll had disintegrated. "No, not a joke," he whispered. "Only the remnants of a dream."

"Your ill-fated dream of regaining your mortality, I hope." Turning his head slightly, LaCroix blew the dust to the floor. He picked up a napkin from the table and wiped off his hand. "Does this mean you've given up this quixotic quest and accepted your true place in the scheme of things? Should I be celebrating the return of my prodigal son?"

Lifting the glass of cow's blood, Nick sipped at it and smiled, ignoring the taste. "I think that celebration might be a bit premature."

"So you're content to wander between their world and our world, belonging to neither," said LaCroix sharply.

"I know where I belong."

LaCroix pushed back the chair and rose to his feet. "Really?" He walked past Nick, then whirled, leaning close to Nick's shoulder. "I've watched you chasing fantasies like this, decade after decade—they've all come to nothing. Why now, after eight hundred years of failure, do you believe you'll be able to accomplish this miraculous feat?"

"Because I have no other choice."

"Then you are doomed to disappointment."

"Maybe." Lifting the glass again, Nick stared at the cow blood, then glanced over his shoulder with a smile. "Or I just might succeed."

With a low chuckle, LaCroix grasped his shoulder tightly, then released it. "Go back to sleep, Nicholas. You're still dreaming."

He relaxed only after he was certain LaCroix had left. With a yawn, Nick placed the glass of cow blood on the table and ran the heels of his palms over his eyes. The blood had offset the worst of the weariness for a bit, but all of that lost sleep was catching up with him. He still had to call Tracy and set things right with her, but it wouldn't hurt to rest his eyes for a few minutes.

Folding his arms on the table, Nick lowered his head and closed his eyes. The music and noise of the crowd seemed to fade around him. For an instant he thought he felt the soft press of lips against his forehead, as a voice whispered,

"Sleep well, Detective Knight. May you have none but pleasant dreams."

Then Nick fell into a soft and comforting darkness, a dreamless, restful sleep, accompanied by the lingering scent of lavender.